★ MAVERICKS

Welcome to Montana—the home of bold men and daring women, where more than fifty tales of passion, adventure and intrigue unfold beneath the Big Sky. Don't miss a single one!

Montana
★ MAVERICKS

HELEN
R. MYERS
The Law
Is No Lady

Silhouette Books

Published by Silhouette Books

America's Publisher of Contemporary Romance

Special thanks and acknowledgment to Helen R. Myers for her contribution to the Montana Mavericks series.

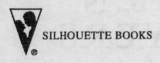 SILHOUETTE BOOKS

ISBN-13: 978-0-373-31030-2
ISBN-10:   0-373-31030-7

Recycling programs
for this product may
not exist in your area.

THE LAW IS NO LADY

Visit Silhouette Books at www.eHarlequin.com

Printed in U.S.A.

HELEN R. MYERS

satisfies her preference for a reclusive lifestyle by living deep in the Piney Woods of East Texas with her husband, Robert, and—because they were there first—the various species of four-legged and winged creatures that wander throughout their ranch. To write has been her lifelong dream, and to bring a slightly different flavor to each book is an ongoing ambition. She admits to a restless nature, but sees that quality as helpful to her writing, explaining, "It makes me reach for new territory and experiment with old boundaries."

Prologue

He didn't want to answer the pounding at his front door. Besides the late hour, the raging storm battering his house was proving that March or not, winter hadn't yet finished with Montana. What kind of fool wouldn't have the sense to stay indoors on a night like this? At the best of times, he didn't have much to say for most people's common sense, and that opinion had recently been reinforced, thanks to his stinging brush with the law down in Whitehorn.

Yet the thumping continued, taking on a frantic urgency that finally had him pushing himself up from his recliner. "Fourth-largest state in the country," he growled, resenting the need to put any distance between himself and the warmth of his wood-burning stove. "And a smaller population than some boroughs in New York City. You'd think a guy could get a little peace around here." If some idiot had managed to get stuck out on the mountain highway, he could go bunk with John Mountain, his sole ranch hand, until the storm blew over. "Damned if I'm going to freeze my butt, or worse, for a—"

As he succeeded in jerking open the door, the rest of his words died in his throat. He stared in mute horror at a snow-covered man who had to use his whole body to bear the weight of an equally frozen, and exceedingly pregnant woman. His mind tried to reject the vision arguing that this couldn't be happening to him; not now, after he'd worked so hard to put his nightmares behind him.

But he was wrong. Again.

"Ethan…"

His sister's pitiful, weak voice yanked Ethan Walker out of his stupor. Lurching forward, he swept her out of Homer Gilmore's grasp.

"What's wrong with her?" he demanded, assuming the old-timer would shut the door and follow him. On the other hand, one never knew with Homer. The prospector was the singular type; the one person in the area with a worse reputation than Ethan's for being unapproachable and eccentric. For all Ethan knew, the restless coot would dash back into the treacherous night, and take off for parts unknown, not to be seen again for days, even weeks.

But apparently Homer had also had his fill of the brutal weather. Ethan heard him shove the door closed and first stomp, then brush, the snow off his boots and outerwear. "Reckon the baby's coming!" he called back.

So much for revelations. Ethan had figured that out for himself the second he lifted Marilee into his arms and felt her writhe and moan. What was more, while genetically the Walkers had always tended to be on the lean side—with Marilee never coming close to outweighing a bushel of twigs in her life—right now her face was the only thing gaunt and fragile about her. The rest of her body reflected a woman ripe and ready to burst with new life, something not even her quilted coat and layers of clothing could hide. What a shock, considering he hadn't seen her in months—not since they'd crossed paths in town and she'd briefly informed him of her pregnancy. He'd just as soon forget *that* episode, considering that right afterward she'd run away, as if ashamed of being spotted with him.

"Found her between Whitehorn and here," Homer continued, the thud of his booted feet signaling that he was following them. "Looks like her car slid off the road. Figured she'd been headin' your way—she didn't have much to say at first, being shook up and all—so I helped her along."

"Don't scold, Ethan," Marilee pleaded, between shallow pants. "Promise you won't?"

Scold? He wanted to roar the roof off the rafters. He wanted to shake Homer until the old weasel's teeth rattled, and then give Marilee a dose for good measure. She was supposed to be in Billings, with her in-laws, for pity's sake! Only her pitiful condition kept him from yielding to his outrage and panic. But of all times for her to decide to patch up their relationship…and just what did she and Homer think he could do for her way out here?

"You should be in a hospital," he muttered, carrying her into what had once been their parents' bedroom. His room now, although he never slept there, because he didn't want to waste the wood it would take to heat that part of the house. And because after Vietnam…after Wayne…he'd found sanity in denying himself such luxuries as beds. But with the door pushed wide, the room would warm up fast and be fine for Marilee. Most important, she would have the privacy this situation called for.

"I had to see you."

"It could've waited. You need medical help." He

thought of the twenty-five miles between his ranch and Whitehorn. In this weather, it might as well be a hundred. Even so, they would provide better care than what he could hope to give her. "Maybe there's time to put chains on the truck."

Marilee clutched at his snow-dampened flannel shirt, only to grimace as new contractions gripped her. "No! I don't want to go back! They'll take my baby! Ethan!"

Despite the prickles at the back of his neck, he told himself that her frantic reaction had to be due to her condition. She'd had a scare, that was all. This was her first child. All women got emotional at this point, didn't they?

"No one's going to take your baby." Good grief, who would dare? he thought, setting her on the mahogany bed. She was a Taylor now. Regardless of how he felt toward her late husband and her in-laws, to everyone else in this area the name personified power and created its own ring of protection. Only a complete stranger would be stupid enough to—

"They will! They'll manage it the same way Clay kept me from you once we were married."

What was she talking about? Was that true? Not caring about the snow that clung to her clothes and boots, Ethan urged her back against the bedding and the pillows. He almost sat down himself; her announcement had him reeling as if he'd taken a kick in the head from one of his cattle.

Kept her away. While all this time he'd believed her happy in her marriage and her life of luxury. So convinced that after Clay's accidental death he'd assumed she was too ashamed to return to the place of her birth. He'd tried to understand, to forgive her for turning her back on him. Social pressure could be an impossible thing. What with so many people in these parts continuing to believe he was a cold-blooded killer, it had only been reasonable to suppose she'd formed doubts herself. But what she'd just told him suggested something altogether different.

An ugly feeling began churning in Ethan's belly. "Taylor kept you from coming out to see me?"

"That's right. When I tried—*oh, God, this hurts*—when I tried, he would get crazy mean. I know it's evil to say this, but…I'm not sorry he's dead!"

Before Ethan could begin to reconcile himself to this latest revelation, a new hammering erupted at the front door. What now? he wondered, glancing over his shoulder at the man standing in the bedroom doorway. He'd all but forgotten Homer.

"Well, don't just stand there. Go see who that is!" Then, muttering an epithet or two, he continued to get his sister out of her wet things.

Muffled voices drifted into the unlighted room, followed by the sound of hurried footsteps. Only at that point did Ethan realize his newest guest was a woman.

"Marilee?"

Lori Bains rushed in and circled to the far side of the bed. She sounded unsure; understandable, since the only light was coming from the lanterns in the main part of the house.

"Oh, no. This is what I was afraid of. I was on my way back from a medical workshop in Butte when I spotted Clay's—I mean your car, in a ditch." She cast Ethan a wary glance, adding directly to him, "Something told me to pull over and make sure she wasn't inside. That's when I saw the tracks heading this way. How far along are the contractions?"

Although he thought it nothing short of a miracle for Whitehorn's own resident certified nurse and midwife to be the one who'd appeared on his doorstep, Ethan paused in removing Marilee's right boot to scowl at the woman.

It was, after all, one asinine question to be asking a bachelor, let alone a man about his sister. "How the hell should I know?"

Somewhere in her mid-to-late twenties, the blue-eyed blonde continued to bear more of a resemblance to a schoolgirl than his idea of an experienced professional. But her answering glare proved she wasn't unused to his brand of ground-zero etiquette, even if he was the area's most recent and notorious jailbird.

Stripping off her own coat, gloves and scarf, and tossing them behind her without so much as a glance of concern for where anything landed, Lori snapped back, "The usual way, Ethan. You *ask* her." But as quickly as she'd lost her temper, she collected herself and asked Marilee gently, "Have you been timing the pains?"

"Before. Not now. Now the hurting's almost constant."

Lori nodded. "Then we can't afford to assume an emergency helicopter can get here in time." Once again she directed her attention to Ethan. "Okay, this is what I need you to do. Light that oil lamp on the bed stand, and the get me whatever other light you can. When you're done, boil some water, and *then* you can call for that chopper. After you're finished with that, we'll need more blankets, and plenty of clean sheets. You have clean sheets, don't you?"

Far too anxious to be angry, or to waste precious seconds by doing more than nodding, Ethan bolted. Something in Lori's voice, beyond her obvious concern about time, had his blood temperature plummeting to match the windchill outside. He could deal with it better by staying busy.

Homer dodged out of his way as he hurried past to put on the pots of water. Then, despite what Lori had ordered, Ethan made the phone call. Although the air ambulance service gave him only limited hope for assistance anytime soon, he felt reassured after that. But his hopefulness lasted only until he started collecting the rest of what Lori had asked for.

Living the life of a thrifty loner had claimed its price; he realized how high of one when he added two more oil lamps to help illuminate the bedroom, then found himself in a fix. Linens. Besides the set already on the bed, he owned only one other change, which he took from the ancient chest across from the bed. Until tonight, he'd considered the supply more than adequate. Now he wished he had more to offer…so much more.

The blankets were in better supply for one reason: A person never knew how cold it could get up here in the winter, or how long a storm might last. No, a rancher never had enough blankets, or enough firewood, Ethan thought as he yanked bundle after bundle from the shelves in the back of the closet, and piled them on the threadbare armchair beside the bed.

"That's good," Lori said briskly, efficiently stripping the wet spread and Marilee's soaked things from under her patient with the minimum of disruption. "Now go make us a pot of coffee. And shut the door on your way out, Ethan. I need to finish getting her undressed. An audience is the last thing she needs."

As he left, he decided Lori had to be referring to Homer, since *he* had been trying his best not to look anywhere near the bed. He found it tough enough listening to Marilee's whimpers and moans; he didn't want the image of her writhing in agony imprinted in his mind, too. Enough ghosts already lived there to last him two lifetimes.

Just as he'd suspected, Homer had resumed his post at the doorway and was continuing to crane his neck for a better view. Firmly pushing him out and toward the warmth of the stove, Ethan shut the bedroom door behind him, leaving the women to their business. Nevertheless, any irritation he felt toward the old-timer was offset by a stronger surge of gratitude.

"Appreciate what you did for my sister," he said, moving toward the kitchen area of the large efficiency-style room. To prove it, he located a bottle of whiskey and a glass from a cabinet. But once he'd set them on the coffee table before the stove, he ignored his companion, preferring instead to pace.

He felt like a trapped bear. A lousy conversationalist at the best of times, he saw no reason to pretend otherwise now—especially not to someone who seemed to suffer from a similar malady. Moving helped, so he piled another few pieces of wood in the stove, and then remembered to put the kettle of water on the propane stove in the kitchen area for instant coffee. All the while, he brooded over what Marilee had confided to him.

How he wished Clay Taylor were still alive. He would have like the opportunity to strangle the last breath out of that sanctimonious, self-serving creep, and hang the consequences!

Poor Marilee. He should have done more for her, tried harder to teach her about men and things. How he'd let her down.

They didn't have to wait long for the screams; they began well before he made it back to the bedroom with the steaming water, a basin, and his small inventory of towels. With Marilee's gut-wrenching cries piercing his eardrums, he raced from the bedroom, snatched up his jacket, and dashed outside to check if the snow had let up at all.

It hadn't. As he ducked deeper into the upraised collar of his jacket, he began doing more than hoping for the helicopter to come. For the first time since Vietnam, he prayed.

Every few minutes he went out to check again. He even took a moment to run to the bunkhouse and tell John Mountain of the situation.

After a while, it did look as if there might be a slowing of the wind and snow, but he still saw no sign of the chopper. It was later, maybe after his third trip into the bedroom, that he realized Homer had vanished, along with the bottle of booze.

Ethan accepted the revelation with a philosophical shrug. Who could fault the old buzzard for pulling up stakes? Hell, if given the option, he would make tracks himself.

Less than an hour later, Marilee screamed his name, and he ran to her side. He let her grip his hand, mumble incoherent things...whatever she needed to do, he stayed with her. It soon amazed him how anyone with chewed-to-the-quick nails like hers could create such deep furrows and scratches in his work-roughened skin. But he also knew he would have suffered much more, anything, for his kid sister. Through the entire ordeal, and feeling thoroughly inadequate, he wiped her feverish brow again and again with a towel dampened in a snow-cooled bowl of water; he promised everything would be all right;
and he kept snapping at Lori Bains, "How much longer, damn it?"

Then everything started happening at once. First there was the faint sound of the approaching helicopter, sweetly underscoring Lori's cry, "Here we go!" followed soon afterward by the announcement "It's a girl, Marilee! It's a girl!"

Ethan wanted to charge outside and guide in the rescue team, but Marilee stopped him. Gripping his hand with a new and different panic, she rasped, "I want to name her Darcy, Ethan. After Mama. Is that okay?"

She was asking *him?* "Sure, kiddo. Whatever you want."

He patted her thin shoulder, ready to promise her anything. "You rest. We'll have you settled comfortably in a hospital in no time."

"Wait!" Again she halted his escape. "Promise me. Promise me if something…anything should happen, you'll take care of her. *You* raise her, Ethan."

He didn't want so much as the germ of that idea to settle in her mind. Didn't she understand he was the last person to be asked to take on such a responsibility? "Nothing's going to happen to you. Don't get yourself all riled up."

"*Promise,* Ethan. You don't know what it's been like for me. Don't let those people get their hands on my baby. Please!"

Lori paused in caring for the newborn and stared. The hum of the approaching helicopter grew into a wall-shaking vibration. Ethan knew he needed to get outside and help or the crew might miss them. Always conserving, he'd only had electricity brought in a few years ago, primarily for the refrigerator and they didn't have any outdoor floodlights. Hell, he didn't even own a traditional lamp yet.

He made the only decision he could. "I promise, honey. Now hush," he added, with a wink and a false grin.

Finally succeeding in easing his fingers from her relentless grasp, he ran like hell. Once outside, he discovered John Mountain had heard the approach, too, and was setting out flares. Together they guided the helicopter in for a safe, if not quick, landing.

In several more minutes, Ethan learned there wouldn't be room for him to accompany Marilee to the hospital. Not if Lori went. What saved him from a new despair was learning that the crew said weather conditions demanded they head straight down to Whitehorn, instead of attempting to reach Helena or Butte.

The closer location was good news to him and, grateful, he found the generosity to tell the nurse that at the moment his sister needed another woman more than a useless big lug like him. Assuring Marilee that he would follow right behind them in his truck, he waved and grinned at her. Then slamming the door, he backed away from the revving aircraft.

By the time he arrived in town the snow had stopped, and six new inches covered the already white landscape. At Whitehorn Memorial Hospital, he parked near the emergency entrance and loped inside. It was well past midnight, and he felt beyond tired—but foolishly cheerful, too. He couldn't get over the miracle he'd participated in. His little sister had given birth to her own baby. That made him an uncle, certified and guaranteed. Who would have figured it?

Just beyond the sliding glass doors, he found Lori waiting for him. It took only a glance at her bloodshot, haunted eyes for the happiness inside him to shatter as if he'd run straight into a pane of glass.

"No."

She took a deep, shaky breath. "Ethan. Come sit down. We need to talk."

"Where's Marilee?"

"She…she didn't make it."

The words didn't register. He refused to let them. He told himself that what Lori meant was that they'd needed to transport his sister to another facility. *That's it. She being such a runt, the doctors probably wanted to make sure—*

"She suffered a postpartum hemorrhage while in transit. Are you listening to me? Ethan!"

What was he supposed to say? Didn't Lori realize she'd just sabotaged the last of his sanity? "Sweet Jesus."

"Please understand. The first hour after delivery is

always the most dangerous." Her tone and expression grew gentler. "Everyone did what they could. But…she was simply too weak. Far too tired to go through the kind of delivery this birth demanded. I'm so sorry."

He stared at her as though she were speaking to him in some unknown language. She might as well have been; nothing she said made any sense. Marilee had only been thirty-two, for crying out loud! How could she be gone? She'd had everything to look forward to. More. She had a child who needed her…needed a mother.

"You're lying." He ground out the words.

"No, Ethan. Please come sit down. I know this is a shock." He wouldn't, couldn't, listen. He didn't dare.

Lying. She had to be lying.

"Marilee!"

Pushing past Lori, he ran down the hall in search of his sister.

One

"Let us pray…"

You go right ahead, pal. For his part, Ethan didn't feel the least bit like praying, not after this most recent spiritual kick in the teeth. To him the service simply reflected another in a series of injustices to have befallen him and his family and he believed it not only logical, but right, for his heart to have grown as bitter cold as the wind sweeping down from the glaciated Crazy Mountains. In fact, he doubted it was possible for a man to get more hostile than he felt.

He shifted his gaze from the alpine backdrop and stared at the spray of carnations on Marilee's casket, already shriveling in the devastating cold. But no matter how hard he tried to ignore all the "should haves" that pounded in his head like toppling tombstones, they wouldn't stop coming….

There should have been a way to save his sister.

His newborn niece should have been allowed to know her mama.

Just once, someone he cared about should have a chance at a full, happy life.

No, he didn't buy into the spiritual fertilizer the pastor from First Christian Church was selling. He'd stopped being that gullible years ago.

Someone cleared his throat, and he glanced up to see virtually everyone on the other side of the casket watching him with varying degrees of wariness and dislike. The Taylor coalition. He scanned the two and a half, nearly three, dozen people surrounding Noble and Ruth. Marilee's so-called mourners.

Most were strangers to him, out-of-towners, from Billings; and judging by the expressions of indifference and resentment on their faces, he would wager the majority had never said more than a dozen words to her in her entire life. Except for Melissa Avery North, who owned Whitehorn's Hip Hop Café, where Marilee had worked before marrying Clay Taylor. She'd been good to Marilee—but Charlie Avery's kid had her own reasons for casting *him* venomous looks.

The rest had to be friends and business acquaintances of her in-laws—a bunch who believed attending funerals was the politically and socially correct thing to do. Considering the number of wreaths and arrangements scattered around, Ethan guessed they'd also sent the prerequisite toasters and can openers to the wedding. Well, the hypocrites had better not get any ideas about sending any sterling-silver baby dishes and junk for Darcy, or he would be doing something besides staring them down. They might find it embarrassing to be asked questions like "Where were you when Marilee was being bullied and heaven-knew-what by her husband?"

A fluttering movement caught his attention. It was the

funeral director, waving at him and indicating the single red rose he'd been handed when he first arrived. The pantomiming and wagging of eyebrows finally jogged his memory. The show was over. They expected him to put the flower on the casket and beat it so everyone else could get back to Billings for the reception the Taylors were giving, which would probably be written off somehow as a business expense against Taylor Construction Company, Inc.

Far be it from him to hold up things. He'd said his real goodbye to Marilee earlier this morning, at the funeral parlor.

He approached the coffin, the snow and frozen ground crunching beneath his boots, and set the rose between two of the pink carnations. The contrast startled him; it reminded him of blood on skin…of why and how she'd died. Swallowing hard, he turned away, only to be trapped by Kate Randall's direct gaze.

She stood half hidden by a hedge of evergreens, as if unsure whether she had a right to be on his side. As far as he was concerned, she didn't. If she belonged anywhere, it was over with the rest of that self-righteous bunch. Noble and Ruth would welcome her with open arms; after all, money and power rarely avoided the opportunity to rub elbows with judicial clout. That was especially true now, with Marilee gone and Darcy's future in limbo. But his bitterness became muddled confusion when he saw the concern and compassion in Kate's clear gray eyes.

What was going on? Weeks ago, if Rafe Rawlings had been a more creative or coercive cop, and there hadn't been scheduling problems, she would have been the one to preside over his murder trial, instead of Matthews. She was certainly capable of such cool dispassion; they didn't call her the Hanging Judge behind her back for nothing. As a result, he had difficulty accepting this performance.

But something still reined in his impulse to strike out at her and he knew what it was. History. Theirs.

Once, in a more innocent time, she'd been his best friend's girl; back a lifetime ago, when she'd wore her hair in a long braid, instead of that prim twist he hated. Try as he did to forget it, memories of those moments the three of them had shared stuck in his consciousness like fresh flypaper. So did the promise he'd once made to Wayne about her.

Damn it all, why couldn't he put all that to rest? She'd proved she didn't need anyone and could take care of herself. Hell, it would take a gun held to his head to make him admit it, but even he stayed a bit in awe of the woman and what she'd accomplished thus far in her life.

Miserable and resentful, he passed her, careful to keep his head down and his stride long. But he hadn't covered much ground before he heard her lighter step behind him. He let her follow, fuming about her nerve. Only when he reached his mud-splattered pickup did he swing around and practically snarl, *"What?"*

"Would you mind some company?"

"What do you think?"

His caustic tone and glare didn't seem to faze her at all. "I'd like to talk to you, Ethan."

"Can't imagine about what…unless your boy wonder Rawlings has cooked up some new theory about how I killed Charlie Avery and you want to find out if it'll stick this time."

The stinging-cold wind whipped free several strands of her dark blond hair and dragged them across her eyes. With leather-gloved hands, she brushed them away, but she didn't shiver, although her slim wool coat and scarf appeared more suitable for Sunday church than snow and near-gale-force winds. Her dressy boots were equally impractical, and it annoyed him to remember what slender feet and ankles she had.

"Don't be an ass, Ethan. I've never been the enemy."

He almost laughed, as much at her opinion of their relationship as at his weakness for making promises he couldn't keep—to a dead man. "Could have fooled me."

She stepped closer. He gave her points for that. Normally women avoided him. That had been the rule long before his arrest. Since his release, things had only grown worse. What made the movement more impressive was that no other single woman he'd ever known—at least none under the age of eighty—had dared to go out in public without wearing full war paint. But, as usual, Kate followed her own rules and stood before him almost bare-faced; what was more, he saw no visible sign of self-consciousness. He couldn't help but admire her for that, as well—and note again that, while not magazine-beautiful, she had a clean, honest something that, combined with her inner strength and professional notoriety, made her a person to be reckoned with. On a good day, he tried to steer clear of her; this was nowhere near a good day.

"I know this is a difficult time for you."

He steeled himself against that calm, low tone that reminded him of brushed suede and quiet moments at sunset. "Do you?"

"Nevertheless, I think it's important that we speak."

Had he described her as strong? Stubborn, he corrected, shrugging deeper into the collar of his down jacket, and tugging the brim of his hat lower. "I have to get home."

"Then I'll follow you there."

He frowned. At home there were things he didn't want her to see, not that he believed for an instant she didn't already know he had the baby.

"At this time the court has no authority to take Marilee's child away from you," she told him, as though his concern were a spoken thing between them. "Nor would I consider it. Yet."

That one economical admission convinced Ethan that he needed to give her the benefit of the doubt. He would be a fool to think Noble had been sitting still and twiddling his thumbs since being chased off the Double N. Ethan wanted to find out what to expect next. Kate's implication that he wouldn't be kept in the dark deserved a gesture on his part. Just as long as she didn't ask for his trust.

"Sure you want to miss the spread over at the Taylors?" he asked, a little annoyed at himself for yielding so quickly. "I hear they're sparing no expense to console all those heartbroken folks who came to mourn my sister."

"I'm positive. Besides, I had my coffee at home, before I checked on the horses."

Ethan seasoned his smile with sarcasm. "Good move, Your Honor. Remind me that you come from the working class, too." As if he ever forgot that, although her learned father had been a judge, it had been primarily her aunt Beryl who raised her, and who was the one to build the reputation of Shadow Ranch as a source for unique saddle horses. The woman had possessed one of the best instincts for character in animals this side of the Rockies, and had been known equally for her gentle hand in bringing out their most favorable qualities. An individualist of the first order, Beryl had never given a damn what people thought of her, and not only had no one dared to call her a spinster to her face, they had never dared accuse her of being a tough businesswoman, either.

Kate was a chip off the old block in more ways than one, except that as much as she loved the animals, the law was her passion. She left most of the training to her foreman, Jorge Cantu, just as she left the general care of her home to his wife, Eva. But there was no denying that she put in her time helping out with the endless chores that went along with ranching. Another reason why he wasn't surprised to see her gray eyes chill to a flinty silver at his remark.

"Don't make me regret coming to see you, Ethan."

Because he knew she'd let him push and provoke farther than most people dared. He shrugged. "C'mon, then, if you're that set on it."

He watched her on and off the entire twenty-five-mile trip from Whitehorn to his place. It helped him keep control of the emotions that kept threatening to burn his eye sockets deeper and a new orifice in his belly. Marilee was gone and he had to accept that. The time they'd lost couldn't be salvaged, nor could the unspoken words of concern and caring be voiced. He would never forget, and maybe he didn't deserve to forgive himself for jumping to too many conclusions; but he couldn't afford to mope about it now. He had new worries to deal with, new responsibilities.

He sighed and scanned the horizon. Since the storm a few days ago, central Montana had a new, cleaner layer of snow blanketing the land, and it visually softened the alternately rolling, then sharp, terrain. As he drove west out of town, he eased around the Crazies, as he called them, the fifty-million-year-old formations that were considered a good twenty million years younger than some of the giants beyond them. To him, the Crazy Mountains always signified freedom; the freedom he felt like a sigh of relief when he was putting civilization in his rearview mirror.

Despite the lingering clouds, the sharp wind off the mountains, along with the traffic, had done a good job of eating much of the packed snow and ice off the roads. It was time to remove the tire chains. Maybe he would get around to it this afternoon. Hopefully. It all depended on how long the twig slept. He could ask John Mountain to tackle the chore for him, but the sooner he got himself organized and adjusted to the changes in his life, the better.

It amazed him how, after only two days of having a newborn under his roof, all his old routines were shot to hell—and it wasn't because of any fear in handling the kid. Shoot, he'd been eleven when his mother gave birth to Marilee, and because she'd had a rough time with the pregnancy, his mother had relied on *him* to fill in wherever possible. If that meant pacing in front of the fireplace with a colicky baby half the night in order for her to get a few hours sleep, he'd done it. He'd changed his share of diapers, too. The way he saw it, there wasn't anything a six-pound-seven-ounce baby could serve up that a calf hadn't presented to him first.

But he was no longer eleven, and Vietnam had changed his sleeping habits; as a result, what rest he usually managed was being cut back by the twenty-inch bundle of energy he'd taken into his home. On the upside, Darcy was already proving to be a cute kid, and while he would have taken a kick in the ribs from an ornery cow before admitting as much, it gave him a strange peace to sit in the recliner with her at night and watch her sleep.

Some might call him a contradiction, but he saw nothing illogical about enjoying having a baby around, and at the same time finding adults more of a hassle than they were worth. To him, life was best if kept simple. As with cattle, babies had fairly basic needs, needs he found easy enough to fulfill.

Grown-ups were another matter entirely. They insisted on complicating everything, and seasoning those complications with ulterior motives and selfishness. Give him solitude over that bunk anyday. His life might not be perfect, but it beat living with ulcers and alimony.

Almost forty minutes after leaving Whitehorn, and a few miles beyond the entrance of Kate's Shadow Ranch, he drove over the cattle guards marking the Double N. Years ago, his mother had insisted on the abbreviation, after his father—unsure of their future as cattle ranchers—dubbed their spread No Name Yet. His mother had been horrified, fearing people would laugh them all the way across the Great Divide, back into Idaho and a tedious existence as potato farmers. She'd never shared his father's sly sense of humor; and despite her willingness to work hard, she'd also been vain about her hands. An accomplished seamstress, she'd much preferred doing custom sewing and alterations after a long day of helping with the stock, if it meant avoiding those potato fields. She'd been an ambitious woman, and Ethan doubted she would have liked the way he'd abandoned her plans for the place.

As he parked before the house, Ethan saw the old homestead through a new perspective—that of a man with an instant family—and his mood grew grimmer. Maybe the compact cabin did look neat enough, but only because there wasn't much to it. It hardly presented the kind of environment wherein a little girl could flourish. The new coat of brown paint he and John Mountain had added last spring helped some, although he now wished he'd chosen a less depressing color. But there still wasn't a tree, or even a shrub, within twenty acres of the house, barn or bunkhouse. If he thought back to how he used to race for the forest at every opportunity with Wayne, he decided anyone with an ounce of Walker blood in him would crave something green and alive to look at while growing up.

Something besides cattle, holding pens and a pair of dust-coated, weather-wrinkled cowpokes. Why not? Maybe, when Darcy got older, she'd like to read while cradled in the arms of a tree. Kate had, when she was a girl.

As she parked beside him, he decided he would take the matter up with John Mountain. It would be a short conversation, but the cowboy had once said that his mother had been gifted with a green thumb. Hopefully some of it had rubbed off on her son, Ethan thought, easing out of his truck. Maybe together they would figure out what variety of tree grew fast enough to keep pace with a little girl.

Kate emerged from her four-wheel-drive vehicle, and once again he found himself noting that she moved with the energy of someone who knew where she was going. In boots she stood an inch short of being eye-to-eye with him. It made him recall that when she was barefoot, her nose would only reach his chin. He hadn't seen her barefoot in…well, almost as long as it'd been since he'd seen her hair down. It didn't seem right or smart to be remembering things like that, especially when he didn't have a clue as to what the heck she had on her mind.

"This feels like stepping back in time," she said, a faint smile on her face as she glanced around.

He hadn't expected her to resist commenting upon the lack of changes. "I know it needs work. Been thinking about it myself. Marilee was always telling me…telling me…" To put in a vegetable garden. Something. *Anything.* "I'll see to it once the ground thaws."

"I'm sorry about Marilee."

Ethan nodded, because he didn't want to risk exposing the true depth of his emotions. It stunned him how deeply he felt the loss of his sister. Because of the eleven-year age difference, he'd felt like both brother *and* father to her.

They'd lost their old man when a freak lightning strike killed him and his mount. Their mother, unable to cope with more than one role in the family, had relied on Ethan not only to watch over Marilee, but to keep the ranch semi-operational, as well.

When he was barely a year out of high school, their situation had become particularly tough when his draft number came up. He could have gotten a deferment by citing the family's hardship status. But Wayne—by then a junior in college—had received his notice, too, and despite being an honor student, had wanted to go. No way had Ethan been willing to let his best friend, his boyhood idol, go into the jungles without him. And although he'd arranged for most of his pay to be sent back home, he still felt as if he'd let Marilee down.

Now they were all gone…his family, his friend. He was alone, except for little Darcy, and…well, he didn't know where Kate thought she fit in.

"Do you think I could see the baby?"

He stared at her for a moment, then felt ashamed for his hesitation and doubt. Whatever their differences, Kate Randall wasn't the sneaky type. If she had anything on her mind, she would come straight out and tell him. He didn't have to worry about letting her have contact with his niece. "Why not? John Mountain's been keeping an eye on her while I was in town."

He led the way inside, where the warmth from the stove and the tantalizing aroma of homemade stew slowly simmering told him that, as he'd expected, the industrious and self-reliant John Mountain had been busy doing more than baby-sitting.

The smaller man had been with him since shortly after his own tour overseas. Ethan had hired him as a result of their brief, emotional discussion about the experience. At the time, he'd wondered about his decision; not because he questioned the ex-tunnel rat's ability to adjust, but because the guy stood only inches over five feet, and was as thin as he was short. Ethan's concern had been whether or not the cowboy could pull his weight.

His doubts, however, had soon been obliterated. John Mountain had proved he worked harder inch for inch and pound for pound than any man Ethan had ever known. That was why he addressed his employee by his full name and made sure everyone else did, too. John Mountain was a rock of stability and support, and the ranch wouldn't have survived this long, or this well, without him.

At the moment, though, the cowboy made an amusing picture, sitting in the middle of the living room floor, surrounded by parts of the crib Ethan had dug out of storage. Without the hat he rarely took off except when sleeping and bathing, John Mountain's balding head reflected the glow from the lamp he'd drawn closer as he pieced things together.

He looked up, and his wise, shockingly old eyes grew watchful. "Boss. Ma'am...I mean Your Honor."

"Kate is fine, John Mountain. This isn't jury duty," she replied, with a warm smile. "How've you been?"

"Good, thanks." He shot a questioning look at Ethan, his screwdriver not quite still in his hand.

"Kate asked to see the baby," Ethan told him.

He was aware that John Mountain tended to be shy and nervous around women, not to mention the law. Unfortunately, Kate represented a powerful dose of both. Ethan had to struggle to ignore his own overawareness as he removed his hat and coat and hung them on the wall rack beside the door. He then had to pretend indifference as Kate unwound her scarf and slipped out of her wool coat, until he could hang up them, too.

Her dress presented more challenge. It was also black, and by most standards demure, but he couldn't help noticing how it seemed intent on caressing her subtle curves. When he thought he would have to face her in court a few weeks ago, he'd thought he might conquer his dread by trying to diminish her psychological power over him by imagining what she was wearing beneath her grim black robe. Now he decided he'd been fortunate that the confrontation hadn't taken place. His strategy would have failed, miserably.

Damn it, why couldn't the woman at least look her age? I sure as hell do.

"I have to check on a few things," John Mountain announced, breaking into Ethan's thoughts. The man rose with his usual agility. "Finish this later. Uh…the stew? It's about ready. Help yourselves."

"I won't be intruding that long," Kate told him as he headed toward the back door. "But it was good to see you again, John Mountain."

He'd already swept up his things from the back rack and set his hat firmly on his head. When he turned back to them, he politely touched the brim, but his eyes remained troubled as they darted from Kate to Ethan. Ethan doubted the man would ever voice the questions in their depths.

"The twig didn't take all her bottle," the cowboy said in lieu of a goodbye. "Reckon you'll hear when she's hungry again."

With that, he slipped out, as quietly as he did most things. In a way, Ethan wished he'd asked him to hang around. The large efficiency-style room seemed to shrink to the size of a coat closet the moment there was only him and Kate left to fill the silence.

"I make him uncomfortable."

"You make most men nervous," Ethan said, having heard enough gossip in town to venture the opinion.

"You included?"

He watched her gaze move over his face and wondered what she saw...and hated himself for caring. "Do you really want to know?"

For a moment, she looked as if she might say "Yes," but she only offered a wry smile and headed toward the baby. "Maybe some things are best left a mystery."

As she crossed over to the tilted-back recliner, which currently served as a bed for the baby, Ethan frowned. He'd never seen her back away from a challenge before. Even when she bent at the waist to peer down at the infant, there was a hesitation, a new tentativeness, in her that was atypical. She looked as if she were trying to figure out something totally foreign to her. Finally, slowly, she crouched beside the chair and sighed.

Ethan edged closer, determined to figure out what was going on, but soon regretted it. He found her tender expression disconcerting, as well. It whispered through him, stirring more old memories, ghostly images he preferred to leave undisturbed, and unanalyzed.

"She's precious."

At least they could agree on that. "Awfully small, though. I was surprised they let me have her as soon as they did."

"I imagine handling her has been somewhat intimidating. But, oh, who could resist? And look at that gorgeous hair... She has Marilee's lovely complexion, too."

He'd never thought of his sister that way, but hearing Kate point it out, he realized Marilee had been pretty, and he'd never told her so. Fighting a new spasm of grief, he retreated to the stove under the pretense of checking on the stew. After stirring it, he shifted the pot to the stack of clay tiles on the corner that he sometimes used as warmers. Kate had already announced she wouldn't be staying long, and it would be some time before his appetite returned.

When the silence grew uncomfortable again, he knew he couldn't put off the question any longer. "What did you want, Kate?" he forced himself to ask.

With a last, almost wistful look at the baby, she rose. But instead of joining him by the stove, she retreated to the front window, where she became a striking silhouette against blue sky and blinding snow. She touched a finger to the frost creeping along one corner of a pane. It once again reminded Ethan of the girl she'd been, her constant fascination with nature, the way she would dwell over a water-smoothened stone found in a creekbed, or the fragile pieces of a bird's egg beneath a tree.

"I was wondering about your plans," she murmured, considering the small peephole the pad of her index finger had burned into the ice.

"Why?" He knew he sounded abrupt, maybe rude; but expecting the inquiry had proved nothing compared to finally hearing it. Bad news was coming; anticipating it strangled what was left of his nerves.

"There's talk down at the café."

"There's always talk at the Hip Hop," he muttered, his mood souring further. "Why do you hang out at that place, anyway? You have Eva to cook for you."

"Sometimes there isn't enough time to go home for lunch. And sometimes I just want a cup of coffee that's not out of one of those awful machines. Besides, my constituents meet there, Ethan. It's the easiest way I know of to learn what's concerning them."

All that interested that bunch was idle, and often vengeful, gossip. That was why he generally avoided the place. That, and who owned it. At any rate, he had no use for hearsay, or the people who spread it. But he knew why Kate had mentioned the place. "So what have you heard about me?"

"Something beyond the usual buzzing and editorializing. Something that smacks of an intentional power play." As if suddenly chilled, she crossed her arms. "It disturbed me, and I wanted to make sure you were aware of it."

Ever skeptical, Ethan lifted an eyebrow. "Should a judge be feeding information to a potential defendant?"

"We've known each other a long time. That has to count for something."

"'Known' is misleading, don't you think?" As he taunted her, he crossed to her side of the room, so that Darcy wouldn't be disturbed by the conversation, which he knew was about to deteriorate. It had to deteriorate, because of who she was and what she had helped put him through by simply existing. "We knew each other because we were in the same grade during our school years. We both *knew* Wayne. But all that's ancient history, and his death changed us forever. It damn sure made it easy for you not to have to deal with me anymore."

That seemed to startle, even annoy, her, and when he stopped before her, although she shifted to lean flush against the door, her gaze held a rebuke. "Believe it or not, I've always considered you a friend, Ethan."

"Sure you have. Because we have so much in common, right?"

Kate shook her head. This was going as badly as she'd feared it might. Granted, she'd expected Ethan to be surprised, even wary of her, at first. He'd always been a loner, and getting arrested and indicted for Charlie

Avery's murder had intensified that quality in him. But the trial was over and he'd been acquitted. Maybe she couldn't expect him to understand what she'd done on his behalf, but did he have to work overtime at being hostile? All that energy needed to be redirected to what might lie before him.

"Why are you being like this?" For her part, she preferred to continue seeing him as Wayne's unlikely best friend, not the caustic stranger he'd become. Sure, there had always been something enigmatic and taciturn about Ethan, even before Vietnam. But she'd approved of and been intrigued by the glimpses she'd had of the person inside.

What would he say if she admitted that he was the only other man besides Wayne that she'd been *both* physically and intellectually attracted to? It was so ironic; after all, the two of them had been physical and emotional opposites. Where Wayne had been fair and brawny, Ethan was dark, taller, and possessed a craggy wiriness. Wayne had been sunny-natured. Ethan was serious, rarely speaking, even when you could tell he had something to say. Wayne had treated her as if she were his sun and a princess all wrapped into one. *If* she'd ever caught Ethan looking at her, it was anyone's guess what he'd been thinking.

But this was hardly the time to dwell on what had been. She'd come because she smelled a legal problem in the wind, one that bore a stench offensive to her respect for right and wrong. If her hunch was correct, the situation would demand her full attention in order to stop it. She would do as much for anyone; and if it meant butting heads with a man who'd forgotten how to accept having someone care about him, then that was his problem.

"Come on, Ethan, answer me."

"*Why* am I being like this? Don't you think I have a right

to be a little bent out of shape?" he replied, seething. "For one thing, I've just buried my sister!"

"This is about more than Marilee. You're angry because of the trial. Ethan…don't you realize that it could have been much worse?" When he ignored her, she made a disparaging sound. "You're thinking Matthews took over your case for me because I was whining about being overscheduled and didn't want it. That's not true. I did. But Harlan Collins is a sharp D.A., and do you know what a public fiasco he could have made if he got the tiniest hint that I had a prejudicial interest in seeing your case thrown out of court?"

Ethan scowled at her.

"Yes, that's right, thrown out. I believed you didn't belong on trial, and I did the only thing possible not to hurt your case. I did some behind-closed-doors negotiating with Matthews, and in exchange for his messy domestic-violence case, he took you on. For pity's sake! Do you realize if you'd ended up with Judge Lessing, you'd probably be in prison right now? The man's a dinosaur who likes female lawyers less than he does short-tempered mavericks. You and Raeanne wouldn't have stood a chance with him."

Of course, Kate knew from conversations with public defender Raeanne Martin that she hadn't been Ethan's choice, but rather his single option when he refused to cooperate in his own defense. Afterward, despite being grateful for what Raeanne had done for him, Ethan had remained cool toward the young but talented attorney, because she'd gotten engaged to Rafe Rawlings. Kate could see he was annoyed at being reminded of all that, too.

"What do you want, my undying gratitude, Your Honor?"

His surly tone made her want to shake him; however, the sound of the baby stirring restlessly warned her to check her temper. She glanced around him at the infant before whispering, "Good grief, Ethan, when did you become a snob?"

"Me?" he whispered back with equal fervor.

"Yes, you! You're subjecting me to reverse prejudice and I don't like it." She watched his icy blue eyes flash with renewed warning, his craggy features grow as threatening as the great mountain range in whose shadow they lived, but she refused to be intimidated. "I may have a law degree and be a county circuit judge, but that hasn't changed who I am inside." Disappointments and heartbreak, maybe, but not her job. She'd refused to let it. She decided to add with a dry smile, "I'm still the person you used to laugh at when we were kids."

He seemed honestly taken aback by that. "I never laughed at you."

"Think harder. You laughed. And being the tomboy I was, I gave you adequate reason to, what with always trying to keep up with you and Wayne, no matter what you were up to. To this day, I can barely resist stopping on my way home from court to join some kids in a snowball fight—though I have to admit, it's not a bad way to ease a day's stress. And do you know that when I'm wearing jeans, I automatically check to see if an integral seam is holding, despite it being years since I slid down a fifteen-foot gully to help rescue one of your wayward calves?"

The memory flickered in his eyes. "Okay. So I jumped to some unfair conclusions. I still don't know what it is that you're driving at."

"You're doubting my motives for being here. You don't believe I'm a friend."

"Look…" He gestured with exasperation. "Back in the old days—neighbors or not, school or not—you would never have hung around me if it hadn't been for Wayne.

Why not admit it? Hell, almost every conversation we ever had stayed mostly between you two."

"Because you were shy."

He snorted. "Right. I just wasn't as fast a thinker as you two were, that's all."

Kate leaned back against the door again, this time crossing her arms beneath her breasts. "Buffalo chips. Wayne used to say that you were one of the sharpest people he knew—and one of the most avid readers."

"Paperback fiction, Kate. That's not exactly law journals and legal briefs."

She glanced over at the coffee table, piled high with familiar publications. "What about those trade magazines?"

"That's work."

"As are my law books and the rest. Trust me, those aren't what I take with me into the tub at night when I'm craving a long soak."

For one instant, she thought he might ask her what she did read there. Instead, he cleared his throat and retreated to the kitchen. "I need a drink. You want a cup of coffee or something?"

Intrigued by the tension she noted in his flannel-clad shoulders, Kate followed. "Actually, I'd love a beer, if you have one to spare." She knew it wasn't noon yet, but she was determined to keep obliterating the false images he seemed intent on having of her. Besides, her throat was as dry as that gully she'd once slid into, thanks to the funeral that had made her ache so badly for him and that poor innocent across the room. Unfortunately, one beer wouldn't stop her from worrying for him, or keep his eyes from looking so haunted and bitter.

If her request surprised him, he hid it well. "Whatever you say." He brought her a bottle from the refrigerator, watched as she screwed off the cap and took a long swallow. The corners of his mouth turned downward. "So what's next? Are you planning to match me beer for beer?"

"If that's what it'll take for you to stop biting my head off and start listening to me."

"All right, if you're that determined to have your say, get it over with. I'm in trouble again, aren't I?"

"Between what I heard in town and what I saw pass between you and Noble Taylor at the funeral, I'd say that's a good guess, yes."

Ethan squared his chin. "Let him glare, and let him threaten. It's not going to change anything."

"Is it true what I heard about you two actually having argued?"

"He first telephoned me at the hospital. I'm not sure who called to let him know what had happened, but I can tell you that his timing was lousy and what he had to say was worse. I thought I'd made my position—along with my opinion of him—fairly clear, but the next day he drove out here."

"Ostensibly to recover Clay's car."

"You heard that one?"

"Stories are spreading all over town, Ethan."

His expression darkened. "I'll bet. But the car was right where Marilee skidded to a stop, not hidden in my barn. And I'll tell you something else—he won't trespass again without a bodyguard and an attorney."

Kate dreaded having to ask, but she wanted facts. "What did he say to set you off?"

"Just seeing his smarmy, self-righteous face is enough to do that." Ethan's disgusted tone mirrored his expression. "But to answer your question, he didn't waste any words of condolences, he simply announced the gospel according to Taylor."

"He told you that he thought it best if he and Ruth became guardians of the baby, is that it?"

"No, he said they *would* be the legal guardians."

"To which you replied—?"

"We'll see each other in hell first. And I offered him a first-class ticket when he tried to come in here and get her."

Kate winced. She knew Noble Taylor more by reputation than from experience, having only met the man at a few benefits. But she understood the shrewd businessman well enough to know you didn't taunt him. "I'm not condoning his approach, but Marilee was living with them, and they are the baby's legal grandparents. Besides that, Clay's death in that jobsite accident in Whitehorn made Marilee dependent on their support, especially for her prenatal care."

"Are you sure of that?"

The change in his tone, as well as his expression, gave her an uneasy feeling. "What do you mean?"

"When Marilee arrived here the other night, she made it clear she didn't want to go back. She was in too much pain to explain much, but I know fear when I see and hear it."

"Fear? About what? Why didn't she say something sooner?"

"How should I know? Maybe she couldn't. Maybe they made certain she never had the opportunity."

"Are you accusing the Taylors of somehow threatening your sister?" Kate asked the question with care, not certain she wanted to hear the answer.

The skin over Ethan's sharp cheekbones stretched impossibly tight. "Not only did she inform me that her great catch of a husband kept us apart, but she admitted he abused her. Since there was no way the Taylors could have missed that, I have to believe they condoned it, and I will *not* have my niece growing up in an environment like that."

This was all news to Kate, but she couldn't have approved more of his fervent protection of Darcy. The problem would be to substantiate such an accusation. As powerful and aggressive as the Taylors were—which often created its own criticism—she'd never heard anything this disturbing about them.

"What a mess…and the bottom line isn't going to please you, Ethan, but because they're one of the most successful business and social families in the state, when they make noise, people listen. That means if they want their grand-daughter, they've every resource available to fight for her."

"Having money doesn't automatically qualify someone to be a guardian," he snapped, his glance slicing.

"I didn't say it did." Regret and weariness washed over her, and she sighed, wishing there was a way to avoid getting caught in the middle of this situation. All of her causes cost her something, but she had a feeling this one would clean her out emotionally. Yet how could she turn her back on someone who had been such a huge part of her past? How could she ignore Darcy's future?

She massaged the ache building between her eyebrows. "Will you at least tell me exactly what Marilee said to you?"

"Are you asking as that so-called friend or as a judge?"

"Both."

He smiled, only it was tight-lipped and reflected little amusement. "You don't see a conflict of interest, the way you did before?"

"We're not in court…yet." She waited, feeling his gaze sweep over her face, her hair. Vanity made her wish she'd used a little eye shadow and more mascara. It was crazy. She was taking on enough trouble without courting this kind.

"I'll give you this," he murmured reluctantly. "You're the damnedest judge I've ever met."

Sharply aware of the male awareness in his gaze, she pointed at him with the long neck of her bottle. "Save the sweet talk, cowboy. Tell me what I need to know, so I can help you."

He exhaled wearily. "Marilee had to sneak away like a criminal to get out of the house even for a few minutes." His grip on his bottle turned his knuckles white. "Apparently life with her in-laws wasn't any closer to perfect than it had been with Clay. The night she ran away, it was because she was afraid they—and I'm assuming she meant Noble and Ruth—were going to take the baby away from her. That's when she made me promise that if anything happened, I would be the baby's guardian. It was as if she sensed something. As if…as if she knew she wasn't going to pull through." He took another drink, this time nearly polishing off the contents of the bottle. "Okay, Judge, you take it from there. What do you think is going to happen?"

Oh, Ethan. Feeling sick to her stomach, and far less in control than she wanted to be, Kate set her bottle on the counter. How much easier her life would be if for once she would mind her own business, maybe be less of a crusader. *Forget about the quiet, serious rebel who'd gone off to war with the man you loved and come back alone…bitter, and more unapproachable than ever.*

She exhaled a pent-up breath and forced herself to meet his wary gaze. "I think the Taylors will definitely bring in the biggest legal guns they can hire and sue for custody of Marilee's child. I also think that if we don't think of some way to stop that from happening, this time I won't be able to keep you out of my court."

Two

"Fine." Ethan shrugged, hoping he looked more confident than he felt. "I'm not worried. Lori Bains was a witness to everything Marilee said. She'll have to vouch for that much, no matter what else she thinks of me. When the Taylors realize they don't have a leg to stand on, they'll be more than willing to back off."

"Will they?" Kate shook her head. "For such a bright man, you're sounding disturbingly naive. Just how apathetic do you think people are?"

He bristled at the idea that she saw him as uninformed. "Given the state of the world in general, not to mention the clowns this country continually votes into political office, I'm surprised you can ask that."

"We're talking about the welfare of a child."

"I'm aware of that," he growled.

"I hope you at least had the foresight to get Lori's statement in writing and her signature witnessed?"

His confidence took a nosedive. "Well, no. But as I said, she—"

"Is simply one witness. And as respected as she may be, under clever cross-examination she could be coerced into sounding as if she'd been made to say what she did to you under duress." Kate tapped a short, unpolished fingernail on the kitchen counter. "Listen, Ethan, there are times when even a written, witnessed statement might not be enough. For example, if it's been only weeks since the principal party has been through an arrest and a murder trial," she added, with a meaningful lift of her tawny eyebrows.

Ethan knew all too well what she was driving at, and his blood pressure soared to its limit. *"I was acquitted, damn it!"*

In the pulsating silence that followed, Darcy uttered a weak, though lengthy, sob. Exchanging guilty looks, he and Kate turned their attention toward the baby in time to see her tiny hands flailing in panic. Silently calling himself several kinds of a jerk for losing his temper, Ethan hurried to the recliner. He hovered close, began to reach for her, then hesitated as the child once again settled down.

Relieved, he backtracked to Kate. But he didn't have a clue as to what to say to her.

"I'm making a total mess of this," she said, offering him an easy way out.

He chose not to take it. "I shouldn't have yelled."

"You yelled because I made you lose your temper. Good grief, Ethan, I'm not so out of touch that I don't know a newborn needs peace and quiet."

Why were they arguing over who should bear the blame, when the kid was already asleep again? "This is nuts," he muttered, frustrated that she could make him feel like a tongue-tied, awkward teenager, just as she had in the old days.

"You're right." Kate set down her bottle and faced him squarely. "What I really came here to say is that I believe in you. If you're intent on fulfilling your promise to Marilee, I want to help you achieve that goal. No doubt it will be in Darcy's best interests, and a good thing for you, too. But please, don't forget that facts are facts, and that, right or wrong, the odds are stacking high against you. It makes focusing and planning much easier if we're starting from a point of clarity, as well as honesty."

Ethan bowed his head, to hide his embarrassment as much as his anxiety for his niece's future. "You don't have to sugarcoat things or beat around the bush. Just say I have a bad reputation."

"Bad? No," Kate drawled, eyeing him with a mixture of thoughtfulness and amusement. "The group of teenagers I had to threaten with reform school earlier this week for vandalizing their high school gym and affixing an unusually generous appendage to the team mascot were *bad*. You're a grown man who's not only built himself a reputation for being antisocial, but fiercely aggressive, even dangerous."

"Dangerous my— That mess with Charlie Avery was twenty-seven years ago! What's it going to take to convince people that the issue is over? Dead!"

"Does that include your feelings for Lexine Baxter? Are they dead, too?"

He stiffened. "I said all I had to say on the subject while on the witness stand."

"Well, under the circumstances, I thought it best to miss out on that. I had to settle for word-of-mouth reports. But may I remind you, mister, that it's a little late to get sensitive? What's more, you opened one big can of worms with that testimony, considering our mystery girl has vanished off the face of the planet." Kate grimaced in distaste. "Talk about dropping a bomb. *Lexine Baxter!* Good grief, Ethan, I could believe Charlie Avery falling for that overpainted, conniving... But you?"

"We were sixteen, Kate." And, if truth be known, it had been sheer loneliness, and having to watch *her,* so sweet and young, but already nuts about Wayne Kincaid, that made him susceptible to Lexine's innocent smiles and experienced ways. "Ancient history," he said, looking away.

Kate uttered a soft sound of disbelief. "All I can say is that you'd better get used to her name coming up again, along with the rest of the past, no matter how unpleasant it is to discuss, because your personal life is all Noble Taylor's attorney will talk about during the hearing." She leaned toward him. "If Raeanne didn't spell it out for you, allow me.

"Your acquittal for Charlie's murder was hardly a vindication, Ethan. It simply means the D.A. failed to show a preponderance of guilt, leaving the jury unable to conclude 'beyond a reasonable doubt' that you killed him. But that also means a fair percentage of the population continues to believe you did go after Charlie when you discovered he was making a move on Lexine—and/or beating up on her—and that you killed him."

Ethan shook his head once. "The one person I felt like striking out against was myself. And that was after I discovered that no-account cattle-rustling jerk was missing, along with Lexine and the money she'd conned out of me."

"Mmm... That sounds good—except there was also the little matter of Nick Dean's car exploding during his investigation of Charlie's remains, and the dynamite being traced back to you."

Ethan stared deep into her clear gray eyes, and looked for a hint of what she believed. As with that horse-trading

Aunt Beryl of hers, with Kate, sometimes you didn't quite know. But although he wasn't thrilled with her in-depth knowledge of his sorry adventures at the hands of White-horn's judicial system, he felt a strong sense of relief that he didn't see condemnation or fear in her, either.

"In other words, you don't think the good citizens of this county are going to stand by and let Marilee's baby stay in the home of a man they believe is a cold-blooded murderer, regardless of what my sister's wishes may have been?" he asked quietly.

"That's exactly right."

He had to shut his eyes to stop the sensation that he was dropping down a bottomless well. "What a fool I've been. You must think I'm the densest thing on two feet."

"I've never thought anything of the kind!"

"Then you should have, because somehow I never figured one situation would affect the other. Hell, I didn't think I needed to do any legal paperwork to keep Darcy. Marilee was over eighteen when our mother died, so I didn't have to deal with that then. As for now, I thought since I was Marilee's closest relative, I would automatically become the baby's guardian. Instead, you're telling me I have to get permission from *you*."

"From the court," Kate replied, clasping her hands together, as if pleading for his patience. "Look, the law tries to cover as much ground as possible, but it's not always up-to-date with citizens' needs, let alone changing social mores. And it's certainly not always fair to all parties."

Ethan wasn't concerned about anyone but his niece. "The point is that Marilee was over twenty-one, and she said what she wanted for her child before a witness. Don't her wishes count for something?"

"Of course they do, and if I have anything to say about

things, they will." Kate laid her hand on his forearm. "But isn't it better to know what you're up against, instead of walking around as if you were wearing blinders?"

For a moment, he couldn't answer, because he was too aware of her touch. Women didn't often make such gestures toward him; as she'd said before, his reputation didn't encourage it. Not from nice women, anyway; and after he realized the truth about Lexine, he'd kept his distance from the not-so-nice ones.

The warmth of her fingers went through him like a late-night whiskey after a long day in the saddle, and a longer evening hunkered over paperwork. It made him resent the flannel between his skin and hers, and reminded him how long it had been since he'd felt a craving for sex, and how much longer since he'd done something about it.

But, damn it all, this was Kate! Never mind that she was a judge and way out of his league, in more ways than he wanted to count. She'd been his best friend's girl. The sweet torment of Wayne's life, because of the three-year age difference at a point when it mattered.

However, she'd become *his* torment, too. It had been hard dealing with the flashes of awareness of her, back when they were barely more than kids. Worse had been having to hide them and his guilty feelings from her and Wayne. He didn't need a crash course in it now. Everyone knew Kate had never married because Wayne had been *it* for her.

He almost exhaled with relief when she withdrew her hand.

"Excuse me," she murmured, in a voice he didn't recognize. "Apparently I'm wrong."

Only when she started for the door did he realize that she'd spoken, let alone what she'd meant. She'd been waiting for him to thank her for her confidence in him, and for him to assure her that he would try to be more patient. "No—wait. Kate!"

He caught her arm before she could reach for her coat. He didn't know if it was centrifugal force or nervous energy; but between her momentum and his, they ended up overcompensating, nearly slamming into each other. They would have, if he hadn't grasped both of her upper arms to steady her and stop himself.

It brought them close, too close for him to avoid filling his lungs with the scent of her understated yet appealing shampoo—or was it her bath soap? In any case, it reminded him that whimsical spring-flower fragrances had never been for Kathryn Lee Randall. No, this was lusher, something that reminded him of evenings and autumn. Wouldn't she laugh in his face if he told her that?

He let her go, but remained close. "I'm not used to being in the position of having to say 'I'm sorry' or 'thank you.'"

"Don't I know it." She spoke as softly as he had. "Maybe you should try practicing when you're alone, and you can try it out on me when we win you permanent custody of Darcy."

"Is that going to happen?" Despite her dry humor, he found himself afraid to hope, just as he couldn't fully understand why she was willing to help him.

"We'll give it our best shot. Will you let me talk to the Taylors?"

"You'd want to do that?"

"A voice of reason seems safest right now, don't you think? If you approached him with your attorney, or they sent theirs to you, that would only alienate both sides."

His attorney? That was rich. The court might have assigned Raeanne Martin to him for his trial, when he refused to retain one himself; but in truth, hiring an attorney for a full custody battle might make a serious dent in his modest savings. Not wanting to dwell on that before he had to, he asked, "What kind of effect do you think you speaking on my behalf will have?"

"Grating, at first." Her grin was brief but irreverent. "We're not that well acquainted, but Noble does pride himself on keeping in touch with the movers and shakers in Whitehorn as much as those in Billings. He's from the school that believes networking is an asset you add to your financial statement when you're hitting your banker up for the maximum line of credit. One of those I'm-not-cheap-but-I-can-be-had types.

"To answer your question, though, I expect him to be a hard sell. However, I'm hoping that once things are whittled down to the relevant issues, he'll see the wisdom in being more flexible."

Ethan lifted an eyebrow, thinking she'd left out a crucial member of the party. "Mrs. Taylor doesn't get a vote?"

"From what I've seen and heard, Ruth is from the old school. In other words, feminists will come and go, but Ruth will always defer to her husband, because that's what she was taught to do, and he likes it that way."

Which left Ethan with only one question, namely the real reason she was doing this for him. Never mind her reputation as a crusader, and her willingness to stick out her neck for nothing more tangible than principle. He understood her sense of obligation, even to old friendships; and, yes, it was possible that it was all for Marilee and Darcy. But he had an uneasy feeling that this gesture went back to the night, when in a drunken stupor, he'd confessed to her that it should have been Wayne who came back from Nam, instead of him. Although he'd never let himself get that lost in a bottle again, she had also never put herself in a position again where he could repeat the comment. Could this be her way of letting him off the hook?

That choice wasn't hers to make. Not his, either. The right belonged to the one person they'd both loved, the one who would never be back to make a choice either way.

"All right," he began gruffly, knowing something needed to be said. "Just one thing—don't jeopardize your career because of me. That would really tick me off big-time."

To his amazement, she leaned forward and quickly kissed his cheek. "Just keep the faith, Ethan," she murmured. "That's all I ask."

He felt the fleeting caress in strange places, lonely places. "Look, I can't let you do all the work. Isn't there something I could be doing in the meantime?"

"How about growing wings and a halo?"

He couldn't find a real laugh, and the brief sound that burst from his lips came out rusty, but it almost felt good. "I wouldn't know where to begin."

Kate briefly glanced around him to the sleeping baby. "Or maybe you've already started."

Kate followed her instincts when timing her meeting with the Taylors. Initially, she'd hoped to hold off for a day or two, out of respect for Marilee. Circumspection held its own value, she'd reasoned. However, a tiny voice warned that Noble wouldn't let that much time pass idly. As a result, she quickly altered her strategy, and had her secretary make an appointment to meet with the Taylors the following afternoon.

Of course, the meeting couldn't take place in her office, as convenient as that would have been. She would manage without the psychological edge of having the signs of her judicial leverage around her.

Instead, she accepted Noble's invitation to their home. The point, she explained in a follow-up chat with a dubious, edgy Ethan, was not to appear threatening. However, her first glimpse of their home triggered the nagging sensation that she'd made a mistake.

The Taylor mansion represented one of the older stately homes. Built only a year or so before women had won the right to vote, the two-story Colonial-style structure stood out starkly from its contemporary neighbors. Kate thought it typified the inhabitants' mind-set: stern in its crisp white and its stark black shutters; predictable as the two chimneys book-ending the east and west sides of the house; and proud as the pilaster-framed doorway crowned with a double set of Palladian windows.

After parking her car along the tree-lined street, Kate entered the wrought-iron front gate, then rounded the circular sidewalk to the pyramid-style front steps. A sweeping glance had her guessing that daylight had never breached the heavy brocade drapes covering the eight front windows.

No doubt behind one pair sat Noble Taylor, ready these past ten minutes or so. She could picture the self-made construction-business magnate settled in a high-backed chair by a fireplace, making a ceremony of drawing out a gold or silver pocket watch that had belonged to someone else's father, or grandfather, to check the time every minute or so. Not that he had anywhere to go these days.

Losing Clay barely eight months ago in a scaffolding accident had cost him more than his only child; he'd also lost his sole heir to Taylor Construction Company. Consequently, it had crushed his drive and his passion for the family business, and the firm's contracts were at an all-time low. Discreet inquiries had confirmed that Noble wanted to sell. Kate couldn't imagine that happening—the Noble she knew enjoyed power too much—but the idea gave her hope. Surely a man in such a spiritual crisis would be less likely to take on something as taxing as a custody battle?

One thing she knew for certain—this was not a home for a child. She decided that as she listened to the door chime echo through the mausoleum-silent house. A little girl needed music and light, a place to run, and the freedom to laugh. She thought of her own childhood, and the racket she, Eva and her aunt Beryl used to make, especially while preparing her father's Sunday pancake breakfasts. The Taylors would never allow Darcy to experiment that way, let alone romp around. They would suffocate her spirit as thoroughly as they'd drained the life out of Marilee. Kate knew she had to remember that as she battled Noble's obstinacy.

The front door eased open, and an elderly woman dressed in a formal black-and-white uniform beamed at her. "Good afternoon, Judge Randall. Recognize you from your picture in the paper." She stepped back to let Kate enter. "It's a pleasure to meet you at last. I'm Norma, Mr. and Mrs. Taylor's maid. You don't know me, but you've met my niece, Iris. Iris Jackson."

The name spawned the image of a vivacious and bright teenager who'd first written her last year seeking educational guidance. "Yes, of course. Well, what a delightful surprise, and how nice to meet you. How is Iris?"

Mahogany-brown eyes glowed with warmth and pride. "She's wonderful, thank you. She's heard back from that college you wrote to on her behalf. Would you believe she's being considered for a *full* scholarship? It's so exciting. We can't thank you enough for helping to give a complete stranger this opportunity."

The woman's shy graciousness had Kate beaming in return. "Believe me, it was my pleasure. It isn't often that I meet someone with her gift for communication and hunger for knowledge. Of course," she added in a loud whisper, "the fact that she cited *me* as an inspiration didn't hurt, either. Please tell her that I said hello, and to keep me posted?"

"Oh, yes, ma'am, Your Honor."

Kate decided to test the friendly woman's observational skills. "Norma, did you know Marilee Taylor well?"

The woman's expression immediately grew sad. "Not really, ma'am. She was a sweet little thing, but she kept to herself, mostly. It was a tragedy what happened to—"

"Norma." A soft but cool voice held a distinct warning. "Mr. Taylor is waiting for Judge Randall."

Disappointed, but hardly thwarted, Kate offered a reassuring squeeze of Norma's arm as she passed her, before addressing Noble's wife. "Hello, Mrs. Taylor. It was so kind of you to see me at this difficult time."

She headed toward the plump matron standing in the arched doorway of the nearest room. Dressed in a navy suit and choker pearls, Ruth Taylor evoked a pleasant image, although Kate guessed her champagne-blond bouffant probably hadn't undergone a color or style change since Clay's days as a high school football star. Yes, Kate thought, she remembered Noble's wife accurately; this was a woman who could be counted on to stay in character—that of the lady of the manor.

Ruth offered a pained smile. "It has been stressful. But welcome to our home. Er, Norma...Judge Randall's coat."

Kate signaled the Taylor's maid not to bother, then slipped out of the wool garment. "I'll set it on this chair, if you don't mind." She draped the coat, along with her leather shoulder bag, on the ornate seat near a door that turned out to be the entrance to the formal living room. "I don't want to disrupt you any more than necessary. Also,

I must confess to having a great deal of work I have to review for court tomorrow, and so it's imperative I get back to Whitehorn as soon as possible."

"Oh, dear. I'd hoped we could convince you to stay for dinner," Ruth replied, with precisely the right amount of regret.

"You're too kind, but I don't dare. By the way, please call me Kate. I try to forgo formality outside the courtroom."

Ruth Taylor inclined her head, although her expression suggested she hardly approved. With a practiced sweep of her hand, she replied, "Then let me take you in to him."

Like the foyer, the living room was wallpapered in a dark, busy print evoking an era when men had paid almost as much attention to fashion and decor as women. With formal, ostentatious furnishings to match, Kate decided that Noble had created his own Freudian slip. He wasn't the laid-back, good old boy he liked people to think. Once again she felt the weight of doubt as she imagined the effect the grim environment would have on a child.

"Judge Randall."

Noble rose from a pewter-gray Queen Anne chair by an unlit fireplace. As he pocketed an ornate gold watch, Kate barely suppressed the urge to cough.

"We're so pleased," he continued, running a hand over his tie. It matched his wife's outfit as perfectly as his suit complemented his blow-dried and spritzed silver mane.

Kate extended her hand. "Surely our paths have crossed too often for you not to call me Kate."

"And I'm Noble. I must admit, after we missed each other at the funeral, it disappointed me to think that those paths wouldn't converge again until the next charity event."

How like him to initiate their meeting with a challenge to her to explain herself for yesterday, she thought as he closed his fingers around hers. Intent on slowing him down, if not stopping him completely, she tried not to miss a beat as she replied, "The funeral was difficult for everyone who cared for Marilee, but you and Mrs. Taylor have my heart-felt condolences. When I saw that you were surrounded by so many caring people, I thought it only right to check on Marilee's brother. You see, I know what it's like to suddenly find oneself without family."

"You must look to us as your extended family."

The prospect felt about as comfortable as the idea of wearing an old-fashioned corset. Suffocating.

Noble wasn't what one expected when visualizing a construction-company executive. Pale and pink rather than sun-bronzed, trim rather than sturdy, as she remembered his brawny son being, he looked more like a successful funeral director than the tough, scrappy businessman who'd helped restyle Montana's skyline for the current generation of homesteaders and pioneers. In fact, he was as much a physical contradiction as a professional one, since his commercial, flashy creations had nothing what-soever in common with the elegant "museum" he lived in. Only his rough, callused hands seemed to offer any link between the two strange personas.

"Now, you must tell me, how's the horse business these days?" he continued, his gaze penetrating. "Your notoriety for bringing those Hollywood people to Montana is certainly gaining momentum."

Kate eased her hand from his grasp, not surprised by this tendency to soothe, then probe, or by the focus of his at-tention. The kind of clientele her business attracted created an ongoing fascination for a number of area residents, and a considerable amount of criticism from others.

It had been her aunt Beryl who first raised West Coast

interest in their stock, when then screen actor Jared Banyon purchased one of her horses after riding him in the Western that ultimately made him a star. From that point on, Shadow Ranch's reputation had spread as *the* source for exceedingly bright, and uniquely well-trained, saddle horses.

Today a single member of Kate's equine family could yield a better price than some local ranchers' entire herds. Her most vocal detractors argued that the attention drew too many celebrity types who ended up buying great chunks of property in the state for private getaway homes, thus raising tax rates to an impossible level for the hardworking year-round residents.

Kate accepted that the theory held a modicum of truth; after all, who could come up here, witness the photogenic valleys, the mystical streams, smell the sweet morning air, or watch stars invade the panoramic sky like hatchling night flies, and *not* fall under Montana's spell? But that was all the blame she accepted.

She gave Noble a cool smile. "It never ceases to amaze me how many people prefer not to see that large corporations are buying up ranches at an even faster pace." What got discussed even less was that the real estate information was supplied by local businessmen interested in finder's fees.

"Oh, they see it, Kate," Noble replied, sounding annoyingly amused. "But they don't mind, because despite the transfer of ownership, the ranches continue to be active participants in their local communities. They don't act like isolationists, the way your people do."

Her people? "You think so?" She knew she could argue until next fall about how that very participation he'd mentioned could turn into control, and she wouldn't get him to admit it. He was obviously one of those poor souls who'd been weaned on the corporate psyche. Any other kind of logic was foreign to him, therefore not to be trusted. "Well, in any case, we're slowly selling off our stock," she told him, deciding they'd parried and thrusted long enough. She wanted to avoid any real antagonism.

"Really? I had no idea."

The truth was, she'd only begun discussing it with Jorge. "It's true. My trainer and foreman is getting on in years, and with my court docket growing heavier, instead of shrinking, we believe it may be the best decision all around."

"Would you be interested in selling your place?"

A hint of the old, ambitious Noble flickered to life. Kate saw it in the eyes that were only a shade darker than Ethan's. "No," she murmured, with a regretful look. "I don't think so."

"Sure? I may know of an interested party. It would be a generous offer."

Wouldn't Ethan love to hear that? "Selling Shadow Ranch isn't part of the plan."

"Well, if you ever change your mind, I'd appreciate you letting me know first."

"Noble, dear, our manners." With an apologetic smile to Kate, Ruth Taylor indicated the straight-backed chair that faced her husband's. "Please excuse him. When he starts talking business, he even forgets to eat. Do sit down. Can I get you a refreshment of some kind?"

"Thank you, but I don't care for anything." However, Kate did sit, inwardly preparing herself to broach the subject she'd come to discuss.

As he lowered himself into his chair, Noble studied her with a new wariness and speculation. "All right then—" he crossed his legs "—we've exchanged pleasantries, and yet as much as I pride myself on reading people, I have to admit I still don't have a clue as to why you asked for this meeting. For some reason, the notion that it has to do with Walker keeps nagging at me. Reassure me, Kate. Tell me you aren't here to champion the man."

She resented the mockery beneath the command as much as she did the order. "I try not to choose sides, Noble. I prefer focusing on issues and principle—in this case your granddaughter. Wouldn't you like to know how she is?"

"*I* would." Ruth leaned toward her husband from her perch on the edge of the nearby love seat. "Please, Noble. Let her tell us about the baby. There's so much to discuss, plans to make. First and foremost, we have to think of a proper name."

Kate couldn't believe what she'd heard. "She has a name, Mrs. Taylor. Marilee's wish was that her daughter be called Darcy. It was the late Mrs. Walker's name."

"Oh, dear." Ruth cast a dismayed look at her husband. "That was a thoughtful gesture, of course…."

"But hardly a suitable name for a Taylor," Noble continued, rising.

He stepped behind his chair and assumed an even more authoritarian pose by slipping one hand into his suit jacket. Kate thought the visual resemblance to another tyrant from generations past an unnecessary but ironic warning.

Ruth nodded in support of her husband. "I'm sure something can be done. How difficult could it be to adjust a birth certificate? Dorothea would be lovely, don't you think?"

"Oh, yes. Darling," Kate replied, with a straight face. "And while you're at it, maybe you'd like to remove all record of the baby's mother?"

The woman was as bad as her husband! Never mind Ruth's ignorance of the simplest hospital policies regarding birth certificates, despite having been a mother herself; the earth hadn't yet begun to settle over Marilee's grave, and the two of them were already working toward remold-ing the child into their own image! Thank goodness Ethan didn't have to hear any of this.

"Now see here..." Noble began. "There's no need for sarcasm."

Kate thought there was every need. "Your granddaughter is adorable. I think she's going to be a mirror image of her mother...a mother she'll never know. How can you consider taking away the greatest gift her mother could give her?"

"We're offering her more. The best of everything," Noble replied, thrusting out his chin. "After all, she's a Taylor, and we intend for her to be raised right."

Right. Now there was an interesting word. Once again, Kate was grateful that she lived in a country where there were laws to override this kind of caprice and willfulness. "Noble, I think you should know Ethan told me about Marilee's wish that he raise Darcy."

"What?"

"He told me yesterday."

"Well, he lied."

"I spoke to Lori Bains, as well. As I'm sure you're aware by now, she was present during the delivery, and she's confirmed his statement."

The man grew florid, and as stiff as a military color guards-man. "I can't believe you mean to buy into that preposterous-ness. You're going to let a few words spoken in a moment of delirium override what's best for my granddaughter?"

What an interesting shift away from the accusation that Ethan had been lying. Kate wondered how deep a hole he could dig for himself, but knew it was up to her to keep things from deteriorating completely.

"I asked for this meeting today to try to raise an aware-ness and compassion for the strain this will cause all parties involved," she told the couple. "*Including* Darcy. And not as a jurist, but as a friend."

Noble grunted. "Yes, but whose?"

She decided to ignore that. "It's my hope that you'll be able to resolve this situation without creating any additional ill will, and at the same time avoid a court appearance."

Her host leaned over the back of the chair. "There damn well will be a custody hearing!"

"Noble, dear…your blood pressure," Ruth murmured, fingering the pearls at her throat.

"Never mind that. Did you hear what she said? Of all the— I was instrumental in putting you in office!" he declared, pointing to Kate.

Could he honestly believe that? "Noble, several thousand voters did that. You aren't even in my jurisdiction." What was more, her concern that someone might attempt to influence her opinions had compelled Kate to reject all campaign contributions at the beginning of her political career. She had the records to prove it. "And regardless of what you think you did to encourage support on my behalf, we both know that it would be unethical of me to allow that to affect or interfere with my responsibility to the bench."

Noble scowled. "You've become quite the maverick, haven't you? Afraid of no one and nothing, because you always get the last word."

Hardly. But he'd obviously decided to disregard the fact that she and her fellow jurists had a higher court to answer to. Any slip on her part, through either an ethical lapse or judicial ignorance, could get a ruling reversed or a decision reprimanded or—to put it bluntly—simply ridiculed. She wasn't, however, going to waste her breath arguing her professional honor with a man who'd been sued on several occasions for various contractual and building-code safety violations, and who'd settled out of court each and every time.

Noble was hardly as restrained. "Let me give you and your friend Walker fair warning, *Judge Randall.* I intend to get full and absolute custody of my granddaughter, and if either of you have any notions about interfering, I suggest you think twice about it. You can't afford the kind of notoriety this case would cause. Think how ugly it could get for you when you come up for reelection. And it's obvious Walker doesn't have a prayer of winning."

"*Is* it obvious?"

Despite the veins bulging in his neck, Noble managed a frigid smile. "He's been accused of murder. He's violent. Heaven knows he isn't one of the most successful ranchers in the area. Under those circumstances, how does he think he can support my granddaughter, let alone afford the attorney fees for a custody battle?"

"On what do you base your opinion that he's an unsuccessful rancher?" That comment had her genuinely perplexed, because she thought Ethan a fine one.

"Well, look at his place. I made the mistake of actually going there, naively thinking I could reason with the man. The cabin is nothing more than a shack, and as for the acreage...well, it's only a fraction of the size of the really successful ranches. In business, you either grow or you stagnate and die."

Kate felt as if she were being yanked down into some intellectual black hole. So much for believing the more-is-better gang had learned to tone down their rhetoric after the financial and economic messes they'd helped create in the eighties.

"The thought of having to live in a world where

everyone's need or ambition was based on being the first, the biggest or the best frightens me, Noble. In fact, I get downright reverential when I meet someone content to live a—gasp, dare I say it?—modest lifestyle. For your information, Ethan lost his father when he was extremely young, and I'd venture to guess most young people would break under the weight of the responsibility he's carried. And let's not forget that he didn't use that responsibility to avoid the draft. He served bravely in Vietnam."

For a moment, Noble looked uncomfortable; however, he quickly recovered. "Fine. But that was then, and this is now. My granddaughter deserves more than modest care."

He'd left no possible negative unexamined. Kate couldn't help wondering if he'd ever expended half as much energy on thinking how to help or encourage someone as he did on pinpointing their flaws or weaknesses.

"Why are you doing this?" Sincerely bewildered, she'd had to ask. "Why do you seem to be resisting an amicable joint-custody arrangement?"

"Because I don't want one. Bad enough for my son to have been hoodwinked by Walker's no-account little sister. I won't have another member of my family tainted by Walker influence. That child will be a Taylor in every sense of the word, or she won't be my granddaughter."

Kate knew she had to get out of there or risk telling Noble in no uncertain terms what an egocentric, mean-spirited man he'd become. As it was, she didn't know how she could break this news to Ethan.

She rose. "Thank you for making your position clear."

"Beating a hasty retreat? That's not like you."

She thought him loathsome, in the way he went from livid anger to cool disdain, but she wouldn't give him the satisfaction of getting to her any more than he already had.

"Any judge will tell you that every dispute has a cost, whether it's human or financial. I believe it would be advisable for us to step back and examine exactly how high a price we're willing to pay."

"We?"

She could almost see the laughter in his eyes, and swore at herself for the accidental, but costly, slip. "Yes, *we*. As in...'We'll meet again, Noble.'"

He nodded. "I think I look forward to that, Kate. Yes, I believe I do."

Three

"Gonna snow again."

Ethan looked up from securing a fresh diaper on Darcy to consider John Mountain, standing at the kitchen window, sipping his second cup of coffee. Dawn was still minutes away, but there was enough daylight for his sleepy-eyed cowhand to see what might be brewing north and west of them. "There's a surprise," he replied drolly.

John Mountain shook his head. "It's taking longer. You noticed? Much as I hated the jungle and the heat, thought I'd never come to resent the cold. But it's happening."

Someone's chatty this morning. Surprised, yet noting that the oddity hadn't affected the man's sometimes frustrating, sometimes amusing, fragmented speech patterns, Ethan replied, "It's been a tough year." In more ways than one. He shushed the baby when she fussed a little louder. "Too much of anything will get to you, and we've sure had our share of cold and snow. On your way over, did you notice if the temperature's dropped below freezing yet?"

"Didn't look. Feels close. And once those clouds building up along the summit start rolling down our way, it'll get worse."

That meant there would be more work for John Mountain, work Ethan wouldn't be able to offer much help with, no matter how good his intentions. As he carefully drew down the baby's sleeper and zipped it shut around her kicking legs, he dealt with a new dose of guilt. Darcy did her best to keep his attention by screwing up her face and squeezing out a temperamental squeal.

"Hey, Little Bit, I thought patience was a feminine virtue." He knew she wanted her bottle; unfortunately, he hadn't prepared it yet. When she first awakened, he'd been busy cooking his and John Mountain's breakfast. As it was, his share was drying out on one of the heated tiles, because at the first opportunity he'd needed to get her out of her soaked diaper. "Just hold your horses. Your old uncle's only got two hands. You'll get your grub in a minute or two."

He hated the fact that he wasn't keeping up as well as he thought he should. Somehow he remembered things being easier when he'd been a boy helping his mother take care of Marilee. It hadn't been a piece of cake, by any means, but, for example, back then a two-o'clock feeding hadn't been nearly the killer it had come to feel like nowadays.

As Darcy's chin dimpled and trembled with the threat of serious tears, Ethan felt a grin building, and a swelling in his chest. The imp was going to wrap him around her little finger, no doubt about it.

He bent to kiss her angel-soft hair. "I'll hurry, sweetie."

After covering her with the baby blanket that had been in the box of her mother's baby things, he joined John

Mountain in the kitchen area. "Once I get her fed," he told the other man as he filled one of the baby bottles, "she should sleep for a good two or three hours. Why don't we use that quiet time for you to drive down into town for those supplies we were talking about, and I'll load a trailer of hay in the barn and check on the stock?"

John Mountain eyed him from beneath the shadow of his brown Stetson's broad brim. "You can't. Too long away from the house."

True, he shouldn't be, but Ethan didn't see how it could be avoided. "I won't go any farther than the herd's closest watering hole. We have to make sure the ice isn't too thick for the cattle to get a drink." Not since he was a kid and juggling school and adult responsibilities had he found it a blessing that his spread was a fraction of the size of the bigger ranches. But, modest as it was, it would take him a good twenty minutes if he was making the ride on horseback—and a bit longer in the tractor, hauling out the hay.

"I'll do it before I go." John Mountain's expression reflected concern as he eyed the whimpering baby. "Just load up what I can in the old pickup. Won't take me any time at all. Then I can give them the rest when I get back."

"That's assuming Old Unreliable's in the mood to make the full trip. But what if she dies on you along the way? You'd have a hell of a walk back in clear weather, never mind a storm."

"Aw, she wouldn't. Knows I'd kick her in her spare tire. Finish off by making a feed trough out of her if she tried it."

Ethan found his longtime ranch hand's obstinacy second only to his own. "Listen to me, you stubborn fool. You can't do both of our jobs!"

"Guess you'll have to give up the twig, then."

Ethan narrowed his eyes, aware of what the cowboy was doing. It didn't amuse him in the least. "Stuff it."

"One stupid comment deserves another," the small man replied, appearing anything but threatened. "Seems to me, we don't have any choice. It's not like I mind. Anyway, you think you could leave her unattended? Sure can't take her with you."

It took only one glance toward the tiny bundle of pink on the recliner for Ethan to know his answer. "I guess not." What was more, he supposed a man who'd survived being a tunnel rat in the war, as John Mountain had, could tolerate just about anything—short of discussing those experiences now, and finding himself in absolute darkness or a cramped space. But that still didn't make it fair; and since Ethan couldn't begin to pay the guy what he was worth, the need to be just, to share fully in the work load, took on a new and deeper importance.

"Okay, thanks," he told John Mountain. "But I promise, as soon as I get this guardianship thing out of the way, I'll look into hiring a sitter for her."

"Lots of luck. Who'll come way out here? I think…I think shifts'll work."

Ethan had only to remember how late John Mountain had come in from the range yesterday to be doubtful. How long could either of them endure that before it became too much, or—heaven forbid—there was an accident, or John Mountain simply quit?

"Soon as the weather warms, you can take the twig with you in the truck," the cowboy added as he set his mug in the sink. "That's when we're busiest, anyway."

He was right. But he couldn't believe John Mountain would tolerate the extra responsibility. "Are you sure?" he asked. "I mean, doing an hour or two of baby-sitting is one thing, but diapers and stuff…it gets old fast."

"Wouldn't have offered if I didn't mean it."

Once again finding himself on the receiving end of generosity and goodwill, Ethan was left feeling awkward, as well as humble. He sighed. "Fair enough. Thanks, man."

Now if only Kate would call. He checked his watch and told himself he wouldn't phone to ask. But why hadn't she gotten back in touch with him?

"Waiting is always the worst."

Something in his tone made Ethan wonder what he was referring to…what he was remembering. John Mountain's comment hadn't just been caused by his awareness that Ethan was worried about the Taylors and Kate's meeting with them. Of course, Ethan knew better than to ask. Unless the information was volunteered, neither one of them ever broached personal subjects.

Instead, Ethan grunted and tested the formula on his wrist, as he'd learned to do years ago. He wouldn't let himself consciously accept that no news might be bad news; however, he was fast learning that he made a lousy optimist.

"Someone's coming."

John Mountain's warning had Ethan setting the not-quite-ready bottle back in the warming water and heading for a front window. "I hear it, too," he murmured, only to feel a jolt of surprise as he looked outside. "It's Kate."

John Mountain immediately reached for his coat. "Good luck."

"You don't have to—" The kitchen door closed behind the cowboy with a soft click that triggered Ethan's nerves. Suddenly abdominal muscles that had been relaxed tensed, and he curled his fingers into tight fists.

He couldn't think of a reason for Kate to come out here this early. Didn't she have to get to court? he wondered, as she brought her vehicle to a halt next to his truck.

Seconds later, she climbed out and reached back inside for... He almost exhaled in relief. Baby gifts. She was bringing out a whole armful, two armfuls, of baby gifts; so many that she had to nudge the door shut with her hip.

He opened the cabin door, sharply aware of how glad he was to see her again. The realization struck as she passed him, buried beneath presents from the waist up and bringing with her a gust of frigid air underscored by the subtle punch of her scent. He'd wanted that fragrance filling his lungs again, he'd missed the challenge of her sharp mind—so much so that if not for his great concern for the baby, he would have forgotten to close the door and followed her into the room.

"I know this is a ridiculous hour," she began, slightly breathless.

"For who? I've been up since two and four."

"Then you're in better shape than me. I haven't been to bed yet."

Now what did that mean? he wondered as she deposited her load on the coffee table and carried a pink stuffed pony to Darcy. "Why, look who's awake. Hi, twiglet! How about a smile for Auntie Kate, hmm? Look what I've brought you."

Twiglet? Auntie Kate?

She set the horse on the chair's raised footrest, then scooped up the baby as if she were hooking herself up to a life-support system. In that instant, Ethan decided he understood her untimely visit. She hadn't come out of friendship or concern for him and his plight. She'd come to get close to the baby.

"You'd probably be more comfortable without the coat," he drawled, brutally tamping down the emotions stirring inside him.

"No doubt. I'll take it off in a minute. How've you been managing?"

If he told her, would she hear him? She hadn't even looked at him when she spoke. As a result, he thought his testy "We're getting used to each other" perfectly justifiable. Of course, the twinge of shame followed anyway.

What the hell—? Jealousy? He felt *jealous* of a helpless infant?

As nuts as he knew the idea had to be, he could neither reject it nor crush it. Instead, it stirred memories of the last time he'd seen a similar expression on Kate's face, the look that said, "I don't want to let you go." It had been the moment she said a final goodbye to Wayne at the bus station. Ethan felt as uncomfortable and locked out seeing it now as he had then.

It didn't help that she looked so good—again, a nutty idea, since there was nothing really different about her this morning. The stuffy hairdo was the same, and so was the black coat. But both seemed to accent her fair skin more today and draw attention to the fine shadows under her eyes that confirmed her sleepless night and gave her an unneeded and unwelcome aura of vulnerability. What was more, the wind had stained her cheeks, and the baby was bringing a tender, soft expression to her face that made her eyes velvet soft and bowed her lips into a too-inviting curve. It left him disturbingly tempted to enfold woman and child in his arms, to soak up some of that tenderness for himself.

He cleared his throat. "I'm late feeding her, so you'll have to help yourself to coffee if you want any."

"No thanks. I've had enough to last me until Saturday."

Once again the reminder of her sleepless night. Why? Was she trying to build up some sympathy for herself before she hit him with bad news or something? That was it. What else would have caused her to stay up all night?

As something cold and sharp took a nasty bite deep inside him, he shrugged off her reply and headed to the stove. "What's in all the bags?" He knew he'd given the question an unnecessary edge, and that she'd noticed, but when he saw the guilty look she sent him, the inner cold turned to dread.

"I hope you don't mind," she replied. "There was this store in Billings that caught my eye. Once inside, I'm afraid I got carried away."

Billings. The situation was worse than he'd thought, he was sure of it.

He reached for the bottle, oblivious of the tiny voice that warned him not to. In the next instant, he flung it into the sink as searing pain raced up his arm. Glass clattered against stainless steel, formula sprayed out from the nipple.

"Ethan!"

He swore and groped for the cold water tap, and succeeded in thrusting his hand under the faucet before the bottle stopped rolling from one side of the sink to the other. The numbing-cold flow hadn't begun to ease the first wave of pain when Kate reached his side.

"It's my fault. I took your mind off what you were doing."

He had no problem with letting her take the blame. It didn't ease his anger, but it helped him bite back the string of curses he wanted to roar. No matter what, he didn't want to upset the baby.

"Can I get you anything?" Kate asked him.

"No."

"Some ice wrapped in a towel. That water might not be soothing enough."

"*Kate.*"

A deaf person couldn't have missed the harshness in his voice. Without another word, Kate backed away, rocking the whimpering baby. Only then did Ethan allow himself to breathe again. The stinging in his hand began to fade, and he could see the damage wasn't anywhere near as bad as it could have been.

He picked up the bottle and inspected it carefully for cracks and chips. Although he found none, he decided on second thought not to take any chances. The crash in the sink had been too violent not to have done some damage, he told himself as he poured the contents down the drain and tossed away the bottle and nipple. Carefully drying his hand, he located a new sterilized one.

It took another five minutes or so, but he finally carried the warmed formula to Kate, who'd removed her coat in the interim. He took one look at her somber but expensive-looking black suit and opted against letting her feed Darcy. She wouldn't thank him if she ended up with formula on her clothes.

"You'd better give her to me."

"I'll be happy to feed her. You go take care of that hand."

Suit yourself, he thought, handing over the bottle. "The hand's fine."

"Let me see. It doesn't—"

"Are you going to give her that, or what?" he snapped.

With another guilty look, she carefully offered it to the excited infant. "Oops…here you go, angel. How about some of this?"

The baby eagerly closed her tiny lips around the nipple. A moment later, her greedy suckling sounds sweetened the heavy silence settling in the room.

"Isn't that one of the most beautiful sights you've ever seen?" Kate murmured, her gaze locked with the infant's.

Ethan turned away from the sight. If he was going to get through what every instinct told him lay ahead, he couldn't look at the perfect picture she made holding the baby. In self-defense, he went to the nearest front window and, staring up at the gray sky, demanded, "All right, how bad is it?"

After only the slightest pause, Kate admitted quietly, "Critical. But not necessarily fatal. I still believe we have a chance."

At least she hadn't pretended not to understand his question. He wasn't, however, wild about how the word *we* had popped into the conversation. "Are you going to tell me about it, or should I wait a few months for the instant book to come out?"

"Of course I'm going to tell you, and there's no need for the double dose of sarcasm. It isn't going to change anything, and it certainly doesn't help this conversation."

He was in no mood for her matriarchal tone. "It'll help me burn up the frustration left over from waiting for your call last night. You remember the call you said you'd make? The one I didn't get?"

"I know what I told you, and I'm sorry. My only excuse—"

"Let the baby breathe."

"What?"

He spun around and forced her to remove the nipple from Darcy's mouth. "Air. It's necessary, if you're going to keep breathing. She forgets, because all she's thinking about is her stomach. You have to do it for her."

Although she turned red and her expression reflected her deep embarrassment, her reflexes with the baby were impressively quick. Immediately shifting to free her hand so that she could gently rub and pat the baby's back and coo reassuringly, she proved to Ethan that her slip had only been that. She knew what to do with that directive. Either that was a result of sometimes having to bottle-feed a colt or filly at her place, or maybe she'd helped out with someone else's baby.

"Okay, go ahead and let her have it," he finally said in a normal voice as he turned back to the window.

She remained silent for several seconds. He could feel her gaze on his back, and knew he'd been unfair and rude, but he couldn't afford to let himself care.

"The only excuse," she continued in her usual calming voice, "is that I needed time to think."

That had him turning around. "Think about how to soften the blow to me, or how to make yourself look better?"

"That's not—"

"Besides rejecting you, me, and my intention to keep my promise to my sister, what else did Taylor have to say?"

Temper finally flashed in Kate's eyes. The smooth skin over her high cheekbones and along her femininely sculpted jaw grew taut. "Couldn't we hold the venom? At least until I've explained things?"

"No. Because I'm the one who's going to have to pay for whatever disaster you're alluding to. Given that, it burns me big-time to know that I'm also the single person who's completely in the dark about what's happened!"

"He was furious, all right?" she replied, with as much low-key testiness as he'd exposed. "I was wrong to think my approaching him would help. Instead, he's accused me of being biased in your favor."

"Boy, was he ever off the mark. Did you finally let him in on the secret that you're actually working for his side?"

"Stop it, Ethan. Jurists work as arbitrators all the time, if they see there's the slightest chance to resolve an issue to the satisfaction of both parties. It can be of great benefit to taxpayers bearing the brunt of litigation costs. But in this case the idea was a bad one, and I've admitted it. You can't possibly say anything that will make me feel worse than I already do."

"Give me a minute, I'm sure I can think of something." Wanting to hit something, hard, Ethan settled for pacing the room.

Why are you surprised? Especially after what you've just been through with the Avery trial? The surprise is that some cop or state official hadn't already knocked on your door, flashed papers at you and taken Darcy away. When are you going to learn, the system works only if you have the bucks to grease the machine?

He was sick and scared, but he had to hang on to the same thing he'd held on to during the trial—the truth. Darcy belonged with him. If Marilee had believed it, that was good enough for him.

He spun around and faced Kate again. "Tell me everything that happened…and I do mean everything."

She did as he asked, while Darcy contentedly slurped and dozed through her breakfast. She repeated the entire experience, from her point of arrival at the mansion, and her hope that Norma might still prove helpful in giving a clearer picture of what Marilee's life had been like as a Taylor, to Noble's final, taunting words. Ethan listened carefully, and in total silence, despite the urge to explode several times. He felt a red tide of fury at the other man's accusations of Kate being guilty of impropriety, and promised himself that the hypocrite would pay for that one. But perhaps the worst moment came when he learned that the human bulldozer wanted to change Darcy's name.

"He's more of a rat than I'd let myself believe," he muttered when she finally finished. "To think Marilee spent all that time trapped in their house, that environment…" He shuddered.

Kate's look held compassion and concern. "Try not to dwell on that. You need to direct all your attention and energy to keeping Darcy."

He watched her place the empty bottle on the counter, then proceed to walk with the baby while gently massaging and patting her back. Yes, she was catching on fast, but he couldn't dwell on that or on her; he had to focus on the uncertain future.

"He's not getting her, Kate. I'll leave the area, move out of state if I have to."

"Don't say things like that!"

"I mean it."

"I believe you think you do, but you're not being rational. Running away would be financial suicide. What's more, what you're threatening is illegal. Good grief, as a judge, do you think that I can stand by and let you break the law, Ethan?" Kate shook her head vehemently. "Please, don't start testing what I can and can't overlook to help you. Believe me, things are getting complicated enough as it is." But as quickly as her temper had flared, she calmed, focusing on his hand. "How does that feel now? Do you think you need a doctor's attention?"

"No. I've had plenty worse."

"Ethan," Kate murmured, edging closer, "I'm sorry for adding to your pain and your problems. Admittedly, what I attempted was risky from the first, but I should have better recognized the potential for disaster because of who we were dealing with."

Maybe he didn't feel like being generous, but he knew she was right about Taylor. Her reputation for being coercive was well-known. If she hadn't been able to sway him, what chance did he or anyone else have?

"I almost have to leave," he told her, inevitably shifting back to his original idea.

"You can't be serious."

"If it's the only way, you bet I am. I won't let Marilee down. Those people have ruined enough lives."

"Didn't you hear what I said? You'd have to virtually abandon your land. The minute you tried to return, *if* you tried, the authorities would lock you up and take Darcy away from you. Are you ready to do that? If so, how will you support yourself and the baby? Where will you live? What about John Mountain? You have to give a thought to him, since he's been resolute in his dedication to you. What do you tell him? There's always work for a good hand, but the day of the cowboy is setting fast. Where will he go?

"Then think of Darcy," she continued, quiet but earnest. "Do you realize you would be committing her to a life of running? That would mean no stability, no friends, no home to call her own. How will you support her? Where will you live? Who will care for her when you're working?"

She hadn't said anything that didn't chip away at his logic, even though he suspected she was talking more as a woman than as a judge. He also didn't have an answer to a fraction of her questions. That irked. "I don't *know*, okay?"

"That's not good enough. Darcy deserves better than that. So does John Mountain. So does Marilee!"

"Well, what do you suggest I do?" he demanded, arms spread wide. He'd talked more in the past few days than he had in years, and he was about wiped out. He *definitely* was out of ideas.

The funniest expression crossed her face. Not funny, exactly, more like uncertain and...wryly amused?

He frowned. "What?" he asked, narrowing his eyes.

"You could marry me."

* * *

There. It was out. In a moment, he would either start laughing hysterically or tell her that he would rather be sentenced to life imprisonment than do something like that, but it was done. The long night of pacing and inner debate had come to an end. Now it was all up to Ethan.

Kate understood the poleaxed look on his face, and sympathized with what he had to be going through. Yesterday, when she finally returned from Billings, she'd believed she would be making this morning's trip to simply deliver the gifts and to apologize. Too wound up and worried to sleep, she'd sequestered herself in the library that had once been her father's, hunting through book after book, searching for a case similar to Ethan's dilemma, some precedent that might give her a foothold. When that proved unsuccessful, she'd begun brainstorming, thinking up various possibilities to suggest to him. None, however, seemed strong enough to offset the fact that Ethan's reputation was still at an all-time low. Unless someone walked forward to confess to Charlie Avery's murder and remove the lingering cloud of doubt over Ethan's head, nothing short of the Taylors' withdrawing their claim would save him from another date in court.

And in that darkest hour of deliberation, the incredible idea had come to her. She could offer herself as a solution to his problems. From the look on his face, she was sure the thought had never crossed his mind.

"Shocked you speechless, did I?" she murmured when nearly a minute had passed and he had yet to make any response.

"Just about." He rubbed the back of his neck, but continued to watch her warily, as though not certain she was through wielding her verbal wallops yet. "That was a joke, right?"

The question stung a bit. She wasn't unaware that some people called her the *spinster* Hanging Judge, and she would even admit that she hadn't had a date since New Year's; however, her lack of a social life was a result of choices she'd made.

At least her proposal had stopped Ethan from yelling at her, she thought, shaking her head to answer his question. "No. No joke."

"You don't have enough headaches in your life, you want to take me on? In case you haven't noticed, I make an albatross look like a canary."

"Try looking at it from my perspective. If I married you, that would automatically preclude my presiding over your custody hearing. Not only would that block Noble's right to make any accusations against me professionally, but you tying the knot with a judge would do wonders to improve your reputation."

This time he lifted both eyebrows. "To who? The divorcée who's been trying to collect child support from her bum of an ex-husband for the past dozen years? The kids from abusive homes? The Native American who couldn't get his medical bills paid by that congressman's kid after a hit-and-run that left the old guy crippled for life? I've seen the articles in the papers, Kate. You don't just operate in court, you're out in the streets straightening out the problems your brethren claim not to have time for. But I've also seen the carefully placed editorials from the headhunters who use every opportunity to paint you as everything from being radical left to fundamentalist right. They already see you as anything but the darling of the judicial system. Can you imagine what they would say if we—"

"Married." Kate wondered if he'd choked on the word

or on the idea that she would be his wife. "I'm flattered that you've been following my career, Ethan."

"Whitehorn's not exactly New York City. It's not hard to do."

"You mean, whether or not you want to, I'm in your face, is that it?" she asked, deciding not to believe him for a second. "Well, I may be considered a bit bold and tough, but when I see an injustice, I like to fix it. What's more, whether or not they agree with me politically, most people admit that I'm honest. Now, would honest Judge Randall marry a man who wasn't innocent? You see? It would be a perfect validation for you."

Ethan made a face. "It sounds more like bad math to me."

"How so?"

"You don't solve one problem by initiating a worse one."

"Ouch—I think."

"Don't play coy. It doesn't suit you. What's more, you know damn well what I mean. My mess—whether you helped complicate it or not—is no reason to turn toward drastic measures such as marriage."

"Look, I know you've probably given up on thinking about that kind of relationship," Kate said, wanting to reassure him that she understood his reluctance thoroughly. "The remoteness of this place, the increasing challenge of scraping out a decent living for yourself and John Mountain…and now Darcy. I know this isn't something you'd ask a woman to endure, let alone share. What you don't seem to understand is that I didn't mean the marriage would be permanent."

"It wouldn't?"

The poor man looked thoroughly mystified now, and she was actually beginning to enjoy herself. "Certainly not. Whatever gave you that idea? As soon as things get resolved, a reasonable period after you won permanent custody of Darcy, we could realize we had irreconcilable differences and file for an amicable divorce. We're talking quick, quiet and painless, because the arrangement would, of course, be in name only."

"Of course."

"Naturally, we'd have to keep the whys and wherefores a secret…and in public we would have to be a convincing couple."

"This is ridiculous." Looking more self-conscious and uncomfortable than she'd ever seen him, Ethan began pacing and rubbing the back of his neck again. "Damn it, Kate, you have your own life to live, a business, a home. Responsibilities."

"I'm not saying it would be easy, but I am good at delegating. The ranch is being ably handled by Jorge and Eva, and will continue to be whether I'm there or not." She glanced around the neat but small cabin. "Would it be a problem having me here with you for a while?"

"You know it would! You'd have virtually no privacy, none of the luxuries you're probably used to at your place, it gets dusty as hell in here because of the wood burning stove… This is nuts!"

She knew he needed time to get accustomed to the idea, and she needed to get to court. "Don't jump to conclusions. That's why I came early. Think about it," she said, setting the baby down on the recliner. She'd already noticed that the crib, while assembled, lacked the other essentials, namely sheets, blankets and such. If she got out of court at a decent hour, she would see to that matter, as well.

"You aren't listening to me! There's nothing to think about," Ethan all but growled from behind her.

Although she felt as if popcorn were exploding in her

stomach, Kate made sure she had a smile on her face as she headed for her coat. "Try anyway."

Before she had one arm in a sleeve, he spun her around. "Why are you doing this?"

At least that was easy to answer—on the surface. "I want to help you. I want to help Darcy. Most of all, I need to do something because I'm painfully aware that I managed to talk myself out of doing enough when Marilee needed help. I could see something was wrong, Ethan. I just convinced myself that she wouldn't have left him."

She knew she wasn't the only one to suspect and do nothing. She saw it in his eyes, along with the raw grief and regrets. Knowing that left them with nothing more to say, she finished buttoning up and left.

He didn't say goodbye as she drew the door closed behind her. It wasn't reassuring in the least, but Kate had known Ethan Walker for a long time, long enough to recognize that he had to make the next step himself. Or not at all.

Four

"Your Honor, I object!"

"You can't object, Harold. This isn't a trial. Sit down and chill out, or we're going to have one of the shortest meetings on record, and mister, I've had some fast ones. It will be in your interest to know that you're giving me my first migraine, and believe me when I say that your client and Mr. Blankenship's hardly seem worth it."

The frazzled young lawyer's eyes looked like painted golf balls behind his thick eyeglasses. But he did sit.

"Now listen up, you two," Kate continued, leaning forward to make sure she had the full and complete attention of both new Whitehorn attorney Harold Massengil and Baxter Blankenship, the opposing counsel in this on-again, off-again, divorce-turned-assault case, which wouldn't come to trial if she had anything to say about it. "It's been a long day, and it's going to be a longer week. The one thing I don't have a stomach for at this point is sitting through another Jenrette-versus-Jenrette mud-slinging party. Is that understood, gentlemen?"

"No, it is not. Your Honor," Harold whined, "my client is in Whitehorn Memorial, with his jaws wired and a future of pureed meals stretching before him, as a result of *Mrs.* Jenrette's violent mood swings."

Without blinking Kate turned to Baxter Blankenship, the debonair younger partner of Blankenship and Blankenship. "Would you like to address that?"

"He shouldn't have stuck his head out the sliding glass door when she was closing it."

Kate shifted her attention back to the indignant Harold. "I think that follows the don't-lean-into-a-punch theory."

"Your Honor," Harold replied stiffly, "Mr. Jenrette demands and deserves the court's protection, as well as release from the purgatory that the state euphemistically cites as his marriage."

Kate bowed her head to hide the laughter that threatened to bubble up out of control. She'd been kidding about the migraine. If it wasn't for these moments of asylum theatrics, she would have few laughs whatsoever. "Harold, if you don't stop reading law novels, I swear you'll put me in the hospital, too. Everyone in Montana except you seems to be aware that Wes and Sugar Jenrette have a particular predilection for using Whitehorn as their personal playpen. They will *not* use the county's courtroom again.

"Gentlemen—" she flipped through her calendar and scribbled herself a note "—tell your clients that they have until Monday to decide once and for all whether they prefer to live with or without each other. On Monday I want either a withdrawal of all accusations and claims, or proper and complete documentation for the dissolution of their marriage.

"Should they decide to remain as husband and wife, I

want notarized affidavits swearing their intention to seek
joint *and* individual counseling. In other words, their days
of acting like preadolescents with money to burn, along
with their complete disregard for the dignity and solem-
nity of this court, are over. Failure to comply will burn my
bustle. Are we clear on that, gentlemen?"

"Y-yes, Your Honor," said Harold Massengil.

"Completely, Your Honor," Baxter Blankenship added,
admiring his manicure.

"Excellent. Then this meeting is over." Kate slapped the
bulging Jenrette file shut. She reached for the hefty rubber
band when it tried to bounce back open.

As Warren Blankenship's younger brother lead the way
out of her chambers, she momentarily thought about
calling him back to ask if Warren had heard from Noble
Taylor. But she knew it would be a tactical mistake. Word
was all over the county that Blankenship and Blankenship
would be representing the Taylors in their attempt to gain
custody of their grandchild. No doubt Warren had told
Baxter to report back on *her* state of mind. It wouldn't do
to let the enemy know you were getting edgy. That was
another reason why she'd decided to put an end to this
nonsense with the Jenrettes. The Blankenships needed to
understand that she had no qualms about playing hardball;
that if Noble Taylor wanted war, she was ready and would
take no prisoners.

Only when she was once again alone did she allow her
fatigue to take over. She buzzed her secretary and slumped
back in her chair. Seconds later, a petite woman stepped
into the room with a gusto that was typical of the redhead's
personality.

"If you don't get out of here now, even your four-wheel-
drive isn't going to help you get up into those foothills," Pat

Fischer warned. "The snow's coming down as if it was one of the first storms of the season, instead of one of the last."

Kate waved to signal her eventual obedience. "Did you get that shopping list taken care of?" she added, her look hopeful.

"Did I ever! You'll never ask me to shop for you again. Everything is in your truck. Be sure a forklift's available when you decide to unload it."

"Have I told you the woman's a saint?" Kate asked, looking up at the ceiling. Then she beamed at the widow, who, like Eva and Jorge, she considered an extension of her family. "Tomorrow's lunch is on me."

"Hold that thought. Tomorrow we may all be under three new feet of snow." The New Jersey emigrant tilted her head, and short curls caught the fluorescent light. "Tell me the truth—is that baby half as cute as I heard?"

Kate knew Pat had a sister-in-law at Whitehorn Memorial, but had a hunch that most of Whitehorn was talking about Marilee Taylor's orphan. "She's a genuine doll. I wish she was part of a litter. That would be one solution for people like us."

"Hear! Hear!" Pat replied with a rueful smile. Then she gestured toward the file-laden desk. "Now, what's most urgent in here?"

As she rose, Kate inspected the mess, too, and shook her head. "On second thought, there isn't anything here that can't wait until tomorrow. Why don't you lock up and head for home yourself? Otherwise you'll have me feeling guilty."

"We can't have that, and you don't have to ask me twice." The trim woman fingered the fringe of hair near her left ear. Her hazel eyes twinkled with excitement. "Um…is this a good moment to tell you that I invited Steve Black Feather to dinner and I need all the time I can get to make a decent impression?"

The pang of envy Kate experienced didn't stop her from being happy for the other woman. Pat deserved some happiness in her life; she'd lost her husband last fall, after a long bout with cancer. Pat lived just south of the Laughing Horse Reservation, and Steve Black Feather was an English teacher at the reservation school. He and Pat had met when he stopped to help her change a flat tire, months before Jerry's death. Even then Kate had recognized the instant chemistry, simply from hearing Pat tell of the experience. Now she was keeping her fingers crossed that things might work out for the couple. The world had too darn little romance, and far too much heartache, as far as she was concerned.

"I can't believe you managed to keep that a secret for this long," she groaned, shaking her head. No wonder Pat looked prettier than ever, and…livelier somehow. She circled her desk to give her a hug. "Well, what are we waiting for? Let's get out of here!"

Her pleasure waned to a wistful sigh once she had the courthouse in her rearview mirror. By the time she turned from Center Avenue onto Mountain Pass, she still felt happy for Pat, but her own life disappointments resurfaced to create a sobering contrast. Suddenly she even felt seriously shortchanged.

"What's wrong with you?" she muttered, turning on the car's wipers to full power against the huge snowflakes collecting on the windshield. She'd never been this negative. She'd always believed in the philosophy that when life handed you lemons, you made lemonade. What was more, she had a lovely house, a demanding but rewarding job— two careers, in fact—and she'd been blèssed to have some fine and occasionally incredible people pass through her life. Maybe she'd missed out somewhat in the romance department—okay, had been shortchanged—but apart from her proposal to Ethan, when had she ever encouraged a man? Since she was eighteen, when...

Focusing on Ethan let a wry smile return. He was, indeed, one of a kind, and she couldn't wait to see the expression on Eva's face when she divulged her latest brainstorm. Over the years, her housekeeper had suffered through some doozies, like the time Kate had brought home a woman and her seven children for the night after the woman's ex-husband went straight from their divorce hearing to torch the family home. Maybe she should have stopped at the Hip Hop and begged one of Melissa Avery's fruit pies to soften the blow. Eva loved the baked goods from there, since making a good piecrust was the one technique she'd never been able to master herself.

Melissa North now.

In a way, Melissa reminded Kate of herself—independent, avoiding commitments, throwing herself wholeheartedly into her work and trying to make it be enough. But Melissa had decided it wasn't. Like a few others lately that she could think of.

Kate couldn't help but wonder if she wasn't subconsciously trying to tell herself the same thing. Had her proposal to Ethan been for reasons other than moral and legal ethics?

"Don't be ridiculous," she finally muttered to herself as she drove over Shadow Ranch's cattle guard. If she'd been interested in seriously pursuing him, she would have started off by inviting the man to dinner, as Pat had done with Steve. She certainly wouldn't have skipped the whole courtship and asked the guy to marry her!

Oh, really?

She'd been trying to tell herself that this was another

case of "Mother Kate" singlehandedly trying to resolve the world's troubles. But this time she'd focused on the one man she wouldn't mind noticing her as a woman. It certainly gave the situation an interesting slant.

If you could be calm and collected about it.

Brooding, Kate drove through a pocket valley and down one small slope, then to another, before spotting the house. Two stories tall, butter yellow, with green shutters, it sat in the snow like a sunny-side-up egg speckled with parsley. Once the snow melted to where it cloaked only the highest peaks, the house would have to compete with a rainbow of wildflowers in the valley.

Who could stay melancholy for long here? she asked herself for the hundredth time, as she eyed the robust curl of smoke rising from the kitchen fireplace. The sight triggered a humorous thought, and she wondered what Eva had cooked for dinner. Something hearty, for sure; they could always count on a hot, stick-to-your-ribs stew or chili guaranteed to increase your weight by three pounds by dawn.

Corn soup, she guessed, once she opened the back door and caught the first sniff of the yummy aroma. She stomped her feet to remove as much snow as possible, and rushed inside.

"Eva, you were reading my mind," she called beyond the utility room. "When it started snowing this morning, I almost phoned and said, 'More than anything I'd like corn soup for dinner tonight.'"

When she peeked into the kitchen, the tiny, robust woman with the adorable face of a Pekinese never looked up from ladling soup into her husband's bowl. "Sure, sure. And Elvis was spotted today in Missoula."

Kate winked at Jorge, who shrugged at her, well used to Eva's drill-sergeant personality. "No kidding?" she replied, pretending to take Eva seriously. "You're the fifth person today to say that. Can spring be far off?"

Eva's expression soured further. "Don't you dare mess my clean floor. Boots off before you eat."

Kate left her briefcase and purse leaning against the nearest cabinet, hung her snow-dusted coat beside Jorge's plaid work jacket and slipped off her knee-high boots. "What a day," she said, rubbing her cold hands together. She headed for the sink to wash up. "How are you two? Anything exciting happen?"

"Are you sure you want to know?" Jorge asked her, with a speaking glance.

"Mind your own business," Eva snapped.

Barely taller than his diminutive wife, and with more hair on his upper lip than his head, he possessed exactly the sweet-natured persona he projected. "I'm not saying another word," he replied, his mustache twitching.

Since he and Kate had always possessed their own shorthand—second only to his talent for communicating with horses—it took a mere lift of his bushy eyebrows, and an innocent look toward the ceiling, for her to figure out that whatever had happened had to do with her, and that Eva didn't like it one bit.

Ethan. Could Eva have found out what she'd done? Already? But how?

"You two stop that this instant, or I'm leaving the room and you can wash your own dishes," Eva warned, letting the ladle drop back into the pot with a clatter. "First you eat. Time for excuses later."

Excuses? Intrigued, Kate took a moment to wash her hands, trying to figure out what that cryptic comment meant.

"Jalapeño corn bread, too," she murmured diplomatically, taking her seat at the head of the table. "It looks and smells wonderful."

Eva returned to the table with the inevitable glass of milk she'd been serving Kate for more years than she wanted to remember. Thanking her again, Kate reached for the soup ladle.

Eva snatched it out of her hand. "All you have to know is that I don't approve. No one has told me anything, and I want to know nothing. I have no desire to get involved."

Kate spread her napkin over her lap. "Okay."

"Don't wheedle. My flexible days are over."

"I must have missed them," her husband murmured into his soup.

Kate nearly choked as Eva swatted him with her dish towel. Dabbing at her mouth with her napkin, she asked, "What have I missed?"

"Your neighbor telephoned."

Eva never could bear to keep a secret, Kate thought with satisfaction. The woman loved intrigue too much, which was why she had a small TV on the kitchen counter so that she could watch all her soap operas. But Kate didn't plan to step into this one too easily.

"Mr. Douglas?" Kate asked, knowing her hedging would upset Eva terribly. She knew, of course, that her housekeeper meant Ethan, and wondered why he hadn't telephoned her at the office.

"Go ahead and pretend you don't know what I'm talking about, but I'll tell you here and now, I don't like the way this feels."

"How what feels?"

"Don't play ignorant with me. You leave here before dawn, and all afternoon he phones."

Startled, Kate leaned forward. "Ethan called? When?"

Eva snorted in disgust. "Look at you, all eager and ready to run to him."

"What time, Eva?"

"Three o'clock. Then at four, and again only minutes before I hear you coming. He's forgotten you work? He thinks you sit at home like some princess, with nothing to do but wait for him? And *you*. What do you think you're doing messing around with that one, eh?"

"Helping a friend through a difficult time," Kate replied, thinking Ethan must have thought the weather would cut things short at the courthouse. Either that, or he'd been too—what?—to call at her office. "Did he leave a message?"

"No."

Impatient, Kate didn't want to accept that. "None?"

"You think I forget when a person hangs up the phone without saying another word? I don't like the man."

"You don't like—you don't know him. You haven't seen him since he was a boy," Jorge offered, a gentle rebuke in his tone.

His wife pointed a finger at him. "And what kind of neighbor is that? He's too quiet, I tell you. You can't tell what he's thinking."

"You married a quiet man." Jorge grinned as he scooped up another spoonful of soup. "You seem to like me well enough."

"Don't talk nonsense, you." She refocused on Kate. "What does he want? You had no role in his trial. He should leave you alone."

Kate took her time selecting a slice of the aromatic bread and adding a dab of margarine to it. "You might as well know something. I wasn't going to tell you unless… Well, the fact is, I've asked Ethan to marry me."

The spoon fell out of Eva's hand and bounced off the side of her bowl and onto the table. She pressed her clasped hands to her lips. "Jorge, pinch me. I don't like this dream."

"I'd be glad to, my heart, but I'm afraid it wouldn't change the outcome much."

The woman pressed a hand to her ample bosom and sputtered a barrage of spicy Spanish at both her husband and Kate. Not inclined to interrupt, Kate waited until Eva ran out of steam.

"They'll take the baby away from him if someone doesn't do something," she explained at last. When Eva refused any sign of sympathy, Kate pursed her lips and told the woman more of his dilemma with the Taylors, and her own reactions to them.

"All right, so the people aren't wonderful," her housekeeper replied. "That still doesn't justify marrying the man."

In other words, she wasn't listening. Kate decided to try another approach. "You should see the baby. She's a delight—tiny, pink, sweet. How long has it been since we had a child in the house? I mean, besides the group social services brings out in the summer to see the horses."

It was the wrong question to ask. For years Eva had wanted her to marry and fill the house with children, having no clue that that could never be.

"I'm too old to care for babies."

When she turned eighty, Eva would have the energy and gusto of someone half her age. Kate knew this posturing merely protected her from her own longing. But as she considered an appropriate reply, they heard a pounding at the back door.

Jorge, Kate and Eva glanced at each other. Jorge made the first move to rise, but Kate motioned for him to sit down.

Her heart pounding, she went to answer the door. She knew who it had to be; she could almost feel him. What she didn't understand was why? Did he feel guilty for the way he'd growled and snapped this morning?

And you could be pregnant by Easter.

Kate opened the door. The picture he made standing on the back steps, his hat low over his intense blue eyes, the snow streaking beneath the rim and sticking to his lashes, made her at once uncertain and tempted to reach out to him. For one of the few times in her life, she decided to be conservative.

"This is a surprise. Come in."

Silent and grim-faced, he did as she beckoned. After shutting the door behind him, Kate turned, intercepting Eva's resentful stare and Jorge's concerned one. The one she sent back said that no matter what reason had brought Ethan here, she wanted to save their neighbor any embarrassment they could.

"Eva, Jorge…you remember Ethan." Without giving anyone time to respond, she asked him, "Are you hungry? Eva's made some wonderful—"

"I need to talk to you."

She gestured toward the kitchen door and led the way down the hall, past the formal dining room that hadn't been used since the reception after her father died. She found the study lights dimmed. For an instant, she considered turning up the brightness, but some impish thought had her leaving the room in its romantic glow.

How much more effective it would have been if she'd let down her hair, changed into jeans and a soft sweater, somehow altered her appearance to make him see her in a different way from the usual, she thought with fleeting wistfulness. She knew her formal outfit made him feel uncomfortable, even though she was in her stocking feet. The house, though subtle in its elegance, had to be making things worse.

"Can I get you something to drink?" she asked, gestur-

ing to the quaint old bar her father had built into the full
wall of bookshelves. "I think we have almost—"

"I still think your idea's nuts."

He could tell he'd shocked her, but he had to steel
himself against regret, since after only a moment in her
presence he could feel her effect on him, the regrets, his
temptation. He wouldn't let her make a fool of him, no
matter what he might end up owing her.

"Correct me if I'm wrong, but didn't you make that
fairly clear this morning?"

She recovered fast. He admired her for that as he
watched her lean back against the huge, ornate desk.

"I wanted to make sure you understood I meant it."

"Message received." Recovering even faster, she
added a spunky salute, touching an imaginary hat.
"Where's Darcy?"

"At home. John Mountain's with her."

"Good. And why aren't you there with them?"

"Because a few hours ago Warren Blankenship telephoned to ask who would be representing me in court."

Kate's expression went from confused to indignant.
"That sneaky, low-down… Of course he would do that. You
can't know this, but his brother was in my office earlier for
something totally unrelated to this. Baxter never hinted that
Warren was up to anything. And since they knew I'd visited
with the Taylors, he could have mentioned his brother's
intent to call you. He should have asked about your
attorney himself."

"Meaning?"

"Don't you see? There was no reason for Warren to
bother you. Except to intimidate. And I see he's succeeded."

He'd managed that, all right. For the first time, Ethan

was feeling the possibility that Taylor did have the upper hand, or at least something more up his sleeve.

"Is that why you're here?" Kate asked gently, breaking into his thoughts. "Do you need me to recommend someone to represent you?"

"No. Well, maybe. Hell, I don't know."

She crossed her arms and her trim ankles. Allowing himself only one sweeping glance, Ethan forced himself to focus on the painting of Shadow Ranch in the spring hanging between floor-to-ceiling windows.

"I can't help you until you decide, Ethan."

"Don't you think I know that?" Damn it all, the angrier he became, the calmer she seemed.

"This is difficult for you—coming here, I mean." She tilted her head in invitation. "Why don't you start by telling me what's bothering you the most about all this?"

Now there was a loaded question. What would she say if he told her to look in a mirror?

He had to suck in a deep breath to clear his head. "You. Me. What you suggested this morning. Do you really think we could fool anyone?" he snapped, annoyed with her serene smile.

"Why not? We're neighbors living well away from town. No one knows what our relationship has or hasn't been over the years, except the people who work for us— and, fortunately, all three are the type who aren't given to indiscriminate gossip."

"And when we get to court? You don't think that one look at us there and it would be obvious we were faking it?"

"It's always a possibility. We'll just have to be convincing, won't we?"

"Am I hearing correctly? Judge Kate Randall is willing to participate in a lie?"

Her gray eyes grew flinty with determination. "Go visit the Taylors' home, Ethan. I know this place makes you itch for escape," she said, nodding around the room, "but this is roast beef to their prime rib. Go listen to them discuss their plans for Darcy as if she were a prize calf to brand and show off. No, Ethan, I have no problem being a bit unorthodox if it means stopping what's clearly a miscarriage of justice."

"I'm not convinced."

She hesitated, her laugh sounding a bit embarrassed— or was that confusion? "Convinced about what?"

"Your ability to pull it off."

"Oh, look who's talking."

He shook his head slowly. "You're out there more than I am, lady. You would have to face the skeptics every day. In court. Out on the streets. You'd be under a microscope virtually every waking hour."

"Are you doubting my ability to convince people that I'm a loving wife?"

She straightened and unbuttoned her suit jacket, not taking her eyes off his face. Then she slipped it off and tossed it over the armchair facing the desk. Beneath the jacket she wore a silk tank top. The stark black made her long, slender throat look deceptively vulnerable. Ethan couldn't decide what he wanted more, to wrap his hands around her neck, or to press his mouth against the tempting column and absorb her heat and taste.

"Yeah, I guess I am," he admitted, torn between focusing on his responsibility and an old hunger.

"Try me."

He stiffened. "Don't make a game out of this, Kate. This is my niece's future you're toying with."

Gray eyes turned as dark as thunderclouds, and fever

pink stained her cheeks. Kate pushed away from the desk and came toward him in what could only be described as a prowl. Ethan knew he'd been unfair and hard, but he wanted to find her boundaries. The closest lines she drew for herself. In all the years he'd known her, she'd never let anyone get that close, not since Wayne. But if he was going to put his future in her hands, he intended to be the one.

"How dare you suggest I would be careless with a child!"

"Not careless," he replied softly. "Convincing."

"I can be convincing." She'd stopped her advance when they were nearly nose to nose, and he watched the melting snow on his hat drip onto the dark gold of her hair. Slowly she reached up to take hold of his jacket lapels. "The bigger question is, can you handle it?"

"Anything you can dish out."

The instant she pressed her lips against his, he felt a flash fire race through him, searing the air in his lungs and stopping his heart in midbeat. As she brought her body flush against his, his blood congealed, crystallized in his ears. In self-defense, he grabbed her wrists, ready to shake her loose, push her away, only to realize he was in deep trouble. Her scent, that damned scent that shouldn't be legal, coiled its way into his lungs, into every pore, and smothered his fury.

In its place, a dormant need roused.

Stunned, he felt his fingers loosen their viselike grip as if they belonged to someone else, slide up her sleek arms and around her back. The silk was like her flesh, warm, smooth, stunningly feminine; it whispered under his journeying fingers, hiding little…not the graceful line of her spine, not the narrow band of her lacy bra. Even as her lips stung his, he knew he wanted to rend the material in two, snap the lace and race his mouth over her until she screamed for him, for more, for everything.

She fed his anger, and he fed hers. Their kiss deepened and became a duel, their hands an assault. Blinded by the red tide of his desire, it was all Ethan could do not to push her back against the desk and take her, let her take him.

He didn't know what ended the fury. Barely able to breathe, let alone think, he was only aware that it vanished as suddenly as it had erupted, leaving them standing nose to nose, so close they were each other's universe. And yet neither of them seemed willing to back down or step away. Ethan searched for words, any words, to explain the moment, and the complex feelings humming inside him.

"So who gets everything right the first time?" she said breathlessly, beating him to it.

He wanted to laugh, but found it impossible. "Nobody, I guess."

But as quickly as her spunkiness surfaced, she grew somber. Sad. "Do you hate me that much, Ethan?"

Hate? He stared as if she'd asked him a question in some language he'd never heard before.

"Resent me, then?"

That seemed closer to the truth, but still not right. Ah, she would never understand. "Kate...do you have to ask such confounded questions?"

"Yes."

"Well, you talk too much."

He initiated their second kiss, and it took her by surprise. He felt it in the catching of her breath, and the way her fingers momentarily tensed on his jacket. Ethan liked the uniqueness, the uncertainty, of it, as much as he liked that she responded as eagerly as before.

She'd always been a physical person, a hugger and a toucher. He wasn't. It should have been impossible for him to let her touch him, explore him, trace the line of his jaw, his throat, to skim her fingers through the snow-damp hair at his nape. But instead of stiffening, he found himself leaning into her touch, wanting more.

"Wouldn't you…be more comfortable without the jacket?"

The breathless question came as he ended the searching kiss to explore the petal-soft skin below her ear. "No doubt."

"Would you like help?"

Reluctantly he lifted his head and forced himself back to reality. "Yeah. You can walk me to the door."

Her expression went from bemused to disappointed. "Am I talking too much again?"

"It's not that." Ethan stepped away from her and tried to concentrate on why he'd come. Blast it, he couldn't even think! This was impossible. "I've complicated things, Kate. I should never have touched you."

"Do you hear me complaining?"

"Well, you should. The situation's a big enough mess without adding sexual attraction to it." He had to say that, no matter how frustrated and needy he was feeling at the moment. Or how insensitive it sounded.

"I told you before, we could have a strictly business arrangement, and we still can." The moment he started shaking his head, she closed the distance between them again, and this time rested a hand near his heart. "Ethan, listen to me. We need to do this because there's another situation coming up that you don't know about. It's a matter that only a marriage between us could help make work in our favor."

Suspicious, he muttered, "What now?"

"Howard Lessing. Remember when I told you Matthews hates to listen to domestic cases? Well, he loathes custody cases even more. If we were married,

Judge Lessing would inherit your custody hearing, and as I said before, that's not great news, except he just happens to be taking medical leave, beginning ten days from now. He'll be out for no less than three months, recuperating from back surgery. In the meantime, Matthews and I will be trying to juggle the work load as best as we can."

"Then what's to stop the Taylors' lawyer from twisting Matthews's arm?"

"I'm telling you, the man's more likely to volunteer for oral surgery. You're even more likely to run for mayor than he is to hear Darcy's case. He'll avoid it, especially if I'm involved. And if you have a good lawyer who can figure out a way to stall Blankenship, that can eat up some time, too. I have someone in mind. I'll give her a call."

Ethan closed his eyes, because as usual she had an answer for everything, leaving him befuddled and unable to think of anything. All he knew was that if he didn't get away soon, he was going to sling her over his shoulder like a caveman and haul her upstairs.

"Do you hear what you're saying? Do you have a professional death wish or something?"

She laughed throatily. "Don't worry. It will all be inside the parameters of the law. I'm simply going to see that the system works *for* you for a change." When he opened his eyes, looked at her and shook his head, she chuckled again. "Why, Ethan, I almost believe I make you nervous."

"I think I'd be a fool not to be."

"The bottom line is, either we try it my way, or you face the probability of losing Darcy. What's it going to be, cowboy?"

Hell, he thought, did he have a choice? He tugged his hat lower over his eyes and glared at her. "I guess you're getting yourself a husband."

Five

"Are you sure we have to do this?"

"No blood test, no marriage license."

"I mean *together.*"

"That's what I adore about you, Ethan, you're such a romantic."

Although she linked her arm through his as they walked up the sidewalk toward her doctor's office on Monday, Kate felt more like giving him a poke in the ribs. It was only the sweat breaking out on his forehead that urged her to forgive his latest lapse in tactfulness.

"This is part of the ritual, *darling.* The ceremonial blood-letting before strangers. It'll help get tongues wagging."

"They do enough of that as it is."

"You know what I mean. By Thursday we should have our certificates, Friday at the latest. Then we can head straight over to the courthouse for our marriage license. I have a call in for Justice of the Peace Monroe Thrillkill to perform the wedding in my office."

Ethan froze, only yards from the front door. "At the courthouse? Why can't we have it out at my place?"

"Even if we stuck bouquets of daisies in your work boots, pulled the curtains to hide one inch of the dust in the place and stood with our backs to your short-order-cook version of a kitchen, I think the atmosphere alone would be too much for this bride to handle."

"You're the one who agreed to live there."

"Fortunately for you, you're gaining more than a bride, you're getting the use of a vacuum cleaner, too."

"Hey, the place isn't that bad."

"Where's your sense of humor, Ethan?"

He grumbled something under his breath, then asked, "Why not your place then?"

"Actually, I thought about that." She'd once fantasized about walking down the L-shaped stairway of her house, and gliding through the double doors of the spacious, guest-filled living room—but to Wayne. She wouldn't do that to Ethan, even if this wasn't going to be a *real* wedding.

"And?"

Kate covered her momentary wistfulness with an airy wave of her hand. "For obvious reasons, having the ceremony at the house is impractical."

"They're not obvious to me."

"You look so cute when you pout." He growled in warning, and Kate laughed softly, feeling another one of those poignant tugs inside that were becoming more and more frequent when they were together. "The point is that we want the news about us to spread fast, remember? What's more, we want people to see how happy and compatible we are, that this isn't a con job."

"What's next, an immaculate conception?"

This time she let the laughter bubble forth, and it seemed

the most natural thing in the world to momentarily lean her head against his shoulder. But, seeing he wasn't enjoying the moment anywhere close to as much as she was, she murmured, "Look, we're here. This is part of the procedure. What's wrong with trying to make the experience as pleasant as possible?"

But as they entered her doctor's waiting room and saw the crowd, she knew Ethan's mood wouldn't be improving anytime soon. She recognized several of Dr. Preston's patients that he would know, too; but even those he might not have met before recognized her. The result was a wave of shocked and speculative glances and murmurs that left even her feeling like an exhibit at a carnival sideshow.

"Is this romantic enough for you?" Ethan muttered out of the corner of his mouth.

Shooting him a dazzling smile, as if he'd said an utterly delightful thing, she tightened her hold on his arm and urged him toward the receptionist's window. "Hi, Maddie. Do you have us on your list? I called Dr. Preston earlier."

"Sure do, Judge Randall. Blood tests for a...wedding license?" The freckle-faced receptionist blushed furiously as she glanced at Ethan, her expression suggesting she might have gotten the message wrong. "Uh...congratulations. If you'll take a seat and, um, have Mr. Walker fill out these forms, we'll be able to take you in as soon as you're through. Dr. Preston's note here says that you would need to get back to court fast."

"I appreciate the consideration, Maddie."

Kate led Ethan to the only available spot in the room, a wooden love seat by the door. They sat touching from shoulder to thigh. Maybe it was their audience, but despite their coats and things, Kate had never been more aware of his masculinity than now.

"Didn't *she* sound sincere," he drawled under his breath.

"If you wouldn't glare at people so, they might not get so awkward and scared when they talk to you," she replied in kind.

"I glare at you, and you don't get awkward and scared."

"That's because way down deep I know you adore me," she replied sweetly, offering him the clipboard and pen. "Do you want to fill out this, or would you like me to do the honors?"

"My penmanship stinks. Go ahead."

She settled the thing on her lap and began filling in his name and address. When she'd finished several more lines, he grunted.

"Now what?"

"How did you know my mother's maiden name, and all?"

"Wayne used to speak about you and your parents…and I'm a good listener."

The mention of Wayne had a strange effect on him. Kate noticed it, because she'd come to the section of the form where she needed his input, and getting the answers proved as difficult as getting facts out of a hostile witness. Finally she handed him the clipboard and pen and told him to finish himself.

"I didn't know you had your tonsils taken out," she whispered to him as he neared the bottom of the check list.

"It happened before I knew *Wayne*."

The implication was unmistakable, and Kate had to wonder if Ethan's sarcasm was directed toward Wayne for discussing him, or her for having been so close to his best friend. In any case, he'd also stopped writing.

"The sooner we get through here," she reminded him, "the sooner you can get back to Darcy."

That brought a new frown from him. "I shouldn't have left her at your place."

"Why on earth not? Eva's taking wonderful care of her…and regardless of how you said she behaved toward you, I know she's having a ball with the baby."

"Gee, that makes me feel better."

Kate touched his thigh to caution him, aware of the way the nearest onlookers were leaning toward them, trying to pick up bits of their conversation. "She's just protective of me, Ethan."

He closed his hand around hers. It was a romantic gesture, unless one noticed his knuckles turning white.

"Yeah, well, do me a favor and fill her in one tiny detail? Remind her that this was your idea."

Wondering if he realized how strong he was, she looked deep in his eyes, willing him to see promised retribution beneath the adoration. "She'll only think you've put a spell on me."

That reached him. She could see it in the way his gaze sharpened, and for an instant it felt as if they were the only two people in the room. Kate thought it such a delicious moment that when someone cleared their throat, breaking the magic, she gave a start, nearly causing her purse to slip from her lap.

"Judge Randall? Mr. Walker?" the nurse at the doorway called brightly. "Please come this way. If you're not through, you can finish the forms in here while we get started."

Kate heard Ethan draw a deep breath as they both rose. Whispers followed them.

"Did you see the way he was looking at her?"

"Married! Can you believe it? Don't you just know her daddy is spinning in his grave."

"Wait until I tell Roy. Imagine, Ethan Walker...and her acting like Miss Hoity-Toity."

"Are we having a good time yet?" Ethan murmured, as they left the waiting room and followed the nurse down the hall.

Kate ignored him. She didn't want him to see her hurt and disappointment in the people she called her own, or her sudden doubt about whether she could make this work. Ethan might not have any faith in the citizenry of Whitehorn, but he had to have at least a little in her to be going through with this.

She had to be strong for both of them. She couldn't let him down.

He'd thought the blood test was bad, but late Tuesday afternoon, as he carried Darcy into the courthouse, Ethan realized that the real circus was only now about to begin. He suspected the place hadn't been this busy since his trial. Unless some other poor fool was being set up on trumped-up charges, word had spread like wildfire over the weekend, and this ant trail of loiterers was here to have a peek at the murderer hitching up with the Hanging Judge.

"Feel like I'm a roach caught in a fruit jar," John Mountain muttered, once they made it into the building and headed for the stairs to the second floor.

"Same here. Sorry." It didn't begin to cover what he owed the guy for agreeing to come and be his witness. No matter how difficult this afternoon might be for the bride and groom, Ethan knew that being exposed to so many people would be a trial and a half for John Mountain.

As they reached the second floor, a man rushed out of nowhere and snapped their picture. Ethan caught a glimpse of a press badge before the flash. Fortunately, both he and

John Mountain had their hats on and ducked enough to avoid the direct glare, and Darcy hadn't yet succeeded in pushing her blanket down far enough to expose her sensitive eyes.

"Gus Muldoon of the *Whitehorn Journal,* Mr. Walker. Would you care to make a statement?"

"Yeah. Do that again in the baby's face and you'll slide facefirst down those stairs."

"It's my job to report the news," the bespectacled man replied with considerable dignity, although his Adam's apple bobbed like a barometer gone haywire.

Ethan exchanged glances with John Mountain, and the shorter man walked up to the lanky reporter and crooked his finger. Suspicious but curious, the man leaned closer.

"This isn't news. This is personal. Last chance. Walk or slide?"

The reporter retreated, trying to look as outraged as possible as he hugged the wall and scurried down the stairs. Once he was out of sight, Ethan cocked an eyebrow at his cowhand.

"They didn't teach you *that* in the tunnels."

"Nope. But if you survived, it did teach you that you didn't have to put up with jerks like that."

"Amen." Ethan tipped his head toward the door bearing Kate's name and led the way to her office.

In the tiny reception area, they found Jorge and Eva Cantu already waiting. They were dressed in their Sunday best and perched stiffly on the couch. Ethan couldn't decide which of them looked more dazed and uncomfortable. For the first time in ages, he felt a twinge of compassion.

Without exchanging more than a nod of greeting with them, he eased Darcy into Eva's arms. When he saw her expression warm a few degrees, he murmured, "I'll go check and see if Kate's about ready."

He reclaimed what John Mountain had been carrying for him and left the group to slip through the door marked Private.

"I can't decide, Pat. Don't you think it's too— Ethan!" Kate froze in the midst of pinning an orchid corsage to her ivory suit.

"Don't you know it's bad luck to see the bride before the wedding?"

Although he heard the redhead, who'd been introduced to him the other day as Pat, chide him while she stepped between him and her boss, Ethan couldn't answer immediately. He was too busy taking in the image of his bride.

Why had he hesitated in calling her beautiful before? He should have remembered that there were different versions of Kate. The one standing before him couldn't be denied the tribute of being termed *stunning*.

Her slender, feminine suit was perfect for her slim, leggy figure, and the soft color and intricate beading added a luster to her skin and hair that he'd never seen before. But it was the hat that transformed her the most. He'd never been wild about hats on women, save the Western variety, but as he eyed the small tilted cap, with its ivory veil sweeping low over her eyes, he knew he'd been too quick to reject them.

"You look…" he began, only to find he couldn't finish.

She smiled. "You too."

That was being polite, that was all, he thought, because beneath his down jacket he wore his only suit, which he'd worn for his trial and Marilee's funeral; also for his mother's; in fact, for every important event in his life. He figured someday he would wear it as his final outfit, too. Cut in a Western style, and beginning to look its age, it was the best he could manage on such short notice. But noting how hard she'd worked to make this event seem real and pleasant for him, he was glad he'd at least splurged on the new tie.

But, eyeing her corsage, he slowly brought forward the bouquet he'd ordered yesterday on a crazy impulse after they collected their blood test certificates and went for the marriage license. "I guess this wasn't such a great idea." Given the short notice, he hadn't had much of a selection to choose from, but he'd believed the spray of roses and the tinier flowers he didn't know the name of suited her.

"Ethan, it's…exquisite." Kate moved in slow motion to accept it. "I'm speechless."

"It's nothing."

"It's everything," she insisted. "Thank you." With a breathless laugh, she spun around and presented her corsage to her secretary. "Didn't I tell you not ten minutes ago that this went better on your dress?"

"Well, you're not going to hear me disagree this time," Pat said teasingly, holding it up to her purple-and-white outfit. Excusing herself, she retreated into the small bathroom to pin it on.

Kate stepped closer to Ethan. "The baby?"

"She's outside with Eva."

"John Mountain, too?"

He only nodded, because Pat returned, the corsage pinned at her shoulder. Beaming at them, she headed for the door.

"Why don't I go finish introducing myself and watch for Mr. Thrillkill? It *is* almost five o'clock."

Ethan thought he would be glad for the privacy, but once the door shut behind the woman, he felt his mind close down, too, and his tongue tangle into a knot. He didn't understand it; worse, the harder he tried to think of something to say, the dumber the idea seemed to be.

"Wouldn't you like to take off your coat and hat?" Kate asked, proving that she wasn't having a problem at all.

Ethan shrugged out of the heavy jacket and slipped off his hat. He set both on the arm of the dark leather couch against the wall, ran a hand over his hair and returned to stand before her. Could she tell that beneath all his gear he was sweating like a stuck hog? The way his nerves were going, in another minute his shirt would be soaked worse than some of Darcy's diapers.

"I have the license ready." Kate motioned toward the desk.

"Good. It's good that you kept it here."

"Well, as I said yesterday, there didn't seem any point to carry it all over."

"No point. None." He fingered the knot of his tie, aware that he was beginning to sound like John Mountain. Kate must have picked up on it, too, because she stepped even closer, her expression concerned.

"You look miserable," she whispered, a slight frown marring the smooth skin between her eyebrows.

"Who? Me?"

"No, the umbrella stand at the door. Of course you. Are you sure you want to do this? Or maybe I should ask if you can bring yourself to go through with this?"

"I could say the same thing to you."

"You're not the one who proposed."

"And you haven't seen how many people are hanging in and around this building. It looks as if there's a bunch of folks who are as eager to see the judge marry the jailbird as there are gawkers to watch the murder suspect marry Wayne Kinkaid's sweetheart."

Kate winced. "Was that necessary?"

"Better get used to it. I have a feeling we're going to be front-page news in at least one paper tomorrow, no matter what we try to do to avoid it."

"Then let's not avoid it." A determined set to her head, Kate went to one of the windows behind her desk. A moment later, her lips parted. "My word…they're doing everything but selling cotton candy and setting up box seats out there, aren't they? I see every gossip in town, including Lily Mae Wheeler. Even Mary Jo Kincaid, for heaven's sake. You know we've caused a buzz when White-horn's answer to Betty Crocker and Bo Peep starts mingling with the curiosity seekers."

Ethan didn't care. He was trying to keep a foothold on his sanity. "You want to tell me again how all that out there is supposed to work in our favor?"

"I told you, it's not just a matter of making people believe it's *real* between us, though that can help sway what the Taylors and their attorney do. It's about buying ourselves time."

"Have you heard anything from Noble's henchman?"

She circled back to him. "As a matter of fact, I did. Just as my last case ended this afternoon. Blankenship came into the courtroom and cornered me, snorting like one of your rejected bulls."

That immediately put Ethan on guard. "Bad news?"

"It could be worse. He'd not only heard about what we were doing, but he also heard about Lessing's leave of absence. Not surprisingly, he's put two and two together."

"You don't seem overly worried."

"Because I'm not. He hasn't succeeded in doing anything yet except blowing a great deal of steam. Another case took him out of town for the last few days, and so he hasn't had an opportunity to file on behalf of the Taylors. Now, with our wedding and Lessing's leave, he knows how much more complicated things will get. He'll probably meet with Noble and Ruth within the next few days and try to think up some new strategy. But by then we'll be married and everything will have changed."

Ethan watched her faint but pleased smile as she admired her bouquet. "Yes…changed."

He must have given away something in his voice, because suddenly she glanced up, met his gaze, and it happened again. The emotions from that night last week were back, the tension and the desire. Ethan felt the pull and yielded to it, as she seemed to. Closer and closer, until he felt a prisoner of the web from which she peeked out at him.

He didn't know whether to swear or sigh with relief when someone knocked at the door. A moment later Pat Fischer poked her head in.

"Excuse me, you two, but Justice of the Peace Thrillkill is here."

Kate looked at Ethan. "Are we ready?"

For a number of things, but this—? "If you are."

Their witnesses and Monroe Thrillkill filed in. They resembled a group of mourners more than they did celebrants. At least Jorge and Eva Cantu did. They went immediately to stand near Kate, while John Mountain hung back, nearer to the door.

If Kate noticed, she didn't let on, instead taking a moment to fuss over the baby and show her to her secretary, then to the J.P. Ethan watched, thinking that with his gaunt, bearded face and funereal black suit and ribbon tie, the guy could have played an undertaker in one of the old Western movies.

Just as quickly as the abrupt, forced chatter and laughter had started, it stopped. Everyone glanced at everyone else, as if to ask, "What next?"

Thrillkill gripped the lapels of his black jacket. "Well, should we have a wedding, folks?"

With a last kiss for Darcy, Kate handed the baby back to Eva, took her place beside Ethan and, as directed by the old man, offered him her hand. Trying to be discreet about it, Ethan wiped his damp palm against his slacks before taking hold of it.

"Dearly beloved…"

How warm and steady she felt in contrast to him, Ethan thought, staring at the book trembling in the justice's hands. At least the old geezer had age to blame for his shakes. He looked down at his and Kate's hands. How real the image seemed, but at the same time dreamlike. No, he still couldn't believe this. Him and Kate. Oh, God. He felt like an impostor, a thief…a traitor to his best friend. He couldn't do it.

"Ethan, do you take this woman to be your lawful wedded wife? To…"

The words pounded in his head, and each one turned his mouth drier and drier, until he knew that when the time came, he wouldn't be able to say a word. He would be lucky to draw a breath. Even his tie was beginning to strangle him.

In a panic, he looked at Kate. That was a mistake. Her profile was a soft cameo against the amber late-afternoon sky, at once stately and ethereal, known and unknown. Soon to be tied legally and morally to him. No one took the law more serious than Kate. How could she join him in this…fiasco? What was she thinking, feeling?

"This is where you say, 'I do,' son."

Ethan felt the reassuring squeeze of Kate's fingers against his. "I do," he managed to rasp.

"Kate!" the old man declared, his enthusiasm rebuilding. "Do you take Ethan…"

When her time came, she looked straight at him. Ethan

absorbed her gaze, letting it warm his quaking insides like mulled cider on a brisk November night.

"I do," she murmured in that velvet voice, letting each word rub the air.

"Then it's time for the ring, folks."

Caught up in the moment and reassured, Ethan dug confidently into his pocket. This he knew how to do. Only his fingers touched nothing but cloth.

It wasn't there. He tried the opposite pocket, then shot an anxious look back at John Mountain. The smaller man motioned to his own inside pocket. Ethan almost sighed with relief when he remembered.

With an incoherent apology, he dug into that pocket and brought out the simple, slender band. Kate had chosen it herself, insisting she preferred it; but he knew she hadn't wanted him to spend too much money on her. That task had been handled yesterday, too, after the stop at the doctor's office. He recalled how she'd also asked if she should get him one, but, already feeling like a cheapskate because of her ring, he'd turned her down, telling her that he would probably lose it while working or something.

All that replayed in his mind as he slipped the band on her finger. And on its heels followed regret, for he knew now that he would have liked a memento of this day for later, once he lost her again.

"Repeat after me…" Thrillkill directed, thrusting out his chest.

"With this ring, I thee wed," Ethan said dutifully, suddenly feeling Kate's hand tremble slightly. Again their gazes met, and this time he squeezed *her* fingers, wanting her to know he understood. God, how he understood this strange, bewildering, magical moment.

"Then I pronounce you husband and wife. Congratulations, Mr. and Mrs. Walker. Er, that means you can kiss the bride, son."

He took hold of Kate's upper arms and angled his head to avoid her hat and veil. From behind the veil—now more like interwoven snowflakes than a web—she watched, her eyes clear, inviting, sexy, willing him to forget that they were acting. He let himself be drawn by her, until their breaths merged, their lips touched, parted, clung. The kiss was so different from the first time, and yet similar in that it was all awareness, sensation, and tethered energy. He wanted more, the rest. So did she. He knew it when she reached up and touched his cheek.

It lasted mere seconds, long enough for someone to whistle, and for Pat Fischer to ask if oxygen would be needed. Then Ethan raised his head, and Thrillkill began drawing him aside, slapping him on the back and congratulating him. He glanced over to see Kate's secretary hugging her while Eva and Jorge exchanged glances. Eva blinked hard and shrugged. It seemed to encapsulate the moment perfectly.

"Okay?" John Mountain asked near his ear.

Ethan hadn't explained much of anything to him, except that he and Kate were marrying. But John Mountain seemed to understand perfectly, which was why Ethan responded with total honesty. "What do you think?"

"You did fine. Like a pro."

It was what he needed to hear to keep his sanity and regain his balance. Enough balance that when Pat insisted they needed a few pictures, he let Kate draw him close, found it easy to slip his arm around her waist and even summon a smile. However, a little of that could go a long way. At the first opportunity, he drew Kate aside.

"Now what?"

The justice of the peace had filled out his part of their marriage license, taken his fee and left. Kate had traded her bouquet for the baby. Ethan thought the two of them made an intriguing picture. When Pat had snapped one, he knew that somehow he would get a copy for himself.

"That's up to you," Kate replied, her expression blushing bride radiant. "Eva brought us a basket dinner along with my suitcases. Jorge's put it all in my truck. We can go anytime you like."

He still couldn't believe it.

"You do remember that part?" Kate murmured, her eyes merry with laughter. "The bride goes with the groom?"

Maybe it didn't make sense, but he felt a bit miffed to be the object of her amusement, or maybe it irked that this performing business seemed to come too easily for her. Whatever the case, he felt himself stiffening. "I just wanted to make sure you're serious about this."

"It's a little late if I'm not. Um, do you think you'll mind driving my truck? I mean, John Mountain can take yours, right? Otherwise, it will look somewhat…strange."

You pegged it, pal. Everything's about appearances now. "We can't have anything looking imperfect, can we? I'll go tell him that he can leave anytime. He looks as if he'd like to get out of here."

Kate touched his arm to stop him from walking away. "Why are you angry?"

"I'm not angry."

"Yes, you are." She kept her voice low, and seemed totally absorbed in stroking the baby's tiny hand. "And it's not fair. You knew what you were getting into, and what it's going to take to pull this off."

She was right. It seemed unfair, not to mention irrational, to treat her as if this were all her fault. But, in a way, she was to blame. After all, if they'd never met, he wouldn't be caught in this twilight zone where she represented both fantasy and nightmare to him. However, he knew that to tell her as much would be inviting even bigger trouble, and so he yielded to his pain and angst.

"I just buried my sister a couple weeks ago," he replied, his whisper fierce. "I'm responsible for a newborn baby that strangers are trying to take away from me, and now I have a wife I didn't ask for, who just happens to represent a branch of the system I've lost complete faith in. If I appear a little edgy and unreasonable, maybe that's because I feel as if I'm trapped in a runaway car that doesn't even have a damned steering wheel!"

Kate lowered her head to kiss the tiny hand wrapped around her thumb, but the look she sent him from beneath her lashes was withering. "Thank you for sharing that, Ethan. Your ability to look at this complicated situation and see yourself as the only one making a sacrifice is truly inspiring. I appreciate being made to feel as if I've not only put my career on the line for nothing, but my faith in you, as well."

"Damn it, Kate."

"Excuse me, please. I have to give some last instructions to Pat, since I won't be in tomorrow."

"If you would just—" Ethan shook his head, wondering if he would ever emerge from the fog he felt lost in. "Why aren't you going in tomorrow?"

Her smile redefined adoration. "When a couple get married, they usually take at least one day off after the wedding. It's called a honeymoon. To ignore the tradition would raise questions I don't think either of us want to answer. But don't worry. I already have my briefcase packed with plenty of work to keep me out of your hair. You'll barely know I'm around."

After that verbal deboning, she managed not to say another word to him until they exited the courthouse and headed for her truck. That space of time gave Ethan yet more exposure to her indomitable spirit—not that he needed the refresher course.

Again and again the lesson struck hard, as when someone in the swarm of curious onlookers called out to her, and then another and another. She waved, stopped every few yards to say something gracious or witty, in her off-the-cuff style. With a few, she shared glimpses of the baby, wrapped snugly against the brisk early-evening air. Always her smile came quickly, and her mood was as bright as anyone would expect of a bride on her wedding day.

Even when the photographer he'd had the run-in with appeared, with a more antagonistic attitude, Kate managed to take a potentially volatile situation and turn it around, so that Ethan almost questioned whether the exchange upstairs had really happened. The guy got his picture, and they made it to the truck without an inkling of noticeable strain.

"You do that very well," he said to her when they were finally in her truck.

After double-checking the special seat she'd bought for the baby during her most recent shopping binge, she secured her own belt. "I don't feel like talking to you right now, Ethan."

"I suppose I deserve that."

Her sidelong look sliced through him. "Let me know when you're sure."

What a difference an audience made. He took extra care in pulling out from her personal parking space, the impulse strong to strip gears and floor the accelerator. *Sometimes the woman's mouth...* But how could he treat his precious cargo with such negligence? Besides, he didn't want to prove Kate right again about his temper. At least not so soon after making a fool of himself.

It took him until he'd gone a few miles up Mountain Pass before he finally calmed down enough to say, "I'm sorry for hurting and offending you."

"It's already forgiven, Ethan."

But not forgotten. That was an important and telling point, and he made a mental note of it. Kate forgave quickly, rarely holding a grudge—which was wise, since behavior like that would probably be professional suicide on the bench—but the offending party would be making a huge error to suppose she forgot. Ethan had first recognized that about her when they were kids.

In high school, she'd rejected the cheerleaders who wanted her for the squad because they'd snubbed a Hispanic girl she'd felt was far more talented. That was another thing she and Wayne had had in common—a fearlessness in standing up for principle, even if it meant standing alone.

How the devil do you hope to live up to that discipline, Walker?

Therein lay a humbling truth. He couldn't. Oh, the alone part he could handle well enough; but he was no hero, and Kate needed to understand that he never would be.

"In case you haven't picked up on it yet," he began, groping for the words to explain it to her, "through the years, when I've made mistakes, I've rarely bothered doing them in a small way."

He thought he heard her chuckle briefly under her breath. When seconds passed and nothing followed, he wondered if he'd imagined it.

"I've noticed," she drawled, at long last. "And I'm still noticing. But don't try the I've-been-alone-too-long-to-change speech. If there's anything more you want to tell me, think of something interesting, like…you sleepwalk in the nude, or something."

"Kate." The woman was working overtime at being provocative. "I'm trying to tell you that I don't know about this."

"It's a little late for doubts, Ethan. The ink's dry on the paper."

"I mean, I'm not sure we can be the friends you seem to think we are."

Out of the corner of his eye, he could tell she continued to look straight ahead at the mountains. The sun had already set, and the sky was now violet and lavender, with only a touch of orange left at the very centermost point. A tiny opening that he felt an urgent need to reach. He wondered at the driven feeling. What would getting there faster do? He still had to face the fact that over the next few months, or who knew how long, he was going to be sharing his small home with a woman who bothered him on too many levels to count.

"You and your speaking silences." Kate sighed and leaned back against the headrest. "You know what? Tomorrow we can butt heads, arm wrestle, or whatever you think is fitting for two cohabitants in our unorthodox position, but tonight… Could we at least try for something more peaceful and harmonious? If not out of respect for the ritual we just abused, then for the baby's sake. She's had a full day, and she needs her rest."

She was right. Again. What was more, he really wanted harmony between them. If it was possible.

"I'd like to try," he admitted quietly.

In his rearview mirror, he saw Jorge Cantu turn off at Shadow Ranch. By the time Ethan drove onto Double N land, John Mountain, who'd been in the rear, had caught up with them and was following down the hard-packed dirt drive.

When they reached the house, his ranch hand waved, but continued driving to the bunkhouse. That gave Ethan considerable pause. He and John Mountain shared many a meal together, and it saddened him to think he'd lost that quiet camaraderie.

"Invite him to join us, if you want."

Ethan hadn't realized she'd followed his gaze. "He wouldn't come. He's reached his limit for socializing today." The bunkhouse had its own stove and a good stock of canned goods. "He'll be fine."

He carried the baby inside, and Kate brought the picnic basket. After placing Darcy in her crib, they finished carrying in Kate's things. When they came over the threshold the last time, Ethan had a flash image of what it would be like to carry her inside.

"Man, you're asking for it," he muttered to himself, thoroughly disgusted.

"Did you say something?" Kate set her briefcase by the couch and began removing her coat and hat.

Ethan hoisted the two heavy cases and headed for the bedroom. "I said Jorge was asking for it when he carried these to your truck. You really loaded them."

"It couldn't be helped. There are some books I need constantly, plus my laptop computer. It was difficult to figure out what I would need and what I could return home to use."

Home. Her real home, no matter what.

When he returned, he hung up his coat and hat, noting that Kate was already working on unwrapping the baby from her cocoon of blankets. "She probably needs changing," he told her. "Why don't you let me do that? You're all dressed up."

"What's that you have on?" she countered, glancing over her shoulder. "Your pajamas? Ethan, you're going to drive yourself crazy if you keep trying to treat me like a combination guest and intruder."

"Yeah, well, maybe it'll sink in that you aren't one—guest, that is—when you don't look ready to pose for some wedding magazine."

"Another clash of wills," she intoned to Darcy. "Okay, how about this? I'm already changing her, so why don't *you* go get comfortable? When you're done, you can add some wood to the stove and unpack the basket, while I get into different clothes."

Ethan didn't need another suggestion to start tugging loose his tie, but he couldn't resist pointing something out to her. "Do you realize you haven't been in the place five minutes and you're already dictating?"

"It must be delirium from hunger."

Just inside the bedroom doorway, he paused. "I know I'm going to be sorry I asked, but when was the last time anyone had the last word with you?"

Her laughter followed him into the dark room.

"Pray for a long life, cowboy. There's always the chance you might be the first."

Six

All grumbling aside, Ethan couldn't wait to change out of his suit. By the time he pulled on old jeans and a comfortable flannel shirt, Kate had Darcy changed.

She would be good with the baby. Not fast, but then she didn't have his experience yet. Still, she had the right instincts, and he had to admit he liked the cooing noises and bits of songs and other nonsense she sang to entertain the child. As he stirred the remaining coals in the stove and added three new logs, he thought about telling her.

"You need some light," Kate announced, breaking into those thoughts.

Perplexed, he paused in sweeping up the ash and bits of log left at the base of the stove. "I have light. When I need more, I just get out another oil lamp."

"No, I mean the kind of lamp you plug into the wall. And you could use a stereo, too."

"I have a TV." He brushed his hands on his jeans and went to take one of the baby bottles out of the refrigerator.

"TV can wait for later. Pat told me about a friend who's a pediatrics nurse over in Helena. She says that babies in her unit seem to cope better if you play them certain types of music."

"Like what?"

"Harps."

"Harps?"

Kate smiled. "Angel music."

Ethan grimaced and put the bottle in a saucepan of water, then set the whole thing on the wood-burning stove. "I don't think I'm ready to listen to this."

"You may be burned and bitter, Ethan, but that's no excuse to deprive a baby of her own kind."

"Her own kind… Could we try to remember that you're a judge? I don't think you want too many people hearing you talk like that."

"Ethan, *I* believe in angels. And this motherless baby no doubt has a double order of them watching over her. She'll need them around you."

"Now what's that supposed to mean?"

"It's too quiet in here. If someone doesn't do something, Darcy might as well grow up in a mausoleum. I noticed it that first day I came in to see her."

Ethan put away the fireplace tools. "Well, I live here, too, and I happen to like quiet. As for Miss Muffet over there, she's too young to state a preference one way or another."

"That's my point. She never will, if she doesn't start hearing something besides her Uncle Ethan snoring." Kate released the first button of her wedding suit's jacket before heading for the bedroom.

"Hey—who said I snore?"

"Well, I'll find out, won't I?"

As she disappeared into the bedroom, Ethan didn't know what got to him more, her teasing or the brief glimpse of the creamy satin camisole as she'd slipped out of her jacket. But, grateful for the reprieve, he concentrated next on unloading the picnic basket.

Out came fluffy dinner rolls, fried chicken and potato salad, and it soon became obvious that if Eva Cantu didn't like him, she didn't believe in showing it by being stingy with food. He also lifted out two other kinds of cold salads before he spotted the bowl of rice pudding.

Kate's all-time favorite dessert, and it had become his, too. He remembered because the year his father died, she'd delivered a big bowl of it on Christmas Eve. It was a memorable addition to the tough elk stew and bargain-bakery bread that they'd been about to call dinner. Ethan had felt as awkward about thanking her then as now.

Lost in thought, he almost forgot Darcy's bottle. He pulled it out, shook and tested it, glad to discover he'd caught it in time. He'd barely lifted the baby into his arms when Kate returned from the bedroom.

"Can I take over?"

At her first mention of changing, Ethan had been relieved, thinking that if she was in casual clothes, he wouldn't be as aware of her womanliness. Stupid thought. This earth goddess in the ivory tunic and leggings, with her hair flowing past her shoulders and her feet clad in thick socks, was every bit as captivating as the formally dressed Kate had been.

She came straight to him, beaming as she had been doing practically nonstop since the ceremony. That vibrant, youthful smile, combined with the brush of her hands across his belly as she eased the baby out of his arms,

forced him to pass over the infant without a word and to
retreat to the kitchen area out of self-preservation.

Terrific. In another minute you'll be drooling.

"Ethan?"

She'd followed him. He spun around, certain she'd
again seen the loss of control in his eyes.

"Bottle?"

Disgusted with himself, he passed it over. "Sorry."

"No champagne, I see," Kate mused, scanning the
bounty spread across the counter once the baby starting
suckling. "I suppose Eva's goodwill didn't stretch that far."

Ethan had thought about it himself, but hadn't followed
up on the idea of getting a bottle, for several reasons. "I
guess you'll have to settle for a beer or whiskey, if you feel
like celebrating."

"Don't you?"

He didn't know what he felt. At least he didn't know
what was safe to admit. "I guess I'll join you."

"Mr. Enthusiastic. Make mine a beer. At least it's a
similar color and bubbles."

Shooting her a doubtful look, Ethan took two bottles
from the refrigerator and then reached up to a high cabinet
for the one long-stemmed glass that Marilee had picked up
at a five-and-dime-store clearance sale ages ago. At dinner
she'd always had her milk in the glass, and in hindsight
Ethan realized her dreams for a better life had been germi-
nating even then.

When he set glass and opened bottle before her, Kate
uttered a delicious moan. "You'd better stop spoiling me.
If you're not careful, you're going to have me eating out
of your hand."

"In that case, I'd better invest in some chain-mail
gloves," he drawled, finishing with the unpacking. To keep

her from noticing his twitching lips, he carried the basket to the corner by the back door.

"You don't have to wait for me to fill your plate, you know. I'll join you as soon as the baby's through."

"That's okay." He returned, poured her drink, then lifted his bottle to take a swallow.

"Wait!"

He drew a long breath. "Now what?"

"We haven't made a toast yet."

He'd been hoping to avoid that particular ceremony. He should have guessed she wouldn't let an opportunity pass to hold to tradition and torment him with rituals he'd been depriving himself of for most of his life. "You're determined to be upbeat and positive about this, aren't you?"

"Call me crazy, Ethan, but I think it beats walking around thumping my chest and sobbing, 'Mea culpa.'"

He succeeded in not swelling up like a blustering rooster, but he couldn't quite keep from clenching his teeth. "Is that what I'm doing? You think I'm playing martyr?"

"I haven't been able to read your mind well enough to make up mine," she replied with a shrug. "Let's just say you could do with some lightening-up."

Since she rarely backed down this easily, Ethan thought that was reason enough to celebrate. Once again he lifted his bottle. "All right, get it over with."

She took her time, first making sure Darcy was ready to take a breather from her bottle. Then she poured her beer and waited for the head to shrink. Finally she touched her glass to his bottle, murmuring a simple "Here's to you... Mr. Walker."

Cute. And she was getting cuter by the minute. Yet, despite his annoyance, Ethan let his gaze wander downward, to the three open buttons on her tunic, the tempting swell of her breasts.

"Mrs. Walker." But as soon as he took a swallow of his drink, he couldn't resist asking, "Have you thought about what you're going to say when people ask if they're supposed to call you Judge Randall or Judge Walker?"

"Tell them the truth…that I'm sleeping on it." She lifted her glass to salute him. "May you get everything you want."

He wasn't about to touch that one, no matter how much she grumbled, and they didn't speak again for several minutes. Ethan figured it was wisest, since she didn't seem capable of saying anything that wasn't provocative.

After Darcy finished her bottle and Kate put her in her crib, they filled their plates. Hoping to continue the silence, Ethan gestured toward the TV. "Do you want me to turn it on?"

"No thanks. I'd much rather talk."

Knock yourself out. Talk— Jeez. He'd lost count of how many knots had formed in his stomach since he'd awakened this morning to the realization that this was his D day. His first beer hadn't done anything to ease them, so he went to get himself another.

"Come on, Ethan," Kate called chidingly after him. "It's been ages since we've spent more than a few minutes in each other's company. Don't forget, if we don't sound as if we really know each other, we're not going to appear very credible to anyone at that custody hearing."

"What's there to know?" He returned to his seat. "I've been working the ranch and you've been raising legal hell. That pretty well covers it."

Kate glanced over toward the crib in the unlit corner of the room where Darcy already slept. "Tell me about your dreams for her. I know you have some. If you didn't, you wouldn't have done all you have so far to keep her."

"I just don't want her to have to put aside *her* dreams."

"The way you did yours?"

Ethan concentrated on scooping a large dollop of potato salad and dropping it next to the two chicken legs already on his plate. "If you want to talk, let's straighten out our schedules and living arrangements. I sleep over on the recliner, so you take the bedroom. Don't argue," he added, when he saw her lips move as if to protest. "I've been sleeping there for years."

That clearly shocked her. "Why?"

"It suits me." The serving spoon cracked against his plate as he misaimed a spoonful of the corn casserole. "The thing is, I have to get up around four every morning, and I'll need to wash up."

"Of course. Don't think twice about coming through. You won't bother me."

"Even so, I'll try not to make too much noise. John Mountain comes in around five. I cook for both of us, to make up for his having to do most of the range work these days. But, uh, if you're going to be here tomorrow, maybe you won't mind watching the baby while I go, too, for a few hours?"

"Love to." Kate reached for a roll and tore it in two. "And I'll make breakfast."

"That's not necessary."

"Nonsense," she replied with an airy wave. "I'm on my honeymoon. I can't think of anything I'd like to do more."

"Very funny."

The *least* she could do was not keep reminding him that they were married, that she was his wife, and that there wasn't any legal reason for him not to follow her to bed tonight. There were plenty of nonlegal ones, beginning with the fact that, as curious as she might have been about kissing him, that didn't constitute an invitation to seek oblivion in her softness and heat.

He had no idea how he made it through dinner. He remained hungry, all right, but not for food; and everything he put in his mouth tasted like cardboard. On top of that, if he did try to hold up his side of their conversation, he ended up feeling like an awkward youth all over again.

When this latest ordeal was over and they'd repacked everything and cleaned up the dishes, a far more subdued Kate finally seemed ready to call it quits, too. Murmuring a good night, she withdrew to the bedroom.

Relieved, Ethan checked on the baby once more, and added a couple more logs to the stove before he started blowing out the oil lamps. Ready to turn in, he realized he didn't have his blanket. Normally he tossed it on the couch, but in anticipation of Kate's arrival, he'd had some foolish notion about straightening up the place and put it in the bedroom.

He went to the door, which wasn't quite closed, and knocked softly. She didn't answer. Small favors, he thought his hopes rising. Maybe she was already asleep. He would sneak in and get out before—

When he was midway into the room, the bathroom door swung open and Kate stepped out, barely wrapped in a towel. Ethan froze. He had a fleeting glimpse of glistening water on her shoulders and her endless legs before he spun around.

"I forgot my blanket," he said to the far wall.

"What are you doing? For heaven's sake, Ethan, I'm decent. Come in and get whatever you need."

He nearly ripped the blanket off the chair in the corner, mumbled, "Good night," and hurried from the room.

Minutes later, as he drew the cover up to his chin and

tried to find a comfortable spot to settle for the night, he couldn't. Why did he have to notice the thing was getting lumpy tonight, of all nights?

He shut his eyes, but found less peace. Against his closed lids, he kept seeing Kate—pale, golden and desirable.

Yep, you're married. He shifted to ease yet another ache in his body. *Don't it feel grand?*

"I bet you're thinking that your Auntie Kate's turning out to be one real nervy lady, huh, twiglet?"

Kate tickled Darcy's chin as she strolled away from the kitchen window. She'd been watching for Ethan, growing concerned now that the sun had slipped behind the mountains. It didn't help that she'd done all she could do for the moment. The baby had been bathed, fed and changed again; she had dinner warming on the stove. With time to pace and think about what she'd been doing over the past twenty-four hours, she was using the baby as a sounding board, and shaking her head a great deal.

"It wouldn't be ladylike for you to mention how long it's been since I flirted like this. And I know you've noticed your poor uncle doesn't know what to do about me, but—" she smiled at the fascinated infant "—all I'm trying to do is give him a hint."

Darcy gurgled contentedly.

"No kidding. I'll say he's a tough customer. Here I am, in the prime of my life, with a man who responds as powerfully to me as I do to him, but getting that grumble bear to acknowledge it…" Kate gave the cherub an owlish look. "Jump in anytime with any suggestions, cutie. That's why we're having this conversation."

Amused at how fascinated the baby seemed to be with her whimsical monologue, Kate returned to the table where she'd been working earlier in the afternoon. She hadn't accomplished as much as she'd anticipated. As she used one hand to negotiate several folders back into her briefcase, she had to admit a newborn took more time than she'd heard. Of course, it didn't help that she couldn't resist holding the darling at every opportunity. But, despite the fatigue that was beginning to settle in after the unusual day, she felt pretty terrific.

"Because you're a doll," she told Darcy, carrying baby and briefcase to the front door, where she set her bag to take with her in the morning. Then she planted what had to be the twentieth or thirtieth kiss on the baby's forehead. "And I wouldn't have missed spending the day spoiling you for anything."

That earned her another tentative, toothless smile. The first had stolen her heart, and she'd nearly gotten teary-eyed, thinking of Marilee, how the dear soul would never know such precious moments. It also made Kate wonder how she'd managed to exist as long as she had without doing something about her own yearning for children.

The back door opened quietly. Oh, darn, she thought, belatedly remembering that she'd been so preoccupied with Darcy and work that she hadn't run a brush through her hair since this morning. It would have been nice to dab a touch of perfume behind her ears, too. Since she'd done neither, she let her smile be her enhancement.

"Hi! I was beginning to worry."

"No need. We were merely catching up on the backlog of chores."

Ethan rolled his shoulders before slipping out of his jacket and taking off his hat. He looked beat, but wonderful.

He sniffed and uttered an appreciative groan. "Man, I thought I'd imagined smelling food outside. What's cooking?"

"Meat loaf, mashed potatoes, and the corn casserole from yesterday. It's not as fancy or pretty as what Eva makes, but I don't think you'll get food poisoning."

Ethan looked both amazed and guilty. "You didn't have to do all that. It meant a lot simply knowing you were with the baby."

"I didn't mind. Where's John Mountain? There's plenty to go around."

"You know he's not going to come over here."

"Because of me."

"Not because of you." Ethan looked at his hands and headed for the sink. "Because he prefers to be alone, and he thinks we do, too."

"Wait a second." Kate hurried to the wood-burning stove, picking up a towel along the way. "I suspected he wouldn't come. That's why I prepared him a plate. Before you wash up, be a dear and bring this to him."

The plate was already wrapped in foil, and the towel made it safe to carry, but Kate was careful to keep it well away from the baby.

Ethan stared at it as if she'd told him it was a four-course dinner. "That's…really thoughtful of you."

The moment he left to carry the food over to the bunk-house, Kate whispered playfully to Darcy. "Did you hear that? He thinks I'm thoughtful. Yesterday I was a rope of chains around his neck that he didn't want to deal with, and today… Isn't it amazing what a modest meat loaf can do."

Ethan soon returned. Because he'd made it clear he was famished, Kate changed her mind about first offering him a drink to unwind a bit. Instead, she placed the sleepy Darcy in her crib and set out their dinner. By the time Ethan had washed up, they were ready to take their seats at the table.

After an initial bite or two, Ethan paused to offer his compliments, then concentrated on his meal. Kate could feel how something else was building in him. She just couldn't figure out what.

"Er...was it tough for you today?" he asked her as he reached for his second roll.

"Different, but I wouldn't say tough. I think Darcy likes our girl-to-girl chats best. She's not wild about the speech I'm writing for the Junior League luncheon in Billings next month."

He didn't respond to her gentle humor; instead, he glanced over his left shoulder at his desk. It was old, like everything else in the small house, and as neglected.

"You should have told me, and I would have made room for you over there."

"That's all right. Anyway, it's a bit chilly in that corner, what with the windows and it being so far from the stove. I worked here at the table."

"Sometimes I notice that myself, but I've always tried to blame it on being tired. Um, did you have problems with the fire?" He checked the stack near the stove. "I should have left you with more wood."

"There was plenty, as you can see."

Kate began to get intrigued. The more agreeably she responded to his questions, the more strained and disturbed he appeared. What was eating at him now?

"I was wondering..." she asked, after watching him stir his mashed potatoes for several seconds. "What will you do tomorrow?"

He shrugged. "Stay here." Once again he glanced around the large room. "See if I can't make this look like less of a dump."

Aha, she thought, finally getting a hint of what was

troubling him. "Your home is not a dump, Ethan. It's spare. Rustic. Utilitarian."

"Right." He made a bitter sound. "I'll bet you haven't missed your place once all day, did you?"

"Am I complaining?"

Her quiet words seemed to inflame him. For a moment, she wondered if he would explode, storm out. But as quickly as the emotion had stirred, he calmed—or rather he rested his elbows on the table and rubbed his face, uttering a weary moan.

"The law's no lady, Kate. No matter how many statues they build to represent her, I've known that truth for a long time. But…you are," he added gruffly. "And I suppose that's proving more than I know how to deal with."

His honesty left her momentarily speechless. Quite a novelty, she mused, searching for an appropriate reply. How much easier it would be if she could simply slip to her knees beside him and wrap her arms around him, but she knew he wouldn't welcome that gesture from her, either.

She could only shake her head. "You give me too much credit, and…Ethan, you 'deal' with me just fine."

He avoided looking at her straight, as if his ability to keep this conversation under control relied on that. "This isn't going to work, Kate. Look around you. My mother sewed those drapes, and they look it, don't they? There's probably two years of dust on them, save the bit I vacuumed off the one or two times I turned on the machine. The furniture—what there is of it—was mostly bargain-basement stuff when *we* got it." His laugh reflected sheer bitterness. "I must have been nuts to think I could close my eyes while you made yourself endure this. I realize now that you'd do about anything for the baby, but I can't watch you…cheapen your own life for this."

She hated seeing him beat himself up emotionally for nothing. And it was nothing to her. But, aware that the matter, his pride, meant a great deal to him, she understood that she couldn't sound flippant.

"What's your solution?" she asked instead, her heart pounding.

He bowed his head. "I don't know."

"May I make a suggestion?" She had to wait for a minuscule nod. "I telephoned Eva today. Well, I would have anyway, because I needed to make sure everything was okay over there."

"There's no need to justify yourself. I understand you have a heck of a lot more invested in your place than I do in mine."

"At any rate," Kate continued, not caring for the sound of that one bit, "I suggested something to her, and now I'd like to run it by you and find out what you think."

As expected, he looked wary. "Go ahead."

"You know I've known Eva for most of my life. I trust her implicitly, as I do Jorge. Today I asked her if—provided we had your approval, of course—she would be interested in caring for Darcy during the hours that I'm working."

"Jeez, Kate…"

"Hear me out, Ethan. That's all I ask. I could take her over in the morning and pick her up on my way home. It's a perfect solution, since most of what she would need is already there. You see, we kept many of my baby things, and Eva's been talking for years about cleaning out the attic."

"You don't think she has enough to do without taking on the care of an infant? And consider her age. She should be slowing down, not getting busier."

"If the baby was older, or this was a long-term situation, I would be more hesitant to suggest it, but you said yourself that this is temporary. As for her age, I think Eva would come after you with her mop if she heard that. Ethan, I make sure she goes in for a yearly physical. The doctor says she's as healthy as I am." Kate leaned toward him. "Think about how this would free you up. It's tearing you apart to see how much you're having to put on John Mountain's shoulders."

Ethan slumped back in his chair. "When is it going to end? Don't you see what you're doing?"

"I'm trying to help."

"You're creating a mountain of debt I'm never going to be able to repay."

It bothered her that he should see their situation that way, and she told him so. "This isn't about who owes whom more, or even *what,* Ethan. You're in the midst of one of the biggest crises of your life. You need help. I can provide that help. That's all there is to it."

"I wanted to be able to do this myself."

"Well, it's obvious that's not how it's going to work out. I believe in life lessons, and I believe you're being challenged with some whoppers, Ethan. Don't fight them. Listen to them. Learn from them. If my hunch is wrong, if things don't work out, we'll try something else. But don't reject the idea because of pride. We simply don't have time for that."

Ethan's strong, sharp features shifted subtly as he worked his jaw. His blue eyes, already dark from fatigue and lingering grief, seemed almost opaque tonight. He was finding it increasingly difficult to hope, Kate saw. And she knew that if he turned her down, nothing would change on the surface; she would continue to work toward helping him reach his goal; but his decision would change something between them forever. Crush the seed she knew wanted to grow.

When she saw his left hand close into a fist, she knew he'd reached his decision.

"Your Honor, after considerable reflection, my client has changed his mind. He wishes to plead guilty and throw himself upon the mercy of the court."

Kate nodded, keeping her eyes on the case notes before her until the urge to laugh passed. "All right, then. Mr. Chester, will you rise for sentencing." As the self-proclaimed poet laureate of Whitehorn stood, she saw from the corner of her eye that Pat was approaching from her chambers. "Pardon me one moment," she murmured, covering the microphone with her hand and leaning back to hear what Pat had to say.

"Sorry to interrupt, but Eva called," the redhead whispered into her ear.

"The baby!"

"She's fine. It's Ethan. He's driving her crazy. He's phoned three times, and a few minutes ago he threatened to drive over to take the baby home because Eva said she was too busy to talk to him. She feels he thinks she can't handle things. She says if you don't do something, she's retiring…without notice."

Kate didn't know whether to laugh or groan. "She's bluffing. That woman took one look at Darcy this morning and it was love at first sight." She did some quick thinking. "Call Ethan, and if you can get through, tell him to stay put, that I'll call him in—" she glanced at her watch "—ten minutes. Then call Eva and let her know I'm handling the situation. By that time, I should be back there to take over."

As soon as Pat started down the bench steps, Kate cleared her throat and leaned toward the microphone again. "All right, Mr. Chester…as much as I sympathize with your frustrations over the mishandling of your property—"

"My book, Judge," the indignant little man said, clutching the remains of his parcel to his chest. "And not for the first time!"

"I understand. However, driving your truck through the plate-glass door of the post office because they'd returned your mangled verse—pardon me, your package—damaged is no excuse for violence. The court hereby sentences you to six months probation, and one hundred hours of community service."

"But, Your Honor—!"

"Court adjourned until eleven o'clock!"

"All rise," the bailiff called, although Kate was already on her way toward her chambers.

Once in the back, she unzipped her robe and detoured to peek at Pat in her reception area. *"Ethan?"* she mouthed to the younger woman, who was holding the phone receiver to her ear.

When Pat nodded, Kate signaled that she would take it in her office. She ran back and snatched up the phone.

"Ethan?"

"Kate, don't lecture. I had every right to check on the baby."

She pictured him standing by the phone at his desk, legs astride, hand on his hip and hat low over his narrowed eyes. Ready for battle. How not to play to his temperament? she wondered, and spun her chair to her view of Whitehorn, and the mountains. "I think you're wonderful."

As expected, her warmth and flattery immediately put him on the defensive. "What do you think you're pulling now?"

"Nothing. We agree, you have every right to check on Darcy, and the fact that you can't concentrate on your own work is so touching, I don't mind at all that I had to stop a trial in the middle of sentencing to keep my housekeeper from quitting."

"Ah. The guilt-trip ploy."

"Not at all, and don't you worry about a thing. I'll call Eva again, and insist that it's more important to take your calls and reassure you than it is to get those eggs colored that we're donating for the communitywide children's Easter egg hunt on Saturday. Or to make an extra casserole for me to bring along when I come home tonight. Or to—"

"I get the message."

The chagrin in his voice assured her. That allowed Kate to feel heartsick for him and for what he must have been going through these last hours. She'd spent far less time with the baby; nevertheless, she'd experienced her own severe pangs when leaving Darcy this morning.

"I knew you would. And you know what else? Darcy is a lucky little girl to have you in her life. Try to believe that if anything, *anything,* occurred, or gave Eva doubts, she would call me immediately, and I would notify you," Kate assured him gently.

"Do you think I'll ever get there?" he said, with a sigh underscoring his doubtful tone.

"I'll bet my name on it," Kate drawled before hanging up.

She was still chuckling over that parting volley when she drove home later that afternoon. Not even the challenging day, the gawking from unscheduled visitors in the courthouse and the occasional needling from regulars like Matthews and Harlan Collins, on top of a busy schedule, could dampen her spirits.

When she reached Shadow Ranch, she thought Eva might try picking up where the others had left off; after all, their conversation following her chat with Ethan hadn't hinted at any mellowing in Eva's attitude toward him or the marriage.

But Darcy had obviously worked her magic. Less than thirty minutes later, Kate left Shadow Ranch with the infant, to the tune of *both* Eva and Jorge demanding reassurances that the child would be back tomorrow.

She returned to the Double N, where this time Ethan was the one waiting with an anxious look on his face. He strode outside in shirtsleeves to help her, and Kate let herself pretend that at least a part of his relief and concern was for her.

Thanks to Eva's casserole, dinner was dealt with quickly. While Kate cleaned up, Ethan sat holding Darcy—who was already showing signs of being a little glutton for attention. Yet somehow the evening flew by.

Before she knew it, Kate was looking for excuses not to turn in. Part of the reason reflected her previous routine; until now, she had never gone to bed before 10:00 p.m., and if she had a speech or conference seminar to develop, it could easily be midnight. But ranch work demanded early rising, so after Ethan covered his second yawn, she gave up.

As she murmured good-night, she told herself not to be disappointed, that they'd reached new ground tonight, and that some of the bumps in their relationship had been smoothed out. She reminded herself that trust took time. But that didn't ease the physical restlessness that struck the moment she drew the bedroom door nearly shut; nor did it keep her warm when she finally crawled beneath the chilly sheets. Once lying there, she got her mind off the cold by reliving moments of the evening, the way Ethan's eyes had gone tender whenever he looked at the baby…how once or twice that tenderness had lingered when he glanced toward her…how they'd actually laughed briefly together over the baby sounds drifting over from the crib. Most of all, the instant of electricity and sharp awareness when they'd both reached for the refrigerator door at the same time to warm Darcy's bottle. The memory of the heat that had swept through her when their gazes collided should have warmed her even now and lulled her into sweet dreams. It didn't.

Minutes dragged into nearly an hour. When she realized she was still shivering with cold and remained as wide-awake as ever, Kate finally flung back the covers and in disgust padded in her socks to the stove to warm up.

"You get any closer to that thing and you're going to burn something personal."

She jumped at the sound of Ethan's low, gruff voice. The stove's window allowed enough light for her to see that he'd sat up and was pushing himself up from the chair. In the past few days, Kate had noticed he slept in just his jeans, and in the amber glow she grew instantly aware of the long, sinewy muscles that sculpted his torso and strong arms, and that without a belt his pants rode low on his hips.

"Sorry I woke you, but I'm f-freezing," she whispered back, aware that she felt anything but apologetic.

"Guess the door needs to be fully open to get any heat in there, but you could dress more sensibly, too."

Kate brushed her hair back as she inspected her thigh-length flannel sleeping shirt and her thick woolen socks. "This is one hundred percent more than I prefer to wear. How anyone can sleep tangled in a bunch of sleeves and whatnot is beyond me. The only reason I am now is so I won't catch pneumonia."

"Thank you for sharing that. Now we can both suffer from insomnia."

"Ha! Listen to Mr. Discipline," Kate said teasingly, her heart beginning to pound.

Ethan shot her a mild look and reached for her hands.

"Knock it off and come here." Then he proceeded to rub her trembling limbs. "Damn. You are cold."

Not for long, she thought as both his heat and the fire's seeped into her, and the intimacy of his work-rough hands created its own furnace. Despite not being a lover's touch, Kate found the stroking powerful. But as a physical, passionate woman who'd denied herself a great deal of intimacy for too many years, maybe she was overreacting?

"You're shaking through and through," Ethan said seconds later, when he noted that her condition hadn't improved. "Here, wrap yourself in this." He backtracked for his blanket, and returned to wrap it around her. "Sit down and I'll go make you a cup of coffee."

"No thanks. Coffee at this hour will definitely give me insomnia. Why don't I go get my blanket, and you can have yours back? Then you can at least try to get some sleep."

"You really think I'm going to rest, knowing you're right here?"

"What's the matter? Afraid I'll watch you?" she asked, only half teasing.

"Would you?"

She expected retreat, at least a wall of some sort. This almost flirtatious reply raced through her like potent wine. "Mmm... Does that bother you?"

"A man would have to be made of something besides flesh and blood not to be affected by having your eyes on him, Judge Randall," he replied, his gaze roaming over her face.

Although his tone was gruff, she knew what he was doing by using her title. "Shame on you, Ethan. That was a cop-out."

Disappointed, she started back to her room, but he thrust out his arm and blocked her way. Once again he searched her face. "What do you want from me, Kate?"

"Why do we have to define it?" she replied, weariness joining forces with her frustration. "We're attracted to each other. You've tried to ignore it. I have myself."

Slowly he reached up and touched her hair. "Maybe we should listen to those inner voices. They're usually right."

Kate leaned into his touch until he cupped her face with his hand. When she felt his thumb brush across her lower lip, her breath locked in her throat; still, she inched closer. "Not always. Who's going to be hurt if we offer and take from each other?"

"Us."

She would have decided for both of them, would have closed the last inch or two between them, made him kiss her. But she wanted him to decide. With a muffled oath, he did.

He fused his mouth to hers, and she eagerly clung. It had been so long since they'd been this close. Too long. What was more, it had never been like this. His intensity triggered a searing but sweet pain that momentarily overwhelmed her. Before she began to recover, he forced her lips wider, all fierce but delicious demand as he explored and claimed.

Kate moaned softly, dropped the blanket and slipped her arms around his neck. Ethan closed her in the vise of his arms and crushed her closer. With another deep-throated moan, he buried one hand in her hair, cupped her head to hold her still, and redefined her understanding of provocation. All the while, he used his other hand to mold her body against his. From shoulder to hip, he learned and worshiped her shape, until their breaths sounded as greedy as the flames devouring the moisture-starved logs. Soon her body was vibrating with pent-up longing, her body liquefying at the pleasure of feeling him center her against his heat.

She had no idea who urged whom down onto the blanket. Her only concern was that he not stop, and he didn't.

He covered her lower body with his and slipped his hand under the flannel. His hand was relentless, his gliding touch sensitive, coursing up her midriff, seeking her breast; when he found her, they both gasped, and he tore his mouth from hers to race it down the side of her neck.

"Ethan," she whispered, unable to remain still, and loving the way the muscles across his broad back tensed under her restless, not wholly gentle, touch.

"Dear heaven, I want you. You're driving me—"

The brush of his thumb across her turgid nipple drew a soft gasp from her and cut off whatever else he might have said. Kate writhed, arched toward him, wanting more, wanting him to give himself to her, and take her in return. The hunger was too compelling, almost raw, and it was long past time that he admitted it.

Instead, she felt him push himself away from her, felt it like a razor slicing across her skin. "Ethan?"

"Damn. Oh, damn…I can't."

"Can't?" The cool air made her shiver.

"Can't, won't, it's all the same."

She sat up, dragging her shirt up over her shoulder and breast, tugging it down over her thighs. "I don't understand."

"I'm sorry. I didn't mean to start this and leave you… hurting."

"I don't want an apology," she managed, her insides still quaking. "I want an explanation."

"It can't be casual for us, all right?"

"It didn't feel as if it would be." She made herself ignore the agony clearly etched on his face. She didn't care that he looked as if one touch from her would make him rupture like skin stretched too tight. Her own pain was too real. "Damn you, Ethan. You owe me more than that."

He sat back on the brick base of the stove and, resting

his arms on his knees, covered his face with his hands. "I wish there was more, but there isn't. I don't expect you to understand, but it all boils down to the reality that I can't change the past. Or the present. I can't change who I am, and you—"

"I swear, if you tell me I'm too good for you, I'll do something drastic."

"Will you go to bed? Please!"

"This is about ghosts, isn't it? About Wayne, and your guilt over surviving, when he didn't. About being able to feel, when—"

"It's not up for discussion, Kate. Just leave me alone."

Aching and miserable, she struggled to her feet. And, not trusting herself to avoid saying something she might later regret, she returned to the bedroom and completely shut the door.

The room's temperature no longer concerned her. Ethan's house couldn't possibly chill her more than the man had himself.

Seven

"So what do you suggest, Kate? Kate?"

Blast, she thought, realizing her thoughts had been drifting again. Giving Harlan Collins an apologetic look, Kate tried to pick up on their impromptu hallway conversation. "I think you're right, Harlan. You have a sensitive situation that under normal circumstances would definitely deserve a formal charge and arraignment. However, considering that two of the three suspects are minors on the reservation, I think we should meet with representatives of the tribal council, bring in the third party's attorney as a courtesy, to protect us from any accusation of preferential treatment. Set everything on the table and see if we can keep this from getting blown up into a media event at the taxpayers' expense. The important thing to stand firm on is that hoodlum behavior will not be tolerated in this jurisdiction."

"Sounds good. I'll get back to you as soon as I have a fix on scheduling." The portly but sharply dressed litigator lifted a stark eyebrow, and a twinkle entered his eyes. "So would it be improper of a well-meaning district attorney to ask a judge he respects how married life and motherhood is taking?"

"Put that way, you may." Kate summoned a grin, albeit a weak one. "As for an answer, let's just say that no astronaut ever went through more intense but sweet training."

"My money's on you. Uh-oh," Harlan added, his voice dropping an octave. "Don't look now, but Warren B. is about to zero in on you, and I see flamethrowers in his eyes. What do you want to bet his business is with Mrs. Walker and not Judge Randall?"

It was going to be one of those days. In the past three weeks Kate had been dodging Warren Blankenship as much as possible, because she'd discovered that his continuing scheduling problems made it impossible for him to instigate a custody hearing faster than he'd originally intended. Now that he was back in town, Kate was relying on her heavier caseload, due to Howard Lessing's leave of absence, to keep him at bay. This time, however, it appeared her luck had run out.

"Mrs. Walker has less to say to him than Judge Randall does," she replied dryly. Of course, what she couldn't let slip was that since the night she and Ethan had fought, she'd avoided thinking of herself as a married woman unless a moment such as this arose. Any reminder of what a fool she'd made of herself was difficult; she still didn't know how she'd gotten through Easter, and particularly the church services that she'd attended with Darcy and an extremely reluctant Ethan.

"May I volunteer myself to hang around and offer moral support?" Harlan asked, with Warren nearly within hearing distance.

As much as Kate admired Harlan the man, she couldn't afford to give the shrewd attorney he also was any free ammunition. "Thanks, but can I have a rain check?"

"Anytime. Blankenship."

"Hello, Warren." Kate exchanged nods with the departing D.A. before giving Warren Blankenship her full attention. "I'm already late for a meeting, but if you need to talk, you can walk me back to my office."

"I need more time than that, Judge."

"Sorry. My schedule is extremely tight."

"See me now, or I'll recommend my client pursues the charge he's entertaining."

The threat bothered her less than his audacity in attempting it. Realizing he wouldn't be so bold if he didn't hold some kind of trump card, Kate opened the door to her office and led the way inside. "Pat, tell the bailiff I need three minutes, no more. And no interruptions while Mr. Blankenship and I are in conference," she told her secretary as she passed the other woman's desk.

The woman's welcoming expression sobered the moment she saw who was following her boss. "Done."

Kate continued into her private chamber, stopped at the door and firmly shut it after the confident and suave attorney. "Now understand this, Warren. If you ever threaten me like that again, particularly in public, I will take great pleasure in making your life a living nightmare."

"A tempting proposition…Your Honor." The tall attorney thrust out his chest and smirked down at her. "But are you sure you can afford to stick out your professional neck any farther than you already have?"

Although she had a good idea of what he was driving at, Kate forced herself to play ignorant. "Meaning?"

"You've interfered with jurisprudence."

"That's an extremely strong accusation, Counselor."

"But an accurate one, though I must admit your marriage to that—" When Kate narrowed her eyes in warning, he paused. "Your decision to wed Mr. Walker stands as a stroke of tactical genius."

"Tactical. You're suggesting I married my husband for reasons other than love?"

Blankenship snickered and stroked his carefully maintained mustache. "Oh, I wouldn't begin to suggest otherwise. Not after you two created such a picture of romantic bliss at church. It's amazing what the love of a good woman can do for a man. Er, how long has it been since Ethan's attended services?"

That episode had been one of the worst ordeals of her life. Still stinging from the night Ethan had rejected her, Kate would have given almost anything to avoid attending the services. But common sense had prevailed and, knowing it was important to be seen as a family, they'd gone. Ethan deserved the accolades, though. He'd proved he possessed an unparalleled potential for performing, by being the image of attentiveness. A hand at her elbow, an arm around her waist, the squeeze of her shoulder when they paused to speak to the minister after the service…one more touch and she would have screamed. She'd almost been relieved when, upon their return to his ranch, he'd changed and ridden out to who knew where. She hadn't seen him again for hours, and hadn't asked where he'd been when he returned.

"You're wasting your three minutes, Warren," she told him, hoping her voice sounded close to unimpressed.

"Then I'll summarize. I happen to know that you made a deal with Matthews not to hear my request on behalf of the Taylors' claim for custody of their granddaughter," the attorney said coldly. "I also know that you two made a deal so only Lessing would hear *your* case—knowing Judge Lessing's unfortunate medical predicament."

"Not that I owe you an explanation, but I'm better acquainted with Judge Matthews than I am with Judge Lessing," Kate replied, matching him stare for stare. "We discussed the matter and agreed that in order to avoid any accusation of impropriety, we should wait for Judge Lessing to preside over the hearing."

Kate crossed her arms, aware of how her wedding band would stand out against her royal blue suit. "All parties agreed. But if you want to suggest that I had other motives for what would intentionally delay achieving closure to an emotionally painful chapter in my husband's life, feel free to make yourself look foolish to your client."

The attorney nodded, conceding defeat. "I'm impressed, Your Honor. You may yet impact the community and convince people that you two are actually serious about your…marriage. But I have one question. How long are you planning to wait after the hearing to file for a divorce from Ethan Walker? And what explanation is the *honorable* Judge Kate Randall going to dream up that doesn't reek to high heaven?"

"Advise your client to do whatever he feels in good conscience he must. As I will. But think about this— I have phoned the Taylors on several occasions in the last few weeks, trying to set up an appointment to bring the baby to meet her grandparents in a chaperoned environment. My secretary can testify to that. However, in each and every case, Mr. Taylor has done more than reject my offer, he's been rude and abrasive."

"Can you blame him? Chaperoned visits— You intentionally insulted the man."

"I'm ensuring the welfare of my husband's niece. Before her death, Marilee Walker Taylor reported prolonged and serious abuse by Clay Taylor. Noble's behavior during our discussions strongly suggests this may be a problem requiring expert psychological input before unmonitored visitation should be awarded."

"What?" For an instant, Warren Blankenship looked as if *he* might be capable of violence. But he quickly collected himself and even managed a cold smile. "It's clear you've won this round, Your Honor. But it's early in the game, isn't it?"

"I don't play games with children's lives, Mr. Blankenship. And if keeping my family whole and safe offsets your own ambitions…tough. Now, this meeting is over."

As the door closed behind him, Kate realized she was trembling. It was a new experience professionally, and hardly reassuring. But she also knew her condition didn't wholly reflect Warren Blankenship's threats; she was beginning to understand the emotional stakes at risk. For her. For Ethan. For Darcy.

"Are you okay?"

She looked up to see Pat easing open the door. Her secretary's look of concern brought her back to reality faster than any internal pep talk could have. "Sure. At least I will be. It's just tiring to dodge accusations and sidestep innuendo when I'd rather be focusing on baby pictures and redecorating."

Pat's expression reflected heartfelt compassion. "I couldn't help hearing what he said. It made me furious. Anyone with one eye can see you and Ethan are a wonderful couple."

A new wave of guilt tugged at Kate for not being totally up-front with Pat. On the other hand, what had been said that wasn't true? She and Ethan *did* make a great couple, and Darcy was thriving in their joint care. The problem was, he didn't see what was before his eyes. No, that wasn't right, either. He refused to see it.

"Blankenship is frustrated and reaching," she replied, as much for her own benefit as for Pat's. "Frustrated people have a tendency to grab at any opportunity to strike out, forgetting that this isn't the only case, and certainly not the last one, we'll have a confrontation over."

"The old lessons about burning bridges," Pat drawled.

Nodding, Kate eyed the view out her window. "It definitely looks like April out there. We should finish up on the Stone case in about an hour. That will give me about a two-hour break before my afternoon meetings. I think I'd like a stroll before lunch. Can I bring you back something?"

"That would be great. I have some calls to make to line up a painter for the house, and won't get away from my desk."

Kate reached for her robe. "Why don't you enlist Steve? I thought you said you two had a great time at that dinner."

"We did. An extremely good time. But seeing how easily things could get serious is making me cautious, know what I mean? No, of course you don't. You knew Ethan all your life as a friend, but when chemistry hit—*wham*. You didn't hesitate taking the plunge, any more than you hesitated letting Warren Blankenship have it between the eyes."

Feeling a bit queasy in her stomach, Kate offered a crooked smile and, reaching for the door that connected her to the courtroom, said, "Just be who you have to be, Pat."

But her secretary's words played in her mind again and again almost an hour later, as she walked out of the courthouse. She was trying to follow her own advice, but Ethan's ghosts were hard competition.

The fresh air buoyed her, however, and the more she walked, the better she felt. She even stopped now and then to chat with several acquaintances, and by the time she reached the Hip Hop, her appetite had almost come back.

The cozy but eccentric café wasn't yet filled with the usual lunch crowd. Kate chose a small wooden table near the window, and offered a tentative smile as Melissa Avery North walked over with silverware and a glass of ice water.

"Am I still welcome here?" she asked, voicing the concern she'd had since her marriage to Ethan. If there was one person who had a right to be upset with Ethan, albeit a right based on misinformation, it was Charlie Avery's daughter. Kate had been too busy to stop by since her wedding, and she had no idea how Melissa had responded to Ethan's acquittal, let alone her marriage to him.

"You know you are, Kate," the younger woman replied, her bright blue eyes as warm as ever. "I may not be crazy about your taste in men, but who has all the answers? How've you been? We've missed you livening up this place."

"Thanks—I think. And I've been well. A bit busier than usual, what with the instant family and all. I've had to pull out of a few social and organizational things, but the trade-off has been worth it."

The spring sunshine pouring through the plate-glass window turned Melissa's wonderful hair a deep rich mahogany, and her eyes a gorgeous azure blue. "I'll bet. How is that precious baby?"

"Thriving. Yesterday Ethan took her in for her second checkup, and she's gained almost two pounds." They'd been worried when Darcy initially lost several ounces, and despite Eva's and the doctor's reassurances that this was entirely normal, they hadn't relaxed until the crisis had been reversed.

Melissa swept her long braid over her shoulder. "I think Marilee would like knowing you're raising her child. I always thought you'd make good mother material, Kate. Hope Ethan knows how lucky he is."

"I doubt he's likely to forget. I remind him at least twice a day."

Melissa chuckled. "That's the way."

"Seriously, I'm the one who's been blessed."

From behind her, she heard a low guffaw. Kate turned and met the challenging gaze of a newer member of Whitehorn's police force, a patrolman who'd testified in her court a few times, and not always well. But seeing that Warren Blankenship sat beside him truly disturbed her. She hadn't noticed him in the corner.

"See there, Blankenship," the cop drawled, "it's not about justice anymore. It's about sensitivity."

"It's become a woman's world," someone else at the table put in. "Give 'em a little power, and they start throwing their weight around worse than any man ever did. Even try to shove some jailbird down your throat."

Anger bubbled up in Kate. About to rise, she felt Melissa touch her arm.

"Let me take care of this." The young woman's long prairie skirt whispered as she moved to the other table. "Boys—and I do mean boys—how about minding your manners, and leaving the locker room behavior out of my restaurant?"

New customers drew Melissa from the area, but things did remain quiet for a while. Kate's waitress came by, and she ordered a fruit salad for herself, and a turkey chef's salad for Pat. Once alone again, she spotted a friendlier group toward the back of the café that waved. She was sobered, however, by the two women nearer to her who sent critical looks her way. They had been among the minority at church on Easter Sunday who looked offended that they had to worship in the same building as a man who'd spent time behind county-jail bars. Never mind that he'd been found not guilty in a court of law. Then she heard Warren complaining bitterly.

"All I know is that a decent couple are being denied their rights, and the judges have my hands tied."

Although she felt Warren was pushing his luck, she knew that she needed to be more than usually careful, because anything she said or did would be analyzed under a very fine magnifying glass by over a dozen pairs of eyes in this room. She did, however, relish the thought that Warren seemed to be forgetting that he would be appearing in her court in a few days to wade through a tricky driving-while-intoxicated case. His client was a well-known doctor's son, and Warren and the doctor just happened to be neighbors and golf buddies. On paper, the son, almost twenty, appeared to be a spoiled brat who'd been saved by his father's financial and political influence one too many times. While Kate would wait to study the young man's demeanor in court, and hear what the D.A.'s assistant had to add to the case, she suspected the outcome would send both the defendant and Warren the message that recklessness of any kind had a price.

"A man's got a right to complain when justice isn't being served," a fourth individual at Warren's table insisted.

Kate recognized the voice. The man was one of the town's insurance agents. A consummate salesman, he drummed up business by getting on any committee or council needing warm bodies. Just recently, as a school board member, he'd helped bring in a vote to approve the building of a new school gymnasium the district couldn't afford. Kate had already heard the complaints that every yea voter was now a customer of his.

If she'd still been single, with nothing to lose but the next election, Kate would have cheerfully taken on this obvious challenge to a debate from the group. However, she had Ethan and Darcy to consider, and Ethan had been right in pointing out that she wasn't without her own detractors. If she could ask him to keep to the straight and narrow path, she had to be willing to follow suit.

Recognizing that would be difficult if she stayed, she went up to the counter, where she paid for her order and asked Melissa to wrap the lunches for takeout. As she stood waiting, she overheard several other people sounding off.

"It makes you wonder. If she can marry him, do we really want her in our courts?"

"I don't know, but I wouldn't want Lexine Baxter's leavings if they handed him to me on a silver platter."

"I'm sorry, Kate," Melissa said, hurrying with her boxes. "Seems that every sour-tongued gossip in town decided to eat here today."

Although common sense told her the younger woman was right, Kate still felt a strong surge of dismay and indignation. "Don't worry about it, Melissa. See you soon."

Kate was relieved to get out of there. Though she was no stranger to criticism, this episode had affected her, because it had been different. The mood had been mean-spirited, and there had been personal attacks rather than disagreements over issues—and that was morally and philosophically wrong. If she didn't do some damage control soon, the momentum would increase until it was out of control. Unfortunately, she hadn't a clue as to where to begin.

* * *

Ethan had just come out of the shower when Kate came in that evening. He'd meant to be quick, but the hot water had been a relief for his sore body, and he'd lingered longer than he intended. After dragging on his jeans, he hooked the towel over his neck and hurried to relieve her of Darcy so that she could drop her briefcase and take off her coat.

"You look tired. Long day?"

"About as long as they get."

It was more than they'd said to each other in days. "Please." "Thank you." "Goodbye." That had been the extent of their conversations since the night he'd come so close to breaking his personal vow of penance. In a way, the reserve made it easier to be around her, to fight the temptation she always presented, and to deal with what-ifs. At the same time, having Kate angry at him had proved almost as difficult as facing a jury that might have slapped him with a murder conviction.

He carried the baby to her crib, finding solace in the delight of her happy recognition. "Hey, sweetheart. How's my little—"

"Your back!"

Ethan heard a clatter as Kate dropped the rest of her things and rushed to him. He barely had Darcy's knit cap and jacket removed when he felt cool fingers run down the six-inch slash along his left shoulder blade.

"What happened?" she demanded, a decided wince in her voice. "It looks like a barbed-wire cut."

"Right the first time. Old Gray picked a bad moment to trip in some abandoned varmint hole, and I rolled off him like some fool who's never been on a horse before. Went straight into the fence."

"Is Gray all right?"

"Fine."

"This needs more cleaning, and some salve. I'll go wash my hands."

The mere thought of her hands on him brought a sweet torment that had his pulse leaping into overdrive and his body tightening. "Don't bother. I'm okay."

"Sure you are. Leave it that way and it'll look like this one," she said, touching the scar higher up. It was the scar he'd brought back from Nam instead of Wayne.

The touch was a mere whisper across his skin, but it went through Ethan like a red-hot knife. In self-defense, he spun around and grabbed her wrist. *"Kate."*

Only then did he see that she looked more than tired, she seemed dead on her feet. He released her immediately.

"I'm sorry for snapping. But you're ready to drop. Don't waste your time on me."

"This isn't about wasting my time, nor is it a maneuver to get you into bed, all right? But I will put on that salve."

Stubborn, mouthy woman, he thought as she slipped off her coat, hung it up, then hurried to the bathroom. He listened to her washing her hands as he finished making the baby comfortable, annoyed that she read him so easily. The cut needed more attention, but he'd wanted to avoid having her that close to him.

"Are you coming, or do I have to call John Mountain and have him hog-tie you?"

He sighed and joined her in the bathroom. She had turned on both the overhead and vanity lights to work by and it gave Ethan a stark view of her.

She'd done more than wash up, she'd slipped out of her suit jacket and heels. Between the oyster-white camisole, the pencil-slim blue skirt and her usually neat hairdo in sexy, windswept disarray, she looked anything but the cool cookie she was trying to portray.

To keep from staring, he gave her his back, but that only gave him her reflection in the vanity mirror. He shut his eyes.

"Would you relax? It's not as if it needs stitching."

It might as well, he thought, resting his forearms on the counter as she urged him to bend. Considering what he would be imagining as she worked on him, a needle and a thread would definitely be less of an ordeal.

Using cotton balls, she dabbed disinfectant gently around the bruised and swollen area. Her touch was feather-light, as fleeting as her teasing kisses had been. He clenched his teeth and forced himself to focus on something else, like listing the tax reports due this week, which he hadn't started.

"You really can't bear my touch, can you?"

Had the woman lost her mind? Gone blind? "Don't start, Kate," he replied, deciding not to pretend. "I appreciate what you're doing, but don't start."

She didn't reply, and that only made him feel more of a heel. It was worse when he saw her reflection in the mirror. She looked as miserable as he felt. He gripped the edge of the counter and sighed. "Don't hate me."

"I don't hate you, Ethan. I just have to wonder why I spend so much of my time reminding myself why I like you."

"It's not me. You have a fixation with people with screwed-up lives." He expected her to counter with a comment about how his messes bore no comparison, a dry laugh, something. "That was a joke," he finally muttered.

"Actually, I was thinking how I haven't done much to help your situation. In fact, I may have made things worse."

He watched in the mirror as she leaned over to drop the soiled cotton balls into the wastebasket beneath the sink. Even as his body heated at the tantalizing view of cleavage, his mind locked in on the meaning behind her words, and her troubled eyes.

"You want to talk about it?" he asked as she unscrewed the medicated ointment.

"Not really. But you have a right to hear it. I had a run-in with Warren Blankenship today. This one almost got ugly. He made accusations. Accusations—there's a laugh. He basically hit the nail on the head regarding us. That's not so bad, I suppose, but when I went to the Hip Hop for lunch, we met again."

She quickly summarized the experience for him. Ethan had a gut feeling that she left out more than she told.

"Needless to say, I changed my order to takeout and went back to the courthouse before they decided I should wear a scarlet letter on my chest."

"I should never have let you get involved in this," he said, as disgusted with those people's behavior as he was concerned for her. "If I had more brains and guts, I'd—"

Kate silenced him with a hand on his uninjured shoulder. "It's done. My concern is that this kind of negativity will somehow bleed back to the courtroom. I've seen it happen. Usually on bigger cases, but public opinion can coerce a judge to change his opinion on something. Especially if he fears a career backlash."

Ethan didn't like what he was hearing. "Are you saying it was a mistake to gamble on Lessing after all?"

"No. That's the problem. Lessing was and is the best, the *only,* choice, despite not being my staunchest supporter. But I had to do something to offset all the criticism. I've been working on it for a while now, and I'm afraid you're going to be angry with me when you hear about it."

Although she was still working on his back, he shifted to look at her. "What?"

"I've been talking to Noble and Ruth. Well, Noble first, but he's refused to listen. Today I approached Ruth, offering to bring Darcy over for a monitored visit."

Ethan straightened and stared at her in the mirror. "You did *what?*"

Kate attached a second piece of adhesive to the gauze pad on his wound. "It's the only fair thing, Ethan. And smart. To cut them off entirely wouldn't look good in court."

"They made my sister's life hell! Their son terrorized her. Do you think I care about *appearances?*" he roared.

"Ethan—the baby!" Kate warned as she heard Darcy whimper.

"I don't care how it looks," he said again, although this time he lowered his voice to an angry whisper. "What right do you have to stick your nose where it doesn't belong?"

She stared at him in disbelief. "Absolutely none," she murmured, and, throwing the adhesive roll onto the vanity, she rushed out of the room.

The haunting image of her anguished eyes, her drawn face, were too much. Ethan lurched after her, barely managing to block her exit at the bedroom door.

"Get out of my way, Ethan. Darcy's hungry."

"No, she's not." Only a week into their new routine, Eva had started giving the baby dinner at Kate's place to save them time.

Her escape plot foiled, Kate tried to sidestep him anyway. He let her, only to grab her from behind, then bring her back flush against him. "Kate." He tightened both arms around her waist, pressed his face against her hair and willed her to be still.

"Let me go."

"Not yet."

He felt, more than heard, her fight back a sob. "You can't keep doing this to me."

"I know." But he didn't release her. In fact, catching the phantomlike whisper of her fragrance, he followed it, ever so slowly letting his lips whisper across the outer shell of her ear, down the side of her neck.

With a sigh, Kate surrendered, letting her head drop back against his shoulder. "I don't know what exhausts me more…fighting you, or fighting for you."

"I'm not worth either." He let his eyes drift shut, let his lips rest against the curve of her throat.

"Don't say that," she whispered back.

"It's the truth. But, God, I love holding you."

"You love turning my mind and my life inside out and upside down," she said accusingly. But she covered his arms with hers.

"In this case, it's deserved. Hell, Kate…taking Darcy to see them?"

"Monitored by *me,* Ethan. You didn't experience what I did today. I admit, after the anger, I felt the first hint of fear. Fear of losing everything. It made me want to try a little harder at compromise."

He didn't want to ask, but, once again touching his face to her hair, he forced himself. "What happened?"

"Nothing promising. Ruth said she would discuss it with Noble. He wasn't home." Kate turned her head until her breath teased his cheek. "Still angry with me?"

Reluctantly he lifted his head. "It's beginning to feel like a waste of time. You'll just clobber me with logic."

She smiled.

He smiled.

Ever so slowly, Kate's gaze shifted to his mouth. "Kiss me."

Dear heaven, he wanted to. His body ached from wanting to. But he didn't want to start something that he wouldn't finish. "Nothing can come of it, Kate."

"Now who's clobbering who with logic?" Her gaze sought his. "I don't care about tomorrow. I'm not asking you for promises. Just…kiss me. Just once more."

In the end, she closed the inch of space between them, touched her mouth to his and edged him closer to madness by using the tip of her tongue to trace the line of his dry lips and beyond. All the while, Ethan stood rigid, throbbing, his fingers biting into the slender span of her waist, because he wanted to fill his hands with her breasts, get drunk on the sweet nectar he tasted on her lips.

Breathing like a freight train and feeling more than one bead of sweat streak down his face, Ethan eased the hold he knew had to be painful for her.

Kate dropped her hands, and as soon as he'd completely released her, she turned to face him. "I'll get dinner."

Not trusting his voice, he settled for a nod. But once he retreated to the bathroom to straighten up, he stared at his harsh reflection in the mirror and whispered, "You son of a bitch."

How much more are you going to take, Kate? How much more are you going to ask me to resist?

Eight

Sexual frustration. Ethan tossed the last three empty sacks of calf-protein pellets toward the burning barrel, only to see all three miss. Cursing the things, his aim, and life in general, he retrieved them and shoved them brutally into the metal drum.

Yes, it was time to admit that was what had him so edgy that he could probably bend a horseshoe nail between his teeth. He was about as tangled up with sexual frustration as a man could get. And there was no end in sight.

"Want a suggestion?"

Ethan turned in time to catch the keys John Mountain tossed him. Only minutes ago he'd handed them over to him. The cowboy needed to drive down into Whitehorn and pick up some feed and supplies. This turnabout confused him.

"What are you doing?"

"You need a break. You go."

"Says who?"

"Me. You haven't been off this place since the wedding. Nearly two months, ain't it?"

Six weeks and two days. Ethan looked up at the blue sky, dotted with lamb-white clouds. May. What had happened to April? He knew what *hadn't* happened. That was the problem. He'd been a fool to think he could share a cabin with Kate and not go out of his mind.

"It's your right to go," he insisted, trying to stay focused on the issue. No matter what, he couldn't deny John Mountain his own break. The guy had few other perks in this job.

"Next time. Now scram. Maybe you'll run into Ms. Kate. Buy her lunch."

Ethan scowled harder. "What are you trying to do, become a fairy godmother in your free time?"

"Nope. But I am tired of seeing Ms. Kate get paler. You getting meaner."

Since when did their resident hermit notice such things? John Mountain worked overtime making sure he was nearly invisible on the Double N. In fact, the harder Kate tried to include him in meals and initiate a friendship, the longer John Mountain stayed out with the herd.

Of course, that didn't mean the concise character study was off. Sure, Ethan knew he'd been behaving more and more like a wounded grizzly. When a man watched his dreams slipping through his fingers, and didn't have a clue as to how to stop the whirlpool that was sucking them away, did anyone expect him to be cheerful?

As for Kate...she was getting paler, true; and he was secretly going out of his mind with concern for her. But when he offered her the only solution he could think of to help her, she'd refused to listen. They were at an impasse, and impasses were always debilitating.

"It's too late for lunch," he muttered, frowning at the keys. "Besides, she's in Billings today."

John Mountain nodded.

That irked Ethan, too. The guy would never ask why, where, or anything. "She's giving another speech."

Afterward she planned to stop by and try to smooth-talk Ruth Taylor into agreeing to visit with the baby. Not because she wanted it, and *despite* his disapproval. At least he could take comfort in knowing that so far it hadn't happened—the Taylors stood firm, wanting everything or nothing.

"There's no reason for you not to go," he insisted when his ranch hand continued to stand there watching him. But as he offered the keys again, John Mountain stepped back.

"Hell's bells, John!"

In the end, Ethan went, if only to get away from John Mountain's stubbornness, and his too-accurate deductions—not to mention his slightly accusatory looks. Once on the road, however, he soon realized he was glad to be going.

The snow had retreated to the higher elevations, and spring had settled in the foothills. Granted, they still had cause to worry about an unexpected, stubborn front blanketing them with a killer snow; last year they'd experienced exactly that scenario. In the process, they'd lost a half-dozen calves and two heifers having difficult births that couldn't be reached in time to help.

For the moment, though, deceptively fragile wildflowers were spreading in the most sunny patches of the brilliant green valleys, and all the wildlife were exhibiting their own signs of renewal. Birds were busy collecting bits of dried grass and twigs for nests, and some were already feeding their voraciously hungry hatchlings. Cattle and horses nursed and groomed their toothpick-legged newborns in the warm sunlight. As he followed a tumbling alpine stream running parallel to the road, he passed the entrance to Shadow Ranch, and his thoughts shifted to his own leggy little miracle.

At nearly three months, Darcy was showing signs of her personality and proving more and more of a delight. Kate kept bringing home book after book from the library on child care and teaching techniques, and while he'd balked at reading them in the beginning, once he'd reminded himself how he'd failed with Marilee, he'd begun to give them at least some consideration. He was, however, most comfortable when he followed his instincts, rocking her to sleep when she was cranky, walking her around and showing her various things that caught her eye. He could already tell she was going to be a remarkably bright little girl. Maybe a singer, he thought, smiling as he thought of the way she'd taken to delivering long soliloquies of gibberish. But thoughts of the future brought him back to the present and the dilemma—dilemmas that wouldn't go away.

Kate. Kate worried him. She was working nonstop, and denying herself too much. True, she bubbled with enthusiasm over Darcy, dropping everything to give the baby a bath or play with one of the dozen stuffed animals that she'd already bought for the child, but he wondered how long the pace could continue. As it was, he didn't know how she managed to be home nearly every night to help with meals or spend time with the infant, and then work until midnight on a speech, or inch through one of the countless folders she brought home, cases she studied prior to scheduled trials.

As he'd always suspected, Kate took every case seriously, following up on women in abusive relationships, runaways placed in foster homes. And still she returned every day to Shadow Ranch to spend time with Eva and Jorge, catch up with business demands there, call clients back.

Not surprisingly, she'd chiseled down her social life to nil. He knew that from how few nights she came home late if court or an appearance hadn't been scheduled. Also telling were the RSVP envelopes that often went out with her as she left in the mornings. He didn't know much about things requiring RSVPs, but after catching a peek at one, he assumed the others were versions of the same thing. Some went as far as California.

He drove himself crazy wondering how many were from men.

Yes, she was pale, pale from burning the candle at both ends and being put through hell by him and his problems. He didn't know how she managed it. But he did understand that she would be in far worse shape if he gave in to what he wanted most from her. He found it incredible enough that he could make her want him, even if he'd convinced himself that much of that was *com*passion, not passion.

Yet he was thinking about that as he gave in to temptation and made an unexpected detour. As a result, it was a full hour later when he finally backed up to the loading dock at the Whitehorn Farmers Cooperative. Several trucks were waiting to be loaded, but the crowd at the counter inside was much worse.

Resigned to a considerable wait, he wandered around the store checking out the new tackle, the inventory of garden seed, which he decided would have to wait another year, the price board for feed costs… He was studying the various varmint traps when he heard footsteps behind him.

"Well, well. What are you doing in town, Walker? Haven't you learned your lesson yet?"

The big mouth belonged to Josh Trask, an old pal of Charlie Avery's. Ethan decided the fewer words that passed between him and the lanky sometime rodeo rider, the better. When he spotted a chance to be waited on, he moved up to the counter.

"What's the matter, Walker? Turning deaf in your old age?"

Bill Frieland, the co-op's manager, pulled a pen from behind his ear. "Trask, I don't need any trouble. Behave or take a walk."

Despite the warning, Ethan noticed *he* was the one who received the wary look from Frieland. It came as no surprise. The authorities had found no new suspects to tie to Charlie's murder; understandably, some still considered him the number one suspect, no matter what the experts had concluded. He was just grateful that Bill had decided to let him place his order.

"Excuse me, gentlemen, could I get through, please?"

Trask tipped his Stetson, and Ethan stepped out of the way of the woman leaning a shovel and hoe against the counter. It was Mary Jo Kincaid. Though they had never been introduced, Mary Jo had faithfully sat through every day of his trial. She had looked as out of place there, with her frilly, garden-tea clothes, as she did now, but Ethan welcomed the intrusion. At this point, a film crew with a bull would work for him if it broke the tension Trask was trying instigate.

"Mary Jo, what are you up to with that?" Frieland asked with a bemused smile. "Gonna do some gardening?"

"I thought I might try a little flower bed in front of the library, Mr. Mills. It could do with some brightening. There's no budget for one, of course, but that's not going to stop me. I plan to donate the expense, and my time."

"Why, that's mighty generous of you, Mary Jo. My wife was saying the other day how lucky Whitehorn was to have you over there." Without asking Ethan if he minded the wait, he quickly rang up Mary Jo's purchase.

She drew out the proper amount from her wallet and handed it to the man. "You be sure to thank her for me. Oh, and do you know who could give me the best advice regarding blooming plants? Especially roses. I'm worried about freeze conditions and maintenance."

Because he was aware of Josh Trask's narrow-eyed stare, Ethan almost groaned at this annoying chitchat. Fortunately, Frieland knew exactly who to recommend, and the woman soon picked up her tools. She cast him a demure smile.

"Thank you so much for letting me elbow my way in."

She really was a pretty little thing, if you liked the frilly type. He didn't, and, barely sparing her a glance touched his hat, murmured, "Ma'am," and turned back to Bill Frieland. It was too much to hope Trask would keep his mouth shut and wait until she was gone to start up again.

"Better watch it, ma'am. Maybe you aren't familiar enough with the goings-on in our little town yet to realize you've been associating with a dangerous hombre. Why, I would consider it neglecting my civil duty not to warn you to give him as much space as possible. The last guy who got too close was a good friend of mine and—"

"Shut your mouth, Trask, or I'll do it for you."

"Tell you what, Ethan," the manager told him, "go out to Will and tell him what you need. I'll bill you."

Grateful, Ethan thanked him. With a curt nod to the wide-eyed woman, he headed toward the loading docks.

He thought he was home free after that. In fact, Will, the order filler John Mountain had mentioned was the most reliable, had him nearly loaded by the time Trask strolled outside.

"Hey, jailbird…where you off to next? Gonna go visit your sweetie?"

Under normal circumstances, Ethan didn't pay attention

to scum like Trask, but the reference to Kate triggered something inside him. Only the thought of what she would say if he landed in a fight stopped him from giving in there and then and knocking the creep off the dock. When Will came along with the last load of fifty-pound sacks, Ethan grabbed the top one and started helping to ensure his speedier departure.

Trask put his foot on the back of Ethan's tailgate. "Yep, it sure did blow everyone's mind when you two got hitched," he said, as Ethan approached his truck with another sack. "What with Wayne Kincaid being her great love and all. Tell me, Walker, when she's crying for it, is it your name she calls or—"

He'd tried. Even as Ethan threw himself at the man, all he knew was that he couldn't let the bastard finish. He would strangle the last breath out of him first.

His first punch went into Trask's belly. It bent the man in half and left him gasping. But when Ethan tried to add a hammerlike blow over the guy's back, Trask dodged out of the way and surprised him with a slice across his cheekbone. Thanks to a rodeo ring, it felt like a knife, painful enough to knock Ethan off-balance.

He shook his head, trying to clear it, then, before Trask could recover himself, once again dived at him. The momentum carried them off the dock and onto the mountain of sacks piled in the bed of his truck. From there they tumbled over the side and onto the packed-dirt-and-gravel driveway. They hit with a merciless thud, and both of them erupted with grunts, groans and curses that would have cleared the area of women and children if there had been any around at the moment. Ethan had a fleeting thought that he might have cracked a rib, and an elbow was in serious question. But having stepped too far over the line of reason, neither of them gave a hint of backing off.

Ethan connected with his next two punches. Trask followed with a uppercut that nearly broke Ethan's nose. Dust and blood seemed be everywhere, but, determined to hear Trask take back the foul words, Ethan snatched up the wobblier man by his shirt and reached back.

He intended to end it, there and then. His thoughts weren't that logical or orderly, but every primal instinct in him was to lock and load. Go for the kill. What stopped him was the view over Trask's shoulder—the glossy but conservative sedan that braked to an abrupt stop in the middle of the road.

Hell and damnation. It was Noble Taylor.

Even in the shadow of the car's interior, Ethan saw the look of supreme satisfaction that spread across Taylor's face. Then the sedan sped away.

Hurting, Ethan hauled Trask up like a rag doll and shoved him against the dock. "You ever…mention my wife again…I'll finish this," he snarled between heaving breaths.

He shoved him away. Then he purged his real anger by kicking a beer can out of his way. Trying to clear his head enough to decide what he was supposed to do next, he wiped at the taste of blood in his mouth and focused on the driver's door of his truck. If he could reach it, he told himself, everything would be all right.

Somehow he did. But as he drove away, his gaze shifted to his rearview mirror, and his thoughts returned to Noble Taylor.

There would be hell to pay. Only right now he hurt too much to care.

"Thank you for seeing me on such short notice, Mrs. Taylor," Kate said, shaking hands with the reluctant woman. "As I mentioned on the phone, I was in town for a speaking engagement, and I thought this might be a good opportunity for us to touch base again."

"And as I told *you*, I'm not sure that we have anything to discuss, Judge Randall." Ruth Taylor kept the handshake short and didn't budge far from the entrance to the mansion. "My husband isn't home, and I wouldn't think of making any decision without his input."

"Nor would I ask you to," Kate assured her. "But speaking woman to woman, surely you agree that if we can't establish an intelligent yet compassionate dialogue, no one can."

That seemed to appeal to Ruth, and she glanced over her shoulder to her housekeeper, who stood aside, looking sympathetic but trapped by her position. "Norma, I think we'll go into the parlor. Perhaps Judge Randall would care for some tea or coffee."

"Nothing, thank you," Kate assured them both. "The idea of visiting for a few minutes would be refreshing enough. You see, I brought some pictures of Darcy that I'd love to share with you."

If Ruth had been hesitant, that remark succeeded in vanquishing her doubts, and she led the way into the first room on the left, which, although smaller, was less stuffy than the living room had been. Kate eyed the seating arrangement of the love seat and chairs and strategically chose the couch. Ruth watched her dig out the photographs from her purse and cautiously lowered herself beside her.

"Er, please don't take this the wrong way, but—is she doing all right?" she asked Kate.

Intrigued by the hesitancy, as much as by the question itself, Kate replied, "She's a joy. She's beginning to make little noises, tiny grunts and cooing sounds. Look. Here she is in her crib. I'm afraid we're inundating her with stuffed animals."

"I'm a fan of dolls myself. I always thought if I had a daughter that I would see she had the dolls I never did. My father was in the military," she explained, when she saw Kate's curious look. "We traveled a great deal, and he thought toys were…superfluous."

"I'm sorry."

The older woman stiffened, as if realizing her slip. "Oh, no. I'm not complaining. Besides, it was a long time ago." But she soon mellowed again. "I did see a doll down at Ivers the other day that I almost purchased on a whim for the baby. Of course, she's too small for dolls, and this wasn't just any doll. Ivers specializes in collectibles, you know."

"Yes, I still have the one my father bought me there when I was four." Kate had preferred models of horses by then, but she still had the doll in storage, respecting that someone, somewhere, would cherish it in the future.

"Four… Well, I suppose I'm too far ahead of myself."

"But it's a lovely thought," Kate assured her. "Maybe if you had a chance to meet Darcy, you'd get a better feel for what she is and isn't ready for."

"You could be right. But of course I would have to talk to— Why, Noble, dear. You're early."

Noble Taylor ignored his wife and stepped farther into the room, staring at Kate. "What are you doing here?"

Red-faced, and more agitated than Kate had ever seen him, he evoked an aura of a man both riding some emotional high and furiously angry. Careful, she told herself.

"I was in the neighborhood, Mr. Taylor. I wanted to see if perhaps—"

"You're trying to brainwash my wife, while your so-called *husband* once again shows his true colors. He may be committing another murder for all I know!"

She couldn't comprehend what he could possibly mean and so simply shook her head.

"I've come from Whitehorn. I saw him myself!"

Ruth did a double take. "Noble, what were you doing in Whitehorn? I thought you said you had to go to Bozeman today."

He clenched his hands at his sides. "Don't interrupt me. Aren't you listening? I saw Ethan Walker, that so-called *responsible citizen* that we're not supposed to be afraid of, beating a man to a pulp."

"Where? When?" Kate demanded, unable to believe what he was saying. It had to be a mistake. Noble must had seen someone who looked like Ethan.

"By the loading dock at the feed store in Whitehorn."

A lead weight fell on Kate's chest. Ethan had said John Mountain would be going to pick up supplies today. Could he have changed his mind and gone instead?

"Dear God." She didn't know what to think, only that she had to get back to Whitehorn. Back to the Double N. "Please don't jump to conclusions," she said, rising. "There has to be some explanation."

"Oh, I've no doubt there is," Noble replied, hooking his thumbs around his suspender straps. "In fact, it's what I've maintained all along. The man you claim is capable of raising my granddaughter is nothing more than a hooligan, a—a sociopath! Now take your propaganda and get out."

Kate didn't need the dismissal. She'd already been shoving the pictures into her purse and heading for the door. In fact, she barely heard him. With a parting, barely coherent goodbye to Ruth, she turned all her thoughts on Ethan.

* * *

The drive from Billings to Whitehorn had never seemed longer. Kate couldn't remember when her nerves had last been stretched to the extent they were when she wheeled into Shadow Ranch and raced to the house. This detour didn't help, but she'd decided she would ask Eva to keep Darcy for the night. She had no idea what she would be walking into over at the Double N, and there was no reason for the baby to suffer.

A short time later, she entered her home, to receive another blow. Ethan had beaten her to it. He'd come by and taken Darcy, despite Eva's protests.

Kate couldn't believe her housekeeper's accusations. "What do you mean, he kidnapped her?" she asked, stunned, as she stared into the empty baby carriage. She shook her head. "Eva, let's not get hysterical. She's his niece. He had ever reason to stop by and take her home with him if that's what he wanted to do."

"Not in the condition *he* was in!"

Kate's heart did a flip-flop. "What was wrong with him?"

"I haven't seen so much blood since I slaughtered my first chicken as a girl."

Ethan was hurt. Although she hadn't touched her lunch at the Billings country club, Kate's stomach rolled threateningly, adding to her unease. "How long ago was all this?"

The corner of Eva's mouth drooped farther as she pantomimed uncertainty. "An hour ago."

"Did he say anything?"

"He told me to mind my own business."

Kate rubbed at the viselike pinch between her eyebrows. "I'd better get over there."

"Stay, child." Eva gripped her arm, intensifying her entreaty. "He's made his decision. Don't let him drag you down with him. How are you going to defend the man? Already his face looks as if a bull used it as a doormat. Who knows what he did before he came here?"

She didn't have any answers to pacify Eva, no possible explanations for what she knew she must do, except one. "He's my husband, Eva. I have to go."

"Go if you must. But do it for the baby's sake, not his." She followed Kate to the door. "And I tell you this—you give your papa no rest in heaven!"

She couldn't have chosen a more cruel declaration; however, rather than get into an argument, Kate muttered that she would be in contact as soon as she could, and dashed back to her car.

As she drove back toward Mountain Pass, though, she put her personal hurt aside. Eva didn't mean half of what she'd said; she simply didn't understand all that was going on. That was *her* fault for not having explained better.

She focused on the baby. Darcy was young enough that she wouldn't understand Ethan's condition. That gave her some reassurance. No matter what this sounded like, Ethan wouldn't endanger a child.

But Ethan... What's happened?

Her anxiety grew as she reached the Double N and drew nearer to the cabin. She felt better when she saw his truck backed up to the entrance of the barn. How badly could he be hurt, how upset could he be, if he could still maneuver the truck for unloading? But her spirits sank again when she realized he hadn't begun to unload, and that there was no sign of John Mountain.

Inside, she found more that disturbed her. Darcy was lying in her crib, screaming her little heart out, and the only sign of Ethan was the sound of water running full force in the bathroom.

"Sweetheart, don't. Aunt Kate's here," she murmured soothingly, tossing her purse and keys on a side table. Quickly shrugging out of the red bolero jacket of her red-and-black suit, she hurried to the crib. "Poor twiglet. Uncle Ethan took you away from all the color and noise of Eva's kitchen. Bet you've been telling him that you don't want to be left alone in this gloomy room. Come on…up you go. We'll make it better."

She lifted the child from beneath the too-warm blankets she'd been wrapped in for the trip and into her arms. Only then did she slip off the baby's bonnet. Dark brown curls clung in damp chaos around her feverish forehead, giving evidence of the baby's overexerted, anxious state. Her small, flushed, tear-mottled face and tiny fisted hands completed a picture that both broke Kate's heart and infuriated her.

"There, there. It's better now," she said in a singsong voice. "Let's go see where that grumble bear is, okay? Bet looking at him gave you a fright."

The chatting calmed Darcy, and it helped Kate, too, giving her a chance to purge some of her tension as she entered the bedroom and circled to the bathroom. However, the lack of sound—save that of running water—disturbed her anew. So did the amount of steam billowing out of the room. If Ethan hadn't been hurt when he went in there, he had to be hurting now, and most likely from second-degree burns!

"Ethan?"

When he didn't reply, she ventured a bit farther into the bathroom. That was when she saw his clothes scattered on the floor where he'd dropped them. Even with the steam, she could see the bloodstains.

"Ethan, it's me. Are you all right?"

She heard a grunting sound—or it may have been a moan—before he shut off the water.

"Go take care of the baby. I'm fine."

He didn't sound fine. "I have the baby. She was blue from screaming when I arrived." Another low sound emerged from the stall, but no real reply. "We need to talk, Ethan."

"Not now!"

"Yes, now."

She only caught the end of the ugly word that erupted from him before he threw the shower door open. It should have come off its rollers from the force, shattered as it hit the jamb. But, to Kate's relief, despite shuddering horribly, it didn't break. Then she saw his face, and concern for everything else shifted to secondary importance.

"Oh…Ethan."

"Satisfied? Can I have my towel now?" He finally took notice of the baby. "For the love of— Get her out of this sweatbox!"

The baby didn't mind the steam, but she took immediate offense at his tone. When she broke into a new heartbroken wail, Kate shot Ethan a scathing look, snatched up the towel from the rack behind her and flung it at him.

"Congratulations. Now you've managed to alienate all of us."

She returned to the living room, where she started preparing Darcy's dinner. She hadn't had time to ask Eva, but due to Ethan's unexpected appearance, she guessed her housekeeper wouldn't have had time to do that. As she went through the mechanics, the sight of Ethan's battered and bruised face remained a terrible thing to contemplate. In her wildest dreams, she'd never have thought anything could make her oblivious of a man's nudity, but that had done it. However, no matter how she ached for him, she was furious with him for what he'd jeopardized.

She'd barely begun to feed the baby when he emerged

from the bedroom. Dressed in jeans that he'd barely zipped, he went straight to the cupboard where he kept his whiskey and poured two fingers' worth into a glass. He downed it in one swallow that left him hunched over and gripping the counter.

Kate watched, torn in two. "Was it worth it?" she finally had to ask.

"That's not the point."

The careful enunciation of each word spoke of how his own nerves were frayed—or else how much pain he was feeling—but Kate couldn't let that matter. "Well, you'd better think of one good one, because I drove here straight from getting thrown out of Noble Taylor's house, and he's crowing with glee at your behavior today."

Ethan slammed the glass down on the counter and started to walk away. In the next instant, he wheeled around and roared, "You weren't there! How can you judge what I do or don't have to defend?" The moment he finished, he realized how loud he'd been, and the look he shot the baby reflected his abject shame. "You weren't there," he concluded heavily.

"For your information *that's* not the point, either," Kate said, keeping her voice so low it shook. "Why did we do this, Ethan? Why did we get married, if you had no intention of trying to help? Why am I driving myself to exhaustion trying to survive, keeping up with two households? Why couldn't you keep out of trouble for a few more weeks—*a few more weeks,* until we got through the custody hearing?"

"I didn't plan what happened!"

The harsh words, as well as the pain they cost him, weren't lost on her. As angry as she was, Kate told herself she had to know everything. "Tell me what did?"

"I don't want to talk about it."

"You don't get a choice. You have to explain it to me so I can inform Joan Nyland," Kate replied, reminding him of the lawyer she'd contacted from Billings to help them with the custody battle. "She needs time to figure out what damage has been done to your position. And I need the information, as well, since who knows what I'll get hit with at court tomorrow?"

He retraced his steps to reach for the bottle again. Then he stopped, and abruptly put it away.

"I was at the feed store," he began a moment later, staring at the cabinet. His tone remained flat, devoid of any emotion whatsoever. "A guy started being a jerk. I left. When I got outside, he followed. He wouldn't give up."

"So you hit him?"

Ethan raked both hands through his hair. "It's not that simple."

"Simple, complicated, right, wrong…do you think Warren Blankenship is going to care? Judge Lessing?" Kate shook her head in disbelief. "You—a man who's already been on trial for a violent crime—you say you were provoked, and despite your precarious reputation in the community, your method of handling the situation was to use violence?"

"He insulted *you!*"

Although barely audible, the words were intense, and his look was feral. Kate was glad Darcy chose that moment to take a rest from the bottle, because her hand suddenly shook.

He'd defended her. Lord, what a mess… But how did she make him understand? "Do you know how many people insult me on a given day, Ethan?"

He made a brief, dismissive motion. "Don't. It's not the same thing."

"It is. They're words, Ethan. Words spoken by angry, small-minded, dull-minded people who want you to lower yourself to their level. And you let him do it."

"Sweet heaven…you're my wife!"

The declaration might have thrilled her, except that a terrible thought came to mind. "Oh, no. That's it? Please say it isn't. Don't try to suggest you were defending me, when what you were really doing is defending your pride."

Nine

Ethan stood at the front window, looking out at the moonless night. The house had never sounded so quiet, not even when he lived here alone. It had been that way for hours, ever since Kate had retreated to the bedroom with Darcy and shut him out.

He felt like slime, an outcast. Unwanted. The feeling closed in on him, forcing up memories of the jungle and how he'd survived its suffocating stranglehold by thinking of Montana. Home.

Where did you go when that home was no longer a sanctuary?

What did you do when you knew you'd done something wrong, but couldn't change it?

He dropped the curtain on the night and returned to the recliner, picked up the large stuffed unicorn he'd brought inside about an hour ago and set it on the floor before him. Another idea gone bust, he thought, remembering the elation he'd felt earlier today, when, on impulse, he'd made the detour to the department store, hunting for something special for Darcy. When he saw the giant stuffed toy in the window, with its soft white fur, flowing silver-thread mane and golden horn, he'd known that, despite being a dozen times bigger than the baby, it was perfect. The toy had brought back all the memories of the day before, when they'd bathed the baby and Kate had entertained them both by singing a song about unicorns and dreams.

He'd wanted to repeat the magic he'd felt with them, if only for a while. He'd wanted Darcy to know that although Kate would inevitably have to leave, her foster aunt would always be part of her life. The toy had been his contract, a reminder that he would suffer anything rather than deny the child Kate's love.

It had been a nice thought—a dream, inspired by a fairy tale, created by a realist. Small wonder that, as impulsively as he'd developed the fantasy, he'd quickly destroyed it.

He couldn't blame Kate for withdrawing from him, for shutting him out. What amazed him was that she hadn't packed up and left already. Yet with each breath he took, he grew more aware that he couldn't go through the night this way. Not this time. Although his face and body hurt like hell, it wasn't all a result of the fight. That pain didn't compare to his inner agony at the thought of all the endless, barren tomorrows without her.

Oh, God. He wasn't even sure he could make it through the night; the feel of her slipping through his fingers hurt too much. Despite the knowledge that he had no right to hold on, would indeed have to let go, something inside him kept demanding, *Not yet. Stay with me a while longer.*

As another wave of despair swept over him, Ethan rose and let his feet carry him to the bedroom. Well accustomed to the darkness, he eased open the door and approached the bed. It was lighter there, thanks to the night-light Kate had purchased for the bathroom. The faint amber glow bathed the woman and child on the bed in an ethereal light.

Ethan stood in silent observance, grateful for the chance to fill his mind with a different vision from what had been festering there. What he saw gave him a quiet joy, but a gnawing envy, too.

Kate lay curled with her back to the light. In the nest of her body lay Darcy, being entertained by some angelic dream. The sweet smile that played across Darcy's Cupid's-bow mouth had him bending low, lower...finally close enough to kiss her forehead. How he yearned for an ounce of her goodness, her pureness of spirit, to seep into him.

Intent on ensuring Kate a full night's rest, he carefully picked up the baby. But no sooner did he straighten than he saw Kate's eyelids lift.

Their gazes met, locked. For a moment, he saw tenderness and more. Then the lingering veil of drowsiness vaporized like morning dew and he saw realization take hold. Doubt, worry and disappointment returned like an overcast sky.

"Go back to sleep. I'll take her to her crib."

He retreated, knowing it was best, painfully aware that to linger and not weaken his resolve would take a stronger man than he. What worked was redirecting the anguish churning inside him into tenderness for the baby as she roused. Since she no longer woke for two-o'clock feedings, he used the opportunity to change her, all the while talking softly to her. It won him a loving smile, which tempted him to show her what he'd bought her today. But, as quickly as she'd awakened, she drifted back to sleep.

The gift could wait for tomorrow, he decided. By then— if Kate was smart and chose to give up on him—he and

Darcy would need all the entertainment he could think of to make up for the loneliness her absence would create in both of their lives.

After he was through, he backed away from the crib, and only then realized he wasn't alone. Glancing over his shoulder, he saw Kate standing in the bedroom doorway. Dressed in the oversize flannel nightshirt he'd once criticized, with her hair in sleepy disarray, physically she hadn't changed much from the schoolgirl she'd been when he and Wayne left for Nam.

But she had changed inside. She'd become much more cautious, even in the past few hours. She was closing emotional doors. It reminded him of a night a lifetime ago, a night as still and stark as this one, when a vow had been drawn from him...

"Promise me, if something happens to me, you'll take care of Kate, Ethan. She won't make it easy for you, she's so independent and spirited, but promise anyway. She's special. I know you see it, too. She has a lot of love to give, but I couldn't stand it if some bastard destroyed that special light in her. Promise, Ethan."

He'd promised, but only to make Wayne stop scaring the crap out of him. And the next morning, his idol, his mentor and pal, had died. That was why he'd come back and, after trying and failing to tell Kate how he'd failed her, how he'd failed them both, he'd given up on his vow.

But how did you stop wanting?

Aware of those old feelings humming in him now, he soothed them by crossing over to her. "I wanted you to sleep," he murmured, letting his gaze caress her face.

"Then you shouldn't have come in."

True. They were growing far too attuned to each other for her not to know if he was close. It made no sense to apologize, either. It wouldn't be sincere, because he liked knowing she could be that sensitive to him.

"How do you feel?" he asked instead.

"Numb."

"Can I get you anything?"

She didn't answer that, but her gaze asked what he could possibly get her that would be a panacea for what he'd cost them. She had a point, but he also knew that if he had to do it over again, his decision would be the same. So there was another dilemma: How did you apologize for accepting your own flaws?

"What's that?"

Her gaze, somewhat bewildered now, had moved on to the stuffed animal hardly hidden by his recliner. "Hell, they say you're never too young to start learning to ride…"

She shot him a doubtful glance.

"Okay, so I was feeling guilty because you've been buying her all these things, and I hadn't gotten her anything. I thought the least I could do is find her something to add toward the collection you started for her," he said, gesturing to the menagerie keeping the baby company in the crib.

Ethan watched her push away from the jamb and circle the decorative dustcatcher. He refused to feel any guilt for lusting after her luscious legs, the silky fall of her hair, the curve of her breast glimpsed in the deep V of her shirt when she stood just right.

"You know she'll toss it out for a water bed in, say… oh, twenty years or so," Kate warned, a husky warmth entering her voice.

"Maybe, but I don't think so. Her aunt hasn't outgrown her love for fairy tales, or her faith in miracles."

She cast him a doleful look. "I'm not in the mood to be charmed, Ethan."

"Stop making me want to try."

As expected, she chose retreat. But, about to circle back to the bedroom, she saw the box on the side table. She stopped.

"What's this?"

She should have missed it. It was a tiny box. But the gold foil wrapping had picked up the light from the oil lamp on the kitchen island.

"A little something for you. I was carrying the toy to the truck when I passed this window and…" He shrugged, preferring to watch what she would do.

She squared her shoulders. "I won't accept it. I can't."

"Yeah, you can. If not as a thank-you for what you tried to do, take it as a thank-you for what I'm about to ask of you."

Some intent must have shown in his eyes, because she suddenly, vehemently, shook her head, and this time she did make it to the bedroom. Only Ethan stretched his arm out across the doorway at the last moment, stopping her.

"Why now?" she whispered, almost beseeching. "Why tonight?"

He almost stopped breathing in order to retain the subtle touch of her breasts against his arm. "It's time."

"No. I'll call Joan Nyland in the morning and tell her not to use me as an intermediary anymore, that you're all hers. This is impossible, Ethan. I thought I could do this, but only a fool keeps banging her head against a brick wall without something giving."

"Give me one more night."

"No."

"I want you, Kate."

"You…" Despite having every right to call him a number of terrible things, she surprised him by falling silent. "Why tonight?" she asked again.

"Because you've finally let go of the illusions you have about me."

"I've never had any illusions about you, Ethan."

"Yes, you have. But now you can see me for what I am."

"Achieving what?"

"Honesty. Complete, total honesty. Enough to admit the chemistry between us. It's time we deal with it." And if she tried to slip past him now and lock that bedroom door, he couldn't guarantee he would let her. Not this time.

Instead, she turned to bring her body flush against his, and looked up at him. "Then say it. Tell me you want to make love with me."

"I want to unbutton that nightshirt, drag it over your head and taste every inch of you. Then I want to rub you all over me until you're closer than my own skin. I want you hard, and I want you soft, and I'll even settle for a little crazy."

"But you don't want to make love to me?"

"No."

"Have it your way," she said, unbuttoning the three buttons on her shirt, then slipping her arms around his neck.

He wrapped his arms around her waist, and locked his mouth to hers. He'd been frustrated, tired, angry with the waiting. Now he knew only the devouring hunger he had to sate. He'd told Kate things would never be casual between them, and he'd meant it. Seconds later, when he felt the first tremors of pleasure begin reverberating from his body and hers, he knew that what followed would be all he'd asked of her, and more. But not casual.

Even before he deepened the kiss, she was his. He felt it from the first instant, and crushed her closer, wanting the imprint of her on him, to know he would feel her hours, days from now, no matter what. He didn't care about the pain settling in his back from his earlier acrobatics, or the ache in his ribs. And, to his relief, Kate gave every evidence of wanting him just as badly. In fact, rising on tiptoe, she held him as tight as she could and pressed herself to him with an urgency that threatened to drain him before they'd barely begun.

Pleasure speared through him, and longing fed him. No matter how and where he touched her, it wasn't enough. He explored her like a blind man, stroking the length of her back, caressing the fine but strong bones of her shoulders, spanning her trim waist, then splaying his fingers to possess the tempting curve of her hips. Dizzy with the heady sensations, he leaned back against the door jamb and tested his endurance further by drawing her between his legs.

When he moaned, she tore her mouth from his. "Am I hurting you?"

"Yeah, but don't stop. It's a good hurt...a very... good..." Frustrated with flannel, he slipped his hands beneath and sculpted her slender, taut curves. If he'd known she felt this good, that she was wearing so little, he might never have resisted her this long.

Wanting more, he cupped her and rubbed her slowly around and around, matching the pagan rhythm of his tongue. Around and around, until a small fire ignited between them and soft, throaty sounds of pleasure whispered in her throat.

When he momentarily clenched his hands, she gasped and tore her mouth from his. "I have...one question," she breathed shakily. "Is this going to happen standing up?"

"Not our first time."

The idea appealed, though. They'd deprived themselves for too long not to claim the right of urgency. He knew she agreed when he slipped his hands to her thighs, and as she hooked a leg around his, he wrapped her completely around him and carried her to the bed.

Lowering her carefully, he eased himself over her. Their gazes held, even when they were once again nose to nose. Slowly she reached up to touch his bruised face.

"Don't keep pretending you aren't in pain. I saw you wince."

"Close your eyes."

"Ethan—"

"Make me forget it."

Silenced for a moment, she searched his face, touched the places he knew would turn him into an eyesore by morning. She then moved those elegant fingers down the taut cords along his neck, across his shoulders, and deliciously down his back, into his loosened jeans.

Her hands on his hot flesh wrenched a deep moan from him. Seeking her mouth again, he resumed the rhythmic thrusts against her to show her what he wanted, and where he ultimately wanted to be.

With that, a sweet wildness settled between them. It intensified like a hot summer afternoon that promised the satisfaction of a saturating storm. The longer the kisses, the more feverish and humid the air became, the more restless and eager their caresses.

They agreed simultaneously that her shirt had become more tedious than temptation, and although Kate began to arch to rid herself of it, Ethan chose to surprise her by sliding down her body, then using both hands and mouth to inch it up and bare her to his view. What he uncovered had him aching all over again.

Pale, shimmering, sleek, she fulfilled every dream he'd had of her. Equal to the need to touch was the desire to taste— at the joint of her left hip, over the shallow valley of her stomach, to the peaks of her surprisingly lush breasts, where she framed his face with her hands and offered herself to him.

The shirt momentarily forgotten, he lowered his head and fastened his mouth to her left breast. Her ragged cry and spasmodic shudder told him what he'd long guessed, that as with him, Kate had denied herself a great deal for a long time. Wanting her to know the same fierce pleasure that knowledge brought him, he did everything he could think of, everything he'd ever wanted to try—not with just any woman. With her.

It was too much, too soon, for her. The way she bowed off the bed, the crescendo of her muted cries, told him so. And he wanted it. He wanted her to come apart for him, because although he hadn't known an excessive number of women, he did recognize he'd been right about her honesty, too. There was nothing she would hide from him, and no one who would prove more generous and willing as a lover. That proved as potent a stimulant as any aphrodisiac could hope to be.

He rose to his knees, helped her sit up, and slipped the nightshirt over her head. Pausing only to shake her hair out of her eyes, she then unzipped his jeans the rest of the way. The briefest brush of her fingers against him had him sucking in a sharp breath. Impatient for more, Ethan pushed off the denim.

"Wait," he said hoarsely as she drew him with her, back onto the bed. "I have to—"

"No, you don't."

"Kate."

"Come inside me, Ethan. It's all right."

He didn't completely understand, and when she closed her hand around him, he almost stopped caring. He could have succeeded if she'd been anyone else. But this was Kate, the woman he'd never been able to drive out of his mind, even when she belonged to another.

His hesitation transmitted his doubt to her. "We're safe," she assured him.

"Not entirely. And I won't put you at risk."

"You can't."

She turned her head away, but he caught the brief glimpse of pain in her eyes that spoke of an old vulnerability. One secret. He wanted it spelled out for him; he didn't want to mangle her feelings any more than he already had.

Taking hold of her chin, he forced her to face him. "Can't?"

"Blast you, Ethan! Why don't we make a big production out of this?"

Taking advantage of his surprise and his bruises, she pushed him aside. She almost made it off the bed, but he was faster, stronger. He had her flat beneath him again after only the slightest skirmish. And he understood. Finally. Thoroughly.

"You can't have children."

"I've changed my mind about this," she said, staring at the headboard. "Let me up, please."

"Ah...Kate." He'd thought he no longer had a heart to break. "I'm sorry."

She turned livid. "Don't you *dare* say that to me! *And get off!*"

Instead, he kissed her, kissed her with a sweet ferocity that announced she couldn't hide from him with this, either, and that it didn't make a damned bit of difference to her desirability to him.

She fought him at first. She punched at shoulders that ached, pushed against ribs that threatened to cut off his breath. Finally, desperately, he succeeded in gripping her wrists and pinning them at the sides of her head.

"Kate, don't. I'm sorry for not having the right words, and even lousier timing. I'm *sorry.*"

She shut her eyes, went completely still beneath him. "I know."

"If you really want to stop, we will. Right now."

She opened her eyes and looked into his. Silently she eased her right hand free, grasped his and drew it down her body, over her taut breast, down the concave line of her abdomen, to the narrow band of material stretched across her hips. "No," she whispered against his mouth. "Help me. Make me stop aching. Let me make you—"

He kissed her before she made him embarrass himself with just her seductive words. Then he slipped his hand inside her panties to that secret place that told him what her eyes transmitted was true. She wanted him as much as he wanted her.

He watched her body tense and arch as he delved into her heat and discovered how hot and sensitive she was. It spurred his own passion, and raced it to a new more dangerous level.

"Yes," she whispered, at his almost desperate movements, when he dragged down that last barrier between them.

He wanted to kiss her there, hear the sounds of pleasure she would make, feel her nails score his back as he raced her toward ecstasy. But she'd pushed him too close to his own edge.

Cursing his own weakness, craving another taste of her passion, he raised himself over her and sought her mouth. Then, slowly, slowly, he lowered himself into her moist heat.

She gloved him with aching care, so thoroughly and deeply they were soon shaking from the hot pleasure. And when he was as far as she could take him, he went still, wanting to feel her heartbeat and let her feel his.

He would have stayed that way forever, if he'd thought he had even a minute chance to make it last; if he hadn't opened his eyes, and seen her face, seen how strain competed with ecstasy. But the sight of her, the feel of finally being inside her, was simply too much.

Too much. All of it. Her. The truth was a scream in his head, and a raging fire scorching every inch of his body. Still, he began the age-old rhythm, a dance she eagerly matched, then reinvented for him. Within a matter of heartbeats, she made him want to swear or pray, he wasn't sure which. But most of all she made him want to watch...watch what was happening between them. It didn't matter that sweat streamed into his eyes, burning them, as he tried. It didn't matter that her short nails were going to leave their own marks on him as she struggled to keep him close. He had to...had to...see.

Kate.

She was his.

They were one...if only for this brief instant.

The image branded into his memory forever, he shut his eyes tight, grasped her hips hard, and raced to end the torment he'd carried in his heart and soul for over half a lifetime.

The first thing Kate realized once her mind began clearing again was that she'd slipped close to the edge of the bed. It seemed appropriate, since she'd already leaped off one precipice tonight. At least the cool air felt wonderful against her scorched skin. She reached beneath her to sweep her damp hair farther away from her nape and fanned it, as well as her equally damp throat.

"And here I thought this room never got above fifty degrees," she murmured, feeling delicious, despite the discomfort.

Ethan remained prone and still beside her, but replied, "If we don't get under these blankets, you'll be saying it again in a few minutes."

"I'll risk it."

"Good." He pushed himself up on one elbow. "That means I get to look at you longer."

Interestingly, the remark didn't embarrass her any more than she thought it might, not any more than his intent gaze did, or his touch as he ran his fingers from the damp hollow of her throat, down between her still-heaving breasts, and beyond, to where they'd been intimately joined only minutes ago. The sensual caress fascinated her as much as it had to discover the sexual side of him.

She'd learned that Ethan approached his sexuality with a deliberate, unapologetic thoroughness, the same thoroughness he applied to most everything else—except maybe relationships. It had made the experience of making love with him one she would never regret, much less forget, no matter what the future held for them. If she'd had a bit more of a clue of this years ago, would she have been able to resist him?

"Did Wayne know?"

Though she was a bit shocked that their thoughts had been running along the same line, Kate had been expecting that particular question. It had her closing her eyes and taking a few seconds to let a familiar wave of sadness sweep over her and recede. She usually handled her grief well. The philosophers were right about time healing even the sharpest pain. But nothing erased it completely, or obliterated the awareness of all that had been lost or denied.

"I was only eighteen when he left, Ethan."

"That's not what I asked."

"No," she said at last. "He didn't know…because we never got that far."

Ethan went still. "You two were nuts about each other. He may have worried about the age thing—"

"He did."

"But no one in all of Whitehorn cared. It was a given. He was the crown prince, you were the princess. You belonged to him. No one would have held it against you."

"He would have held it against himself. That's the kind of person he was. We didn't, Ethan."

He was silent for a long time. Heaven only knew what he was thinking. For her part, Kate concentrated on keeping the past where it was, but not too successfully. How could she, when Ethan was staring at her as if he wanted to attach her to a lie detector.

"Would you have told him?"

What was it she heard in his voice? Shame? Jealousy? "Of course. It would have mattered to Jeremiah. He wanted grandsons, and even though he liked the idea of a Kincaid and Randall union, that little technicality would definitely have changed his mind."

"Wayne would have handled him. He was the only one Jeremiah couldn't dictate to."

Kate knew the late patriarch had idolized his oldest son, as had most everyone else, but even handsome, strong, and ever-charming Wayne wouldn't have been able to budge his father on the sticky issue of the purity of the Kincaid family tree. But there was no need to argue the point with someone who'd known Jeremiah's headstrongness as well as she had.

That was why she'd always known that, as much as the head of the Kincaid clan might have approved of *her,* he hadn't been wild about Wayne's closeness to Ethan. That had been proved upon Ethan's return from the war. He'd tried to pay his respects to Jeremiah, but the grieving and bitter man had chased him off the ranch, shouting hideous accusations and insults.

But she hadn't treated him much better back then, had she? She hadn't let him talk, because she'd been locked up in her own pain.

And she'd been afraid that if he looked at her even close to the way he was looking at her now, she would embarrass them both with her willingness. No, her eagerness.

"When did you find out you couldn't have kids?" Ethan asked thickly.

Kate sighed and covered her face with her hands. "Don't, Ethan. This isn't something you need to hear, any more than we should have brought Wayne into bed with us."

"Tell me."

She couldn't, not if she had to look at his grim, battered face, which reminded her so acutely that their problems were far from over. Rolling onto her stomach, she bowed her head and focused on her loosely clasped hands.

"I wanted to get pregnant before he left. Wayne refused. He worried that if something happened to him, the pressure and responsibility might be too much for me. He didn't want his father pulling what Noble did to Marilee. Don't get me wrong, he loved Jeremiah. But he also understood what a bastard he could be."

"He never stopped thinking of other people. Especially you," Ethan said, his voice gruffer than usual. "He wanted to take care of everyone. Make everyone happy."

"That was his gift. And I wanted to give him one back, but it wasn't to be." She tried a shrug, but failed.

"How did you find out, Kate?"

The man was relentless. "Have I ever asked *you* about your sexual initiation? Never mind," she replied when he lifted an eyebrow. Once again, she sighed. "After we got the news, I went back to college and…I did something stupid, okay? I got scared, went to a doctor, and the rest is history. I can never get pregnant, okay? Damn it, Ethan, you know yourself from being on that witness stand that confession is *not* good for the soul."

To her amazement, he reached forward and stroked her hair.

"That must have been tough news to bear alone."

She closed her eyes, wanting to resent him for his generosity. Why wouldn't he call her half of the names she'd called herself?

"Wayne wanted children as much as his father did," she said, trying to remember the innocent she'd been then. "Probably more than me at the time. Do you realize, if things had turned out differently, I would have had to make him see that he belonged with someone else, who could give him babies? If that didn't work, I would have told him that I'd had second thoughts about marriage. That I wanted a career instead."

Ethan made a low negative sound. "He would never have believed you."

"Maybe. Look at me now. At any rate, I would have tried. I probably would have asked you to help me, too."

With an oath, Ethan sat up and combed his hands through his hair. Kate sat up, too, hesitantly touching his broad, scarred back. "I'm sorry. I know you would rather have taken a bullet yourself than do anything that hurt him."

"Don't give me credit I don't deserve," he muttered. "Wayne was the hero. Not me."

She thought about arguing the point, about finally letting him tell her whatever it was that brought such a look of anguish to his pale blue eyes whenever anyone mentioned Vietnam. She'd seen it the first time their paths crossed after his return, and he still carried the look today. But she hadn't been able to listen back then. At any rate, the past couldn't be changed, she insisted to herself for the hundredth time, and nothing could be gained by reopening old wounds.

"So," she said instead, "now you know why you needn't worry about me muddying your life with more unwanted complications."

He surprised her by turning around. "But it doesn't explain why you let me complicate yours."

She should have known he would go for the jugular. First he'd knocked her off-balance with his passion and openness as they made love, and now he wanted to refuse to let her sidestep her deepest thoughts and feelings. "I thought we'd covered that weeks ago," she said, hedging.

"I'm talking about what just happened between us."

"You asked me. Or rather," she added throatily, "you told me."

"If you'd said no in any way, shape or form, I would have stopped."

Because he was edging toward dangerous territory, Kate chose to retreat. "I'd like to go freshen up now."

"Not yet," he said, suddenly pushing her flat on her back. He kept her there with his own body.

"Ethan!"

"You know what I think? You were trying to purge something. What was it, Kate? Or were you punishing one of us? Who was it? Me? You? Or were you getting back at Wayne for dying on you?"

"That's a horrible thing to say!"

"The truth often is."

"You don't know what you're talking about. You certainly don't want to deal with the truth."

"Try me."

Her heart pounding, her body once again reacting to the

power of his, Kate let her emotions take control. "Which truth, then, Ethan? The truth about lust? That I wanted you to carry me to this bed, and have wanted it for a long time? That it shames me not to care about anything right now except that you make love to me again? Oh, excuse me. You don't want to hear that word. But I don't use another word for this feeling, because no one has ever made me feel this reckless, this hot, this needy, before. *No one,* do you understand?"

"That's not what I—"

"Oh, yes, it is what you wanted to ask. Just as you wanted to know how you ranked against Wayne, but would never say it because it would be committing the ultimate sin against a man you held as close as a brother!"

"Stop it, Kate!"

"Just as I'm afraid to ask if once was enough for you," she concluded softly, wanting only to know his power and heat again.

Ethan uttered a soft curse. Then he whispered, "No, it's not enough," and silenced anything else she might have said by hungrily locking his mouth to hers.

Kate reached for him as he pressed her deep into the bedding, aware of his agitation as much as his desire. She understood those warring emotions well. They both had to deal with the guilt of being survivors.

"Come inside me again," she told him as she felt his arousal, hot and demanding, against her thigh. "Let's stop stirring up memories and hurt. Let's not think about yesterday or tomorrow. Let there just be *this.*"

He gave her what she wanted, his entry fast and as breathtaking as the kiss that accompanied it. In a matter of hours, they would have to go back to analyzing, planning, negotiating, and dealing with the countless demands that filled their days. But this was the eye of their storm, a temporary oasis in the middle of an unforgiving spiritual desert.

Kate wrapped herself around Ethan and reached for the oblivion only he could provide. Then she dared him to follow.

upholstery, light curtains. There was a lawyer, Josh? John—
someone—who would handle the legal papers and the deed.
Kate wasn't afraid of this man. Sadness filled her. So little
while in your life, and you've already thrown it away.

Ten

"Would you please repeat that?" Kate said, unable to
believe what she'd just heard.

The sound of Sheriff Judd Hensley clearing his throat
came clearly over the telephone line. "I know this is not
the kind of news you need to start your morning, Judge,
but it's true. Josh Trask wants to file assault charges on
Ethan. I was hoping you would ride out to the Double N
with me when we go pick him up for questioning. Ethan
might take the news better if you're around."

"This is insane. It's been nearly a week since that
episode. What's the man been doing since then?"

"He says he's been home recuperating from his injuries.
He does look a mess, Judge."

"So does my husband, but he hasn't filed assault charges
on anyone."

The lawman sighed heavily. "I didn't say I agreed with
what's going on here, but I do have an obligation to follow

the law. Especially when the guy walks into my office with his attorney."

Kate's heart did a nosedive. This was serious, if the man had already contacted a lawyer. All Judd had to tell her next was that Trask's doctor had also concocted a serious injury for the guy to make his claim more believable. "Who's his legal counsel?"

"Baxter Blankenship."

She gripped the locket she'd accepted from Ethan the morning after they first made love. "Why am I not surprised?"

"I had a feeling you would say something like that. Can I count on you, Judge?"

"You realize this is a farce?"

"You bet I do. Trask has spent more than a few nights behind bars for disorderly conduct and a few other things, so I'm not wild about what smells like a waste of taxpayers' money. But I have to honor this accusation, because this county can't afford any lawsuits from citizens who feel their rights have been violated."

Dear Lord. Poor Ethan. How was he going to bear this? "Give me an hour, Judd. I have to cancel a number of appointments."

"I appreciate it."

With Pat's help, it took her less than ten minutes to clear her calendar. She tried to call the ranch right afterward, but, as expected, Ethan wasn't in, which canceled her hope of warning him about what had happened. Then she decided that might be good news.

It made her sick to her stomach, but she focused on using the extra time to detour by the offices of Blankenship and Blankenship. Inside, she spotted the brothers in a glass conference room, and she wasted no time in waving off a secretary and barging inside, getting straight to the point.

"Plotting how to next accuse my husband of abducting residents of Whitehorn on behalf of aliens, gentlemen?" she asked as they reluctantly rose in greeting.

The two exchanged sly grins. "This is an unexpected but delightful surprise, Judge," Warren said, gesturing to a chair. "Care to sit down?"

Kate ignored the invitation. "I want you to know I'm aware of what a sham you're pulling, and think it's despicable. It's one thing for a relative to contest the custody of a child. But to try to add leverage to your case by what amounts to nothing more than a provoked situation is reprehensible behavior."

Unintimidated, Warren sat down again. "Your Honor gives us too much credit. Baxter was just now informing me of the unfortunate situation. But I must say I understand your distress. Your husband can't seem to keep out of trouble, can he?"

Kate wished she could reach across the conference table and tip his coffee mug into his lap. "This is going to backlash on you two. At any rate, be assured I will have the charges dropped, and there will be nothing on the books for you to even allude to at the custody hearing."

"Don't be too sure," Baxter replied. "I think my client has a right to be concerned for his safety. After all, Charlie Avery had a disagreement with Ethan Walker, and look at what happened to him."

"Baxter, try it and you'll be lucky to walk behind an ambulance in the next parade, let alone chase one." Kate decided she needed to make one more stop, at the feed store. She needed a reliable witness who would make Trask look as if Ethan should have filed charges against *him.* "But I'm here to give you a chance to withdraw your charges while you still have time."

Warren turned to his brother. "See what I mean? She's terrific. Understands the best defense is a strong offense. You're a worthy opponent, Your Honor. But this time you're shooting in the dark. Ironic as it may seem, one case has nothing to do with the other."

"Have it your way," Kate replied, with an indifferent shrug. But she walked out before her act of bravado slipped, out of fear for Ethan.

To say she'd expected a different response from the brothers would have been an overstatement, but she'd had to try to appeal to their conscience if nothing else. Now all that was important was to get to Ethan. She needed to phone Eva, too, in case anyone called from the press.

Preoccupied, she almost collided with an attractive blonde who, laughing throatily, backed out of the small conference room. Kate sidestepped her, guessing by the woman's attire and the folder in her hand that she was on the staff, but she stopped short when she saw the man she was talking to.

Noble Taylor.

And Warren had the nerve to suggest the Trask situation had nothing to do with Darcy's custody case. Disgusted, especially since the businessman had a decidedly guilty look on his face, Kate shook her head. "What won't you sink to?"

Without waiting for a response, she stalked out of the building.

At the feed store, she spoke quickly with Bill Frieland, who not only agreed to be a witness for Ethan, but gave her a list of names of people who might also testify should she need more. Then he brought in Will. The loading dock worker admitted he had some concern that Trask might come after him, but agreed he would testify if his boss did.

Kate was almost ten minutes late arriving at the sheriff's office, but she felt much better. She found Judd Hensley on his way to his patrol car. When he spotted her, he tugged his Stetson lower over his dark eyes and gave her one of his long speaking looks.

"You gave me a few minutes of doubt—especially when I phoned your office and learned you'd left there quite a while ago."

"Don't tell me you thought I'd hightailed it to the ranch without you?" she replied, lifting an eyebrow. She liked the no-nonsense lawman; a man of few words, in some ways he had much in common with Ethan. They'd both been through some tough times. "And then what?"

"Yeah, that's what I told myself. But was it smart going face-to-face with the Blankenships?"

She refused to ask how he'd heard about that. Secretly, however, she knew she should be glad they hadn't filed a complaint against *her*. "Maybe. It resolved any doubts I had regarding this being a setup."

Judd nodded, indicating this came as no surprise. "Hop in, and you can tell me about it along the way."

"Expecting company?"

Ethan looked up from the ancient water pump he and John Mountain had been trying to overhaul and felt a prickling at his nape. He'd seen the sheriff's truck, with its overhead lights, too often not to recognize it without having to see the official decal on the side.

"No."

He tossed the wrench into the tool chest and reached for the rag hanging out of his right hind pocket. And here he'd been thinking life had been almost sweet these past several days. Wiping grease from his hands, he wondered who was gunning for him now. When he saw Kate in the passenger seat, his self-pity turned immediately to concern for her.

Since the night they'd made love, he'd made every excuse to keep his hands off her, doing paperwork he'd put off for months until she went to bed, staying out late to work on one piece of broken machinery or another...and although he had a feeling Kate knew all that, she seemed willing to let him decide what their future held.

Well, this was obviously it. Judd Hensley's arrival was exactly why he'd been keeping her at arm's length. Who did he think he'd been kidding, to hope he could have a normal life and a real relationship? But if anyone had tried to hurt Kate, they were in for it, he vowed, striding for the truck, which stopped a few dozen yards away. He headed straight for Kate's side and jerked open the door.

He helped her out, then gripped her by her upper arms to search her face. More than anything, he needed to know she was all right. Instead, he noted how clean and elegant she looked in her green-and-blue suit, which conservatively hid both lush and lithe curves that could make his mouth go dry and desire charge through him like a high-voltage current.

God help him. It shouldn't be possible to be thinking about what he was thinking, with trouble looming so close he could smell it in the air.

"What's wrong?" he demanded gruffly, his gaze searching her face.

"Ethan...there's trouble, darling."

Her own gaze spoke volumes. Asking him to be brave, it prepared him for the arms she slipped around his waist, and for her tender kiss. Despite the dread of the unknown, the gift of having her this close had Ethan's pulse racing.

"Sweetheart, you'll get filthy."

"I don't care."

Wishing he could kiss her properly, he looked over her shoulder at Judd, who was rounding the truck. "Sheriff. What's up?"

"I won't beat around the bush, Ethan. Josh Trask has filed assault charges against you. I've come to take you in."

"Oh, no." If it hadn't been for Kate holding him tight, he didn't know if he would have believed what he was hearing. "No way. You'll have to bring in your whole department to get me downtown again."

"Ethan, Judd is on your side," Kate assured him. "He agrees that this is nonsense."

"Then he can let me be," Ethan replied, speaking directly to the lawman.

"He would, darling. But he has to follow the rules."

"Rules." Ethan's world turned dark. "I'm sick to death of rules. Why is it that everyone ignores them until they want to get at me? Was Trask obeying any so-called *rules* when he insulted my wife? What was I supposed to do, stand there and let him get away with it?"

"I've talked to Bill Frieland, Ethan," Kate said, laying a calming hand against his heart. "He says he'll vouch for you. Will agreed, too. They're going to meet us at the station. And Bill gave me several other names. Judd thinks we'll have this cleared up in a few hours. But if not, I've already made arrangements for a bond, and if you do get booked, I'll get you out right afterward."

Booked. He briefly shut his eyes. He couldn't deal with the humiliation and shame again. He wouldn't stand for Kate seeing him that way. "How much more are you going to put up with? Don't you see it's over! I can't win."

"Stop it. What are you going to do, let the Trasks and the Taylors of the world win?"

"Honey, they already have." He put her at arm's length and turned to John Mountain, who'd been standing by and listening, his expression enigmatic, as usual. "Guess you know the routine by now."

"I'll be here. You listen to your lady."

Surrounded by people who thought he was a bottomless pit of faith, he thought with frustration. Well, he wasn't. He focused on the sheriff and offered his wrists. "You need to cuff me?"

Judd grimaced sourly. "Just get in the damned truck before I forget who I'm really ticked off at."

Ethan expected at least a few members of the press to be waiting at the station when they arrived, especially after Kate and Judd Hensley filled him in on what they knew.

"Baxter Blankenship must have been doing some phone calling," Kate said with disgust as the small group swarmed the truck.

Just as he had in the old days, Ethan coped by turning into himself, making fewer and fewer responses, the closer they got to town. By the time he exited the truck, he was totally within himself and barely heard anything the demanding reporters yelled at him. Nor did he blink as a persistent photographer tried to get a full-face photograph.

Only inside, as Kate tried to follow him into the sheriff's office, did he momentarily flounder.

"Go away, Kate."

"I'm staying with you."

"No. I don't want you to. Go away and do what you have to do. I know you're putting off meetings and work for this."

She stared at him incredulously. "Do you think I could work, knowing *this* was going on?" She stayed right at his side. "I'm with you in this, Ethan. Get used to the idea."

"But I don't want you here!"

He'd been too loud. People turned and stared. Others whispered. One or two elbowed each other. However, none of that bothered him as much as seeing Kate's hurt. If it hadn't been for Judd Hensley, he might have made an even greater fool of himself by reaching for her. Then it would have taken a cutting torch to get them apart.

"He'll be fine," the lawman assured Kate with a sympathetic look. "But you may want to use the office next to mine to call his lawyer, just in case. Keep everyone happy."

"Joan Nyland does need to be informed of this. I'll be back soon," Kate told them both.

Ethan thought she sounded far more subdued than usual. And the kiss he turned away from in self-defense barely skimmed his chin.

"Ethan…"

He knew she was worried about him, maybe a bit angry, too, but he couldn't reassure her. Hell, he couldn't get past his fear to reassure himself.

"…and I asked Eva to watch Darcy tonight," Kate said as she sped past Shadow Ranch's entrance.

It was early afternoon. This ordeal had taken longer than she'd anticipated. But through a tremendous amount of work, and even more willpower, she'd managed to turn a potential nightmare into a closed matter. Ethan was free. Witness after witness had come down to the station at her pleading, cajoling, arguing and, yes, even threatening, to tell of what they'd seen. By the time Judd Hensley had heard the same story a half-dozen times, he'd had a deputy haul Trask in and demanded he stand before those witnesses and defend his own story. The man had squirmed and whined, and finally had pointed a finger at Baxter Blankenship— who'd also been ordered to the station—

for talking him into filing. When Baxter shrugged and pleaded a loss of memory regarding how he'd learned about the fight, Kate had challenged him by bringing up Noble Taylor's name. Not only had the man had the audacity to insist he didn't know what she was talking about, he'd pretended to be offended at Trask for using his good name to waste everyone's time, and magnanimously assured Judd that he considered all of Trask's charges dropped.

Kate was exhausted, but very proud. On the other hand, she remained extremely worried about Ethan. The Blankenships had succeeded in achieving what they'd set out to do. He had been totally humiliated once too often. But Kate knew what had shamed Ethan the most. It had been Trask's taunt about her and Wayne.

Kate winced, thinking about it now. What man could have dealt with hearing that? She wished she could take back what she'd said that evening she'd come home and found him all bruised and bleeding. No wonder he'd gotten that terrible look on his face.

And now he'd gone through the ordeal of hearing Trask's taunt repeated and repeated in Judd Hensley's office before all those people. It had been a nightmare, but the expression on Ethan's face had been even more frightening. He'd virtually removed himself spiritually from that room, and now she didn't know if she could get him back from the dark place he'd let himself slip off to.

"Turn around."

Because they were the first words he'd said since leaving Whitehorn, Kate nearly pulled over. Then she realized what he meant, and changed her mind.

"No. You need the time alone to rest and regroup."

"I'm not abandoning my niece."

She gripped the steering wheel more firmly. "No, you're

not. You're letting her stay with a couple I trust implicitly. Don't try to pull that argument again, Ethan. Eva may give you heck because you scare her, but she adores Darcy, and the baby will do better there than if she's listening to you rage throughout the night."

"I haven't said anything yet."

But he would. He needed to, if he wanted to get beyond this and prepare for their next challenge. Whatever it would be. Whenever the Blankenships or Noble Taylor got creative again.

Once they arrived at the house, however, things got worse. Ethan didn't go in. At first, Kate wondered if he might hop in his truck and go after the baby himself, or Trask or the Blankenships. But, to her relief, he strode over to the bunkhouse.

Hoping he might sit and talk things out with John Mountain, Kate went into the cabin and changed from her business suit into a terry robe and let down her hair. She was pouring herself a glass of wine and thinking of indulging in her first bubble bath since moving in when Ethan came in through the back door.

"Hi," she said, offering a soft smile. "Want to join me in a glass?"

He shook his head.

"Are you hungry? There's some roast beef and cheese. I could make you a sandwich."

He shook his head again.

Kate drew a deep breath. "How can I help you?"

"You mean you haven't performed enough miracles today?"

She knew he didn't mean it, but she had to bite back her own sarcastic retort, nonetheless. Damn it, she'd suffered today, too, and she'd asked for nothing from him except to let her stand by him so that she could get him back here and safe. In order to achieve peace, did she had to force a war with him?

Apparently so, she concluded, seeing his resolute expression.

After taking a last sip of her wine, she set down the glass and focused on him completely. "What Trask said that day at the feed store was tasteless and disgusting, but the only reason he said it was to provoke you. After what we shared that night, after what I told you afterward, how can you let his words have any power?"

"It's not what he said, it's that *every damn person* in Whitehorn heard him, all right?"

Now they were getting somewhere. "I may be wrong about this, but I'm fairly certain that my secretary and a few other people don't know, because they weren't there. And I doubt John Mountain knows, because he wasn't there…"

She spoke gently, and with a coaxing smile, but Ethan remained aloof and unamused. Hands clenched, jaw working, he glared at her.

"I'm taking a shower," he muttered abruptly, and walked away.

Kate decided to let him go. She might have struck out in this first attempt, but maybe the shower would help him scrub away the memories of what he'd been through today.

She picked up her glass and sipped her wine. Then she began pacing around the room, listening to the water run and run.

She tried to fill her time by phoning Eva and checking on things. But when she hung up minutes later and the shower was still going, she wasn't worried about him running out of water—they gravity-fed from a large storage tank out back, and the hot-water heater operated on propane—but she understood Ethan wasn't even beginning to champion his demons. How long should she wait for him to call to her for help?

Under the circumstances, he wouldn't let himself.

Determined, she placed her empty glass in the sink and headed for the bathroom. Untying the sash of her robe, she slipped it off and laid it on the vanity. Then she slid open the shower stall door.

"What do you think you're doing?"

He'd been leaning back against the fiberglass wall, eyes closed, simply letting the water spray over him. The steam was so thick, Kate thought it a miracle he could breathe.

"I got lonely and decided to join the party," she replied, closing the door behind her.

"Don't you understand? *I don't want you here.*"

He meant to be cruel, and his words sliced at her, but Kate focused on the desolation she felt emanating from him. "Shut up, Ethan, before you hurt my feelings. And turn around. I'll wash your back for you."

She would have smiled at his stunned look, but she knew better. Just as she knew that, when he turned, it had more to do with not wanting to look at her than with any submission. She picked up the washcloth and soap he'd dropped on the built-in seat and began massaging his back.

"I know what you're doing," he said, bracing his hands against the wall. "It's not going to work."

"That's a boy. Stay tough. Go down fighting. Don't even open your eyes to figure out who's the enemy and who're the good guys. Just punch everyone's lights out."

She thought his spine would snap, he went so stiff.

"You think you're cute, don't you?"

"Ethan, I'm an only daughter and an only child. I'm not only cute, I'm downright incorrigible."

He wanted to continue to fight her. She had to wait for a small eternity for him to change his mind, before she felt his shoulders relax and saw his head bow. Kate used the time to massage the stiffness out of him, kneading and rubbing as she would one of her weary horses after a torturous workout.

But this wasn't methodical routine to her. She was fighting for the heart and soul of the man she loved.

She loved Ethan's body, the strength and spareness of it, and with water sluicing off him in long streams, he looked like a finely molded sculpture. The brutal scars that marred the beautiful lines broke her heart every time she saw them. As tenderness merged with sensuality, she leaned forward to kiss the deepest, oldest injury. Hearing his breath catch, she did it again.

"When we're done, I want you to climb between the fresh sheets I've put on the bed. You need to be able to stretch out and relax," she murmured, caressing him more slowly and rhythmically now.

"Kate…stop."

"Fat chance, cowboy. I'm not going to let you forget what you've achieved today."

"Nothing. You're the one who did everything."

"Only because you were in the right. What's more, you didn't lose control when things got tense in Judd Hensley's office." Kate knew that even though she'd been instrumental in getting the charges against Ethan dropped, she couldn't have succeeded without his cooperation. "I'm very proud of you."

He whipped around, grabbed her wrists and growled, "Damn it, will you stop it?"

She lifted her chin, but her gaze relayed a sensual invitation. "Make me."

Aware that he needed release of some sort, she offered herself, not caring at all that he recognized her motive and that he wanted to resist. When he shifted his hold to frame her face, she saw the internal battle. Touching him as gently as she would have the baby, she slid her hands along his arms, then across his broad shoulders and downward, downward, until she cupped his taut buttocks and brought her hips flush against his rigid body.

With a groan of surrender, Ethan locked his mouth to hers. Expecting anger, she was astonished by his urgency and tenderness. He used his thumbs and lips to award the same caresses she'd bestowed across his back, relaxing her and seducing her into a long, explorative kiss that became more like an erotic feast with every second. Then, using his tongue, he initiated a sinuous stroking, tempting her to participate in a sign language as explicit as any words could be.

By the time he slipped his arms around her and drew her more tightly against him, she throbbed all over. But that was only the beginning. He continued to move against her, letting her grow more and more intimately aware of his aroused flesh. Finally he cupped her hips, and soon their bodies matched the erotic rhythm of their kiss, melting away all thought, as well as all patience.

Wanting him more than she could have told him, Kate rubbed her thigh intimately against his. Ethan reacted immediately, turning her until she was flush against the wall. Expecting him to lift her, she found herself the recipient of even more passionate loveplay as he bent to lick the wild rivulets of water coursing across and down her breasts. First her right, then her left… He paid both the same intense attention he had her mouth, until her nipples thrust toward him in hard, aching points. All the while, he let his right hand bury itself in the golden curls between her thighs. His touch was amazingly gentle and generous, and knowing he could feel her melting for him, Kate dragged her mouth from his to rest her forehead against his shoulder.

"Bed," she breathed.

"Too late."

This time he did lift her. As careful as he was, it was still an impaling as he lowered her onto his burning-hot flesh. She balanced herself with his strong shoulders and arms, while inside she felt him turning her core into a liquid heat. Ethan felt it, too, groaning softly.

"Ah, Kate…Kate. Am I hurting you?"

"No. I can't believe—" She bit back a cry as he taught her a new pleasure. "Ethan, I'm so full. I need…I need…"

"I know it. It's the one thing I can give you, sweetheart. Come on, Kate. Burn for me. Then I'll burn for you. And maybe, if we try hard enough, we'll hold back tomorrow for a while."

Something about his words troubled her, but caught up in his passion, and driven by a current she couldn't control, Kate quickly pushed her doubts aside.

He wanted her. He couldn't seem to get enough of her, just as she couldn't satisfy her curiosity and pleasure in touching him. It was going to be all right, she thought, feeling the tremors that began crescendoing at her core.

She would make it all right, she promised, as he cried out and went rigid in her arms.

Ethan reluctantly let Kate ease down his body until she stood on her own two feet again. Her breath was still coming in shallow pants, and his wasn't much better. But he knew he already wanted her again, and this time he intended it to happen in bed.

He adored her for trying to make him forget the nightmare of today, and for ignoring the countless differences between them. There would be plenty of time to mourn the fickleness of fate in the empty expanse of the years ahead.

Tonight, and for however many nights she would give him until the end, he would stockpile the memories he could. And he would try to show her at least a trace of how much he loved her.

After shutting off the water, he grabbed the towel over the door and wrapped her in it. Then he lifted her into his arms as he'd wanted to the evening he brought her here as his bride.

"I could get used to this romantic streak," Kate murmured, using the tip of her tongue to absorb a droplet of water that had been streaking down his jawline.

He carried her to the bed, stretched himself beside her, and then rolled them around and around until she lay stretched over him. "I don't know anything about romance, Kate. I just know that I still want you all over me, closer than a rash."

She smiled, settled herself more intimately over him and laughed softly as he quickly sucked in his breath. "So where do you want to itch first, cowboy?"

His heart stopped. "I'll show you."

Eleven

He knew better than to let himself get seduced into believing that maybe, just maybe, as they'd worked things out
with Trask, he, Kate and Darcy would make it as a family.
Happiness lured him into believing in tomorrows and
tricked him into a severe case of myopia.

Through June, their world settled into a near normalcy.
He called it "near" because living in the cabin continued
to be problematic for them. No matter how organized she
managed to be, Kate still had her hands full, ferrying her
belongings between their homes. He tried to help by doing
more to make her situation easier, even started picking up
Darcy at Shadow Ranch on evenings when she was out of
town or would be delayed at the courthouse.

Nevertheless, the work load continued to grow, and the
strain was often more than he thought she could manage.
But she never complained; in fact, she seemed to be blossoming with every day, adding to the temptation to trust in

hope. If they had a future, he began to tell himself, he could do more to make her life easier. Add to the cabin, for one thing. And put in central heating and air conditioning for another.

How Kate managed to structure her evenings so that there was playtime with Darcy, he didn't know. But he loved to watch her with the child, and it hurt like hell to think of all the years she'd lived with the double grief of having lost Wayne and learning she would never have a child of her own. He even fantasized about the doctors being wrong, about them discovering he'd planted his own seed inside her. They were both still young by today's standards.

Most of all, he lived for the hour when he could lead his wife to bed. At first, as he'd feared, he couldn't sleep there; and he thought it would be as it had been when he first came back from overseas. He'd tossed and turned, and he'd about given up and retreated to his chair when Kate began talking. It had been her voice, that velvety, soothing tone, that slowly but surely numbed whatever psychological mine fields he'd created for himself, and let him sleep.

The next night, she'd done it again. He'd soon learned she didn't even have to talk about anything sensible or logical. One night she'd actually drawn him into a conversation about saddles, of all things. Soon, between the pleasure of holding her love-sated body against his and their friendly banter about the slope and length on saddles, stirrup preferences and whatnot, he'd drifted off to sleep again, and for the first time hadn't awakened until morning, when he felt the cramp in his shoulder from the unnatural sleeping position. Kate had laughed all the way out the door at what she called his "poleaxed" look.

It became their ritual, and a way for them to get to know more of the little things about each other. He soon learned that she was delightfully ticklish, that she had never enjoyed skiing as much as Wayne did, that she loathed the taste of fish, but had always wanted an aquarium, that she dealt with the stress from her most traumatic cases by once a month renting a bunch of three-hankie movies from the video store and then watching them over a weekend until she was cried out...and that she was a tireless, adventurous lover, eager to try anything if she thought it would bring him pleasure.

But not all of their bedtime chats were amusing or teasing. One night, after a tranquil evening when they'd finally convinced John Mountain to come sit out back with them and share the homemade ice cream Eva had sent over, Kate had asked him if he knew about John Mountain's experiences in the war.

At first, he'd worried that this was a prologue to questions about himself and Wayne. Selfish or not, he didn't want the subject arising at this stage of their relationship. But he'd soon realized she was simply trying to understand the man who moved like a benevolent shadow through their lives, to respect his indescribable need for space and privacy.

"He was a tunnel rat," he'd begun one night, resting his cheek against her soft, fragrant hair. "As best as I can figure it, they were mostly reconnaissance and intelligence people, a branch of the engineers who went down into those countless miles of tunnels the Vietcong built to transport troops and supplies, and basically did what they had to do to stop them."

"Dear Lord. Little John Mountain?"

"They had to be the smaller guys, sweetheart. We aren't talking about something the size of the New York subway. It was all volunteer duty, too. No officers allowed."

"I can't imagine him down there in such a dark, confined place all by himself."

"Well, they usually operated in groups of three to six, but I guess there were times that didn't seem reassuring, either, considering the limited amount of equipment they took with them. I know I'd want more gear with me than a pistol, communications wire, a knife and a damned flashlight. John Mountain's the only one I ever spent any time around, but I knew one guy who said he'd met a couple. From what he told me, they make me sound like a party animal. The guys tend to be pure loners. Not the type for long-term relationships."

"It sounds as if it was a suicidal job."

"There were a lot of top brass that agreed with you. In fact, they started using something called a Rome plow instead, that caved in the tunnels. Later they figured out that a flight of B-52s dropping a couple hundred bombs each could be even more expedient."

Kate had stopped him there. She'd buried her face in the curve of his neck and muttered that she would never again ask another question about the war. It had reminded Ethan of her block about listening to certain things in the past, and for the first night in several days he hadn't been able to sleep.

By the following night, however, the bliss had returned, and it had stayed. That was why he wasn't prepared for Kate's arrival from court the Friday before the Fourth of July weekend.

They were planning a relatively quiet few days, except for the customers coming out to Shadow Ranch, which would take her away overnight—Saturday into Sunday morning. But the idea of having her to himself for an entire Sunday and Monday filled him with an almost boyish pleasure. They'd even talked of driving out with the baby to one of the larger creeks that ran through Kate's spread for a picnic. Then he walked out to meet her as she pulled in Friday evening.

He took one look at her pale face as he opened her door and forced himself to ask, "What's happened?"

"So much for thinking I have an indomitable poker face," she replied, attempting to brighten her tired smile. She kissed him tenderly and motioned toward the back seat. "Why don't you get our little charmer back there, before she starts blowing out your eardrums, too."

"She's not sick, is she?"

"Hardly. I'd wager to say she's getting a bit spoiled from all the attention she gets. She thinks she should have driven over here sitting on my lap. Riding in the back in a boring old carrier is for other twiglets."

Ethan knew this forced chattiness covered something serious, but he let her get away with it, aware that she wanted to choose her own time. When she uncorked the barely touched bottle of wine in the refrigerator, even before changing out of her work clothes or kicking off her shoes, Ethan knew it was time to force the issue. He put Darcy in her crib and set her stuffed unicorn close, so that she could gurgle at it and reach for it between the bars. Then he went to find out what was troubling Kate.

He came up behind her, wanting badly to wrap his arms around her waist, to bury his face in the silky softness of her hair. But, sensing that this might be the news he'd been dreading, the beginning of his end, he asked, "Is it about the case?"

She didn't beat around the bush. Putting down the bottle without pouring, she said, "Howard Lessing is recuperating in record time. He came by my office this afternoon— a courtesy visit to let me know that he's going to be hearing cases beginning the fifteenth. He's scheduled Darcy's custody hearing for the sixteenth."

"Two weeks." After waiting for so long, willing it to be over, now he wanted it postponed for…twenty years and about eight months.

"I phoned Joan to fill her in," Kate continued. "She's put us on her calendar."

Ethan glanced over to the baby. "We're just getting to know her, getting a glimpse of her personality. She's identifying her toys, the people she loves…"

"Please don't. Not tonight. For one night, please don't assume you're going to lose at the hearing."

"I don't want to have the hearing at all. It's not fair that it happen."

"I know."

"You told me that just the other day you were in Billings again and tried for another meeting with Ruth Taylor, and it didn't work." He turned away and ran his hand over his hair. "Does that sound like a person who'll do anything as long as she can spend time with her grandchild? They don't want her. They want to win a power play."

"It'll all be brought up. Joan will see to it."

But her flat tone, and her failure to turn around and face him, finally got through to him. "What aren't you telling me?" When she didn't respond right away, he took hold of her shoulders and carefully forced her to face him. "C'mon, babe. Out with it."

"Blankenship is causing trouble again. This time he's setting fires at the county clerk's office. As a concerned taxpayer, he's saying that since we're married and I'm living here, I should no longer be able to claim a homestead exemption on Shadow Ranch."

Ethan grimaced. "The guy is unbelievable."

"The *guy* is dead meat if I ever get my hands on him. He didn't even try to hide the fact that he was the one raising the question."

"Did they give you an idea how long you have to do something about the situation?"

"If I remember correctly, it's prorated between the months I lived there and how long I lived here. The thing is, they want me to select one to make their bookkeeping easier."

As much as it stuck in Ethan's throat, he had to say it, though he had to let her go and step back from her to manage it. "Well, maybe it'll work out soon. As you said, a few weeks after the hearing, you can, uh, set things straight with them."

She frowned. "Set things… Oh. I see." She looked to her left, to her right, everywhere but at him. "Yes, no doubt you're right."

"Kate, look at me. I didn't mean I wanted to— I'm not in any rush to annul our marriage."

"*Annul?* Oh, God." She touched a hand to her head. "You'd better stop while you're ahead."

Ethan tightened his abdominal muscles against the pain he felt at her cold response. How could this be happening? Why now, when things had been perfect? "Look, I'm sorry. The news about the hearing date being set, and this tax thing, just rattled me, that's all." But her expression remained closed. Offended. "How did I become the bad guy here?" he asked, sincerely at a loss. "You're the one who told me this arrangement would be temporary."

She laughed mirthlessly. "You're absolutely right. No one can fault *you* for being inaccurate." She circled the island the long way, to avoid touching him.

"Kate. Don't walk away angry. Doesn't the fact that we're lovers count for something?"

"We have sex, Ethan, remember? You're the one who made it clear what you did and didn't want from me. And I'm going to go get some aspirin for this headache before you redefine another word I used to think I understood."

Kate didn't know how she made it through that night or through the long weekend. It helped to have to get back to her place for the couple from California who'd come to look at her dwindling stock. She'd dealt with them before and enjoyed the husband's comedic flair in film. Nevertheless, entertaining them overnight when she was juggling these new problems, not to mention certain heartbreak, wasn't the easiest thing she'd ever done.

In the end, she and Ethan didn't go on the picnic with Darcy. They didn't go down into town for any of the celebratory activities, as they'd discussed. Most hurtful of all, she and Ethan didn't touch again, and Ethan had returned to sleeping in his recliner.

The one thing they didn't stop was making sure that Darcy had plenty of attention and fresh air. But they didn't do it as a couple, or as a family. Either Ethan took her with him in the truck for a drive to check on his herd, or she spread a blanket on the floor and played with the baby, flipping through colorful magazines, reading her children's books, or playing make-believe with all of Darcy's stuffed animals.

Emotionally exhausted, she dropped Darcy off with Eva on the fifth. She wasn't at all surprised when the older woman took one look at her and shook her head.

"I didn't want to believe you were in love with him when you two first married. But I realized not even my Kathryn would do something so bold, so crazy, as to play house with a man she didn't care for. Now your heart is breaking. Don't deny it. I have eyes. What are you going to do, child?"

"I don't know," Kate admitted. "And I don't have time to worry about it, either. There's too much else to focus on, and Judge Lessing isn't going to be fooled if I walk into his court looking as if I'm in mourning."

"I think your so-called *husband* is a fool for not seeing what's in front of his face."

No, Kate thought as she drove toward Whitehorn a short time later. It was her fault for being too good an actress. She'd even fooled herself into thinking her attraction to Ethan was primarily physical, and would stay that way. From the beginning, when she hadn't let him tell her about Wayne's death, she'd given him all the signals that she would always keep him at arm's length. How could she blame him for doing exactly what she'd wanted?

Her only escape came through throwing herself into her work. During meetings and phone calls, she managed to push her personal crises far enough in the back of her mind to retain a hold on her sanity. And yet she even failed to fool Pat.

"You keep looking like that, and Blankenship is going to claim success before he ever gets to court," her secretary warned her late that afternoon.

"I know. There's a saying I like in one of my meditation books for women that goes, 'This revolution of women is the only revolution where the outpost of the enemy is in our own heads.' Whoever said that knew what she was talking about, because I'm a prime example." Kate sighed and scrawled her name on the bottom of the letter Pat had handed her. "If we're caught up, I'm going to call it a day. I'd like to detour by the cemetery, since I didn't get into town over the holiday. Why don't you take off, too?"

"Thanks, boss. Steve and I are refereeing a volleyball game for some of his students, and I don't have anything to wear."

The unlikely comment gave Kate the laugh she needed. "You'd better hustle, then. We can't have our ref looking scroungy," she said teasingly, reaching for her purse.

The Kincaid family was buried at the town's older cemetery, on Willow Brook Road. Kate didn't come here often, because she didn't like to think of Wayne here. It reminded her too much of the pain he might have suffered. The place she felt him most was in the mountains they'd ridden in together, often with Ethan. But she'd come today because there would be no opportunity for a long ride for some time yet, and she needed the unique spiritual grounding that Wayne had always provided to anyone in his presence.

There were several small flags by his headstone. That didn't surprise Kate. A great many people had cared for him. Life did, indeed, go on, but no doubt a whole generation would have to pass before his loss would stop being felt so poignantly in Whitehorn—especially since his nine-months-younger brother, Dugin, was proving such a disappointment these days.

As far as she was concerned, Dugin's most recent disturbing move had been to marry Mary Jo Plumber two summers ago. Most everyone else in town seemed to like Mary Jo well enough; she was described as sweet and demure by those who thought she was a salvation to the children's section of the public library, but Kate's feelings toward Dugin's attractive wife weren't dissimilar to how she'd felt about Ethan's former flame, Lexine Baxter. As far as she was concerned, the old saying about butter not melting in her mouth applied to both women. However, if Dugin was happy, she supposed that was all that mattered.

"You see why I needed to visit?" she murmured, with a

sad smile at the headstone. "I'm pitying Dugin, while my own life is a disaster and a half."

With a sigh, Kate wrapped her arms around her waist. "What am I going to do, Wayne? I love him. I've tried to ignore it, ignore him, for years. I've achieved everything Dad and Aunt Beryl always wanted for me, except to experience a loving relationship with a man and have a family of my own. And I know you want it for me, too. Ethan's the one. We both know that. But I can feel my chances with him slipping through my fingers, the same way I felt it when you said goodbye that last day."

She looked up between the branches of a great ponderosa pine to gaze at the brilliant, cloud-dotted sky. No sudden solutions or reassurances popped into her head; nor had she expected any. But a feeling of deep peace and reassurance slowly embraced her, a feeling that gave her the strength she needed to return to her truck and head for home.

Focus on the positive. Kate told herself that no matter what, Ethan would want her to continue being an important part of Darcy's life. If she couldn't share her life with him, she could share in a part of the life that brought him such joy.

As she drove away from the cemetery, she didn't know what made her look at the small house on her right. It was the last of three modest bungalows that some young upstart builder had designed to launch his career, in a rural area where land costs were significantly cheaper. The elegant sedan parked behind the compact automobile in the driveway definitely didn't fit with the middle-class aura of the house. It also looked extremely familiar, but she didn't remember why.

She drove on, turned onto Mountain Pass, only to pull over and wait for an eighteen-wheeler to go by. Then she made a U-turn. Something about the car bothered her, and she wanted to take a second look.

As she drove past the house that second time, it still didn't trigger her memory. Annoyed at herself for wasting time, she turned at the church and accelerated to make up for lost time.

Just as she was passing the third house, she casually glanced over. The front door opened, and she saw a man and woman embrace. As she began to glance away, she suddenly did a double take. "Good...*grief*," she whispered, and barely recovered in time to brake for the stop sign at the corner.

She drove in a blur all the way to her ranch, where she barely could talk to a concerned Eva. Pleading a headache and a preoccupied mind, she went on to the Double N, with at least one conflict before her.

Did she tell Ethan what she'd seen?

Needing time to think, she couldn't deny being relieved when she discovered he hadn't come home yet. After changing, she carried the baby outside for a walk, to show her the pasture where Ethan kept his new mother cows and their calves. But as the baby cooed and fluttered her hands at the romping calves, Kate's thoughts were focused elsewhere.

She was still brooding when Ethan and John Mountain pulled in a short time later.

As usual, John Mountain tipped his hat and retreated to his quarters. Ethan came over to her and, with a brief look of longing, took Darcy from her. "How are you?"

"Okay."

"Are you sure?"

Shaking her head, Kate admitted, "No. I've just seen something that would guarantee you getting custody of Darcy, but I'm not sure I can tell you about it."

Ethan stood watching her for several seconds before drawing off his hat and wiping at his dusty brow. "I don't think I'm ready for this. Are you saying we could put an end to this fiasco, and you're going to keep it a secret?"

It sounded horrible to hear it said back to her, but Kate had to nod.

"Would you mind telling me why?"

"Because I don't approve of the tactics the Blankenships and Noble Taylor used. And to participate in the same kind of manipulation as a defense to win your case wouldn't be making the point you're trying to establish."

"Since this argument ceases to make sense to me, what is that point?"

"That you're the choice Marilee made when she debated on who should raise her child."

"I thought we agreed that if I'm going to rely on my reputation and good intentions, I don't have a prayer."

"You don't know that."

"Oh, yes, I do. Which is why, if I'm out of options, I want the information."

"I'm sorry. I have to think this over."

With a parting look of rebuke, he started for the house. After a few steps, he turned around. "Let me ask you one more thing—whose side are you on?"

Stinging from his cold rejection, Kate watched him walk away. She yearned to follow him, to tell him what she knew. But he'd already told her what he would do with the information. Kate couldn't give him that ammunition, because she believed in her heart that responsibility stood before convenience.

Ethan didn't understand that there were more futures than his at stake here. Noble had seen to that. If Joan could establish Ethan's case on its own merits, then sharing this damaging information would serve no purpose except to hurt and humiliate an innocent woman who'd believed in her husband's fidelity.

If a case couldn't be raised in Ethan's favor...well, she would have to deal with that when the time came. But how to explain that to Ethan and ask for his trust, his faith?

She didn't ask him for anything, nor did she give him the information he wanted. In fact, over the next week, Kate made a point of keeping out of his way, to avoid another outburst between them. At one point, he wanted to order her to leave. In the next hour, he feared she might pack her things and go. It was the longest week of his life, so much so that when the day of the hearing arrived, he was more than ready to have it over with.

He dressed in the suit he'd worn for his last court appearance. Because he finished early, he stopped by Shadow Ranch to spend a last few minutes with Darcy, just in case. Eva eyed him with skepticism, Jorge with caution; but when she saw him fumbling for his handkerchief on his way out, she stopped him and gave him an impulsive hug. Then Jorge shook his hand.

The hearing was closed to the public, but word of mouth had lured quite a few of the curious. He endured a considerable crowd on his way inside, to Kate's office, where he met up with her and Joan Nyland. Even then he hoped Kate would give him some signal to let him know he could embrace her, and tell her the truth—that he was afraid, for all three of them.

His new attorney reminded him of an older version of his wife—sophisticated, sharp, and with no patience for fools. The look she gave him asked if he was going to be an asset or a liability to her.

Kate saw no reason to remain in her office, and they moved to Lessing's courtroom shortly thereafter.

Soon afterward, they were joined by the bailiff.

In about ten minutes more, the judge walked into the large, quiet room.

He moved slowly, his recent surgery still showing its effects on him. It took him almost another five minutes to get up to his bench and settle himself, at which point he was sweating profusely and cussing almost as badly. His secretary placed a folder before him, and a glass of ice water. After shuffling and muttering for another moment, he looked at the table to the left of theirs.

Now what? Ethan wondered, staring at the old man.

He sniffed and coughed and scowled down at the folder before him. "We have a small problem, ladies and gentlemen. Just before entering this court, it was brought to my attention that Noble Taylor has suffered a stroke."

Twelve

"Thank you for coming."

The woman before her represented a shadow of the Ruth Taylor Kate had come to know over the past months. Pale, her hair still that perfect champagne blonde, but no longer coiffed to bubble perfection, her attire a simple cotton top and slacks instead of a designer suit and pearls, hanging on her drained and aging body. Ruth had met this latest challenge in her life, but was floundering. It compelled Kate to reach for the woman's hands and lead her to the couch in the intensive-care unit's special waiting room.

To offer regrets and condolences over Noble's devastating condition would have been hypocritical. Kate avoided that by replying, "What can I do for you?"

After Judge Lessing's shocking announcement only hours ago, which had included a startling notation that Ruth Taylor wanted the custody hearing to continue and for Ethan and Kate to be awarded custody, Kate had quietly told her husband to go home. She had wanted to come here to Billings. She wasn't sure why, but she felt it…necessary.

"I appreciate the gesture, Your Honor…."

"Oh, heavens, Ruth. Call me Kate."

"Kate…I'm so ashamed," Ruth whispered, as soon as she sat down.

As she bowed her head, Kate wrapped an arm around her shoulders and lowered her head to the older woman's. "No. The problems we went through are in the past. Done."

"It will never be done. You see, I knew what he was doing. I knew about—" Ruth drew a deep breath and somehow reclaimed her dignity. "You and I need to talk, Kate. The doctors say it's unlikely he'll recuperate to a fraction of who he was. It's our punishment for his infidelity as we were inflicting our rigid ways on others."

Once again Kate hugged her. "This isn't the time."

"It is. You tell Ethan…you tell him Marilee was a lovely girl. Being simple and undemanding shouldn't be a crime, and I'm ashamed that I didn't speak up when I should have. When it would have saved her some pain. It's bad enough I stood by and let Noble's selfishness and cruelty ruin our son. You see, I've been a coward, thinking only of protecting my marriage.

"But I'm speaking up now. I only cared about being a model wife, and that wasn't enough. Or maybe that was too much. I think it would take someone of this younger generation to explain it to me."

"The fact that you recognize your mistakes is the beginning of change, Ruth. The rest will come."

"Will it?" Ruth stared at her with pain-filled eyes. "I'm almost alone now. My days will be long, and often empty. Would it be too much to ask if once in a while you might bring the child to visit me?"

This was beyond Kate's expectations. And yet she'd seen miracles happen in her own court. But each time they were new and special.

One question remained, though. Would Ethan be gracious in victory?

Kate thought of his expression when Judge Lessing had awarded custody of Darcy to him...and seconds later, when Ethan had turned to her. He hadn't said anything, they hadn't touched. It had broken her heart, because she'd needed him so much.

But, for Ruth, she would dare to have hope.

"Let me know when you're ready," she told her.

They spoke for several more minutes before Kate, deciding the exhausted woman needed some rest herself, hugged her again and made the long trip back to White-horn. She passed Shadow Ranch, because she'd already phoned Eva and Jorge and warned them she would probably be returning later that evening. But, knowing she would need to finish things with Ethan first, she drove straight to the Double N.

She found him sitting at his desk when she entered. One look at the crib, and she froze. "Where's Darcy?"

"With Eva. I asked her if she minded, because I thought we needed to talk."

Kate nodded and dropped her things on the couch. "You're right. I suppose you know I went to Billings?" When he inclined his head, she continued, "Naturally, it will be days before they're certain of the severity of Noble's stroke, but considering what they know so far, and his age, Ruth's been told she'll have to hire a full-time nurse to help her out."

After a long pause, Ethan looked out the front window. "If you're expecting me to offer some token sympathy, you'll have a long wait."

"I'm not asking. I didn't have much to offer myself. I went to thank her for the decision she made."

"Almost too little, too late."

"Ethan."

"What? Do you think this cleans the slate as far as them trying to ruin my reputation?"

Kate moistened her lips. "I should tell you that Ruth asked if I might bring Darcy over sometime for a visit."

"Absolutely not."

"Ethan, please hear me out."

"No, *you* listen! They were out to destroy me. Ruin my reputation. Get me thrown back into jail. Make it impossible for me to see my niece, not to mention ruining your life."

Kate kept nodding until he was through. Then she crossed the room and leaned her hands on his desk. "That was Noble and Warren Blankenship. I told you before that Ruth was a good wife. She didn't challenge him. Even if she secretly disagreed, she would never have challenged him. If you want to judge her for anything, judge her for that."

"And you think because the old buzzard is hooked up to life-support now, anything's changed?"

"Yes. Because she's decided she no longer owes Noble that kind of allegiance."

He studied her for several seconds, narrowed his eyes and demanded, "Meaning what?"

"She discovered that Noble was having an affair with one of Blankenship's paralegals." As concisely as she could, Kate told him about what she'd seen the other day, then how that had triggered a memory of when she'd been in Blankenship's office last month and seen them together. "I'm not saying that she's the only one Ruth was referring to, but there you are."

"There you are," Ethan murmured, looking a little dazed. "That's what you were holding back from me?"

"Yes."

"And when were you going to tell me?"

"As I said before, I wasn't—unless the hearing was handled badly or there was a strong suggestion that Judge Lessing was going to decide in favor of the Taylors. This was a matter of a marriage, Ethan. I didn't know whether Ruth did or didn't know about it, wanted to condone it as long as it was kept quiet, or what. We had no right to intrude on that."

"Why not? They didn't hesitate intruding in my life. *And* yours." He rose, furious. "What if you'd waited too long? What if Lessing didn't want to listen to you? What if Blankenship had managed to convince Lessing that you were making it up?"

As he spoke, he circled the desk. Now he was face-to-face with her, his expression evoking a man pushed to his limit, but Kate refused to back away. In fact, she was getting fed up with these accusations altogether.

"I'm going to explain myself once, and then, as far as I'm concerned, the matter is closed. It was my call, Ethan. And it wasn't one I made lightly, regardless of what you're obviously thinking. *I* read the situation. *I* have the experience. I made the decision to leave them room to do the right thing, for once in their lives. And Ruth did."

"In other words, you didn't think I had the discipline to resist going for Taylor's jugular. Thanks for the vote of confidence, Your Honor."

He said that quietly, which made the inference sting all the worse. "If I'd been in your shoes, Ethan, I'm not sure I wouldn't have done anything to keep that child away from Noble."

"It would have been nice to have been given the benefit of the doubt. All you managed to do was prove you don't trust me."

She couldn't believe he was pushing this hard. Exhausted, disappointed, she wanted to end it. "That's why I married you. Why I'm risking my career, my reputation, my *safety* if you ask some people…and my heart to a child I'll have to withdraw from, to an extent, once we separate. Absolutely, Ethan—I had no faith in you at all."

Maybe it was those words, the fatigue in her expression, or the tremor in her voice, but Ethan suddenly seemed aware of what he was doing—and stepped back, looking ashamed. "Hell, Kate…I don't know what I'm saying anymore."

"Forget it. Let's just stop. This is supposed to be the happiest day of your life."

"I know." He sighed. "Then why do I feel caught in limbo?"

"Because we're still supposed to play house and keep up appearances. But…I don't know if I can anymore."

He bowed his head. "I didn't thank you enough for putting up with the primitive lifestyle, let alone taking the risks."

"Yes, you did. That's not the point."

"Then what is?"

"That too often you made me forget about the risks."

"Did I?" he asked huskily. When she nodded, he took a step closer. "What if I wanted more?"

If he didn't stop doing this to her, she was going to have to sit down. "I'm not sure I know what you mean."

"Was everything you did just for Darcy and—?" He held up his hand. "And the fact that we make great lovers."

He'd said the word, at least. It was better than simply being sexually compatible. And Kate knew what she wanted to say, what she thought he wanted her to say, but she'd stuck her neck out for him so much already. She needed him to let her know that he would be there to catch her if she went any further. "What is it that you're asking for?"

"I want you as my wife. Permanently." He exhaled shakily. "I've tried to think of a day when you wouldn't be in my life, and I couldn't. I don't want to." He closed the space between them and took her face in his hands. "I... love you, Kate."

She searched his face. "Why was that so hard for you to say?"

"Because I know I'll always be number two in your life, and I had to believe I could handle that, that it wouldn't matter, coming in second to a ghost."

"Wayne's dead, Ethan," Kate whispered. "I faced that a long time ago."

"I know that's what you want to believe, but you were at the cemetery the other day, when you saw Taylor. That doesn't sound like a woman who's put the past behind her."

"You and I had fought, Ethan. And I was struggling to figure out what to do next. Of all the people who knew you, I believe he understood you best. It may sound crazy to you, but I was there hoping that being closer to him would make me understand you better. I was there because of *you*, Ethan."

For a moment, he looked hopeful. His thumbs even stroked her cheeks, as if he were about to kiss her. But in the next instant he shook his head. "Then why haven't you ever let me talk about him? About what happened to him?"

Now it was her turn to shake her head and retreat. "I was afraid of what you'd say. He was gone. What did it matter how or— No," she said, turning to face him again. "I was afraid you would say something that would take you away, too."

"So instead we wasted all these years circling each other like wary combatants?"

"They weren't wasted," she replied, seeing it more clearly now. "I think we needed the time to heal, and grow, because we were three parts of a whole...and we always will be. But one part of us was cut away, and we needed to learn that he's still an integral part of who we are."

"Some of us are still trying to heal, Kate," Ethan said quietly. "You've found your peace. I still need to find mine, and I can't if you don't let me tell you about that day."

Could she bear it? She had to, if they were going to move on together.

Slowly she nodded. "Go ahead."

He walked to the window, his shoulders squared, his head high. "Our platoons had both suffered heavy casualties after this push to take a village, so they put our two groups together. I hadn't seen him in almost two weeks, and so we stuck together as we entered the village.

"Wayne spotted the little girl before I did. She'd been injured, and she was huddled against a hut that we needed to check out. At the same time, a kid came out of the woods. Wayne yelled, 'Take him!' But I told him he was just a kid. No more than thirteen."

Ethan sucked in a shuddering breath. "Before I knew it, the kid had thrown a grenade at the hut. It would have killed the girl. Wayne knew there was no time to get her away, and he leaped, yelling, 'Take him!' and threw himself on it."

He let his head fall back and groaned. "It should have been me."

"You can't say that," Kate replied, swallowing her tears.

"I hesitated with the boy, and I lost my best friend. It should have been me."

Kate rushed to him, grabbed his arm and swung him around. Despite her own anguish over Wayne's terrible death, it was Ethan's self-loathing that tore at her heart. All these years, she'd made him carry that grief, when she could have given him release from it, only she hadn't wanted to know, to protect herself.

"Ethan, listen to me. He made a choice. You said it yourself, he was always concerned with fixing things and making people happy. Do you think he could have stood it if he'd had to look at that mutilated little girl? Or *you?*"

"Oh, God, Kate."

Ethan reached for her, and she wrapped her arms around him as tightly as he held her, absorbed the shudders of his work-hardened, grief-racked body.

"I'm so sorry," she whispered again and again. "But, Ethan, there was nothing you could have done. Let it go. He'll always be a special part of both of us, but let it go. Let him rest now."

They stood together, clinging and holding, something silent and sweet seeping from one to the other, easing the old pain, offering something new and hopeful in its wake. Finally, when she felt him relax and press a kiss to her brow, she leaned back to gaze deeply into his eyes.

"I love you, Ethan. *That's* why I married you. That's why I fought so hard for you. That's why I want to spend the rest of my life with you and Darcy."

His eyes grew bright and intense, his hold tighter. "Say that again. The first part."

"I love you."

"And I love you. I always have."

Kate nodded. "I know. Now."

He framed her face with his hands, caressed her with his thumbs, his look as relieved as it was worshipful. Then he closed his mouth over hers for a kiss that sealed their hearts as their vows had linked their lives. They'd never held each other with more care or with more joy. Their kisses had never offered sweeter promises.

"Your heart's pounding like a sledgehammer," Kate said, when she could speak again.

"So's yours." But, as quickly as he'd grinned, Ethan sobered. "Damn, Kate. Are you sure? I'm more of a liability than an asset—"

"You're everything I want."

"And this isn't exactly a paradise," he added ruefully.

She shrugged—as much as he would let her—and lifted her mouth to his. "We'll work on it. Together."

"Together," he agreed, holding her fast to his heart.

Epilogue

"Have one more pancake."

Kate held back a grin until Eva had added it to Ethan's plate and returned to the stove. Shifting Darcy on her lap, she leaned over to whisper to him, "I think she's definitely getting to like you."

"Either that or she plans to do me in with kindness."

But there was only amusement in Ethan's eyes as he winked at her and attacked the rest of his breakfast. This late-morning meal together was a treat for them, after the past several weeks' hectic pace;
however, life was tasting very sweet indeed.

Only a few days after the hearing, they'd discussed their future and the cabin. Although he'd been hesitant at first, Ethan had agreed they would all be more comfortable if they moved to Kate's house.

Between the move, decorating the baby's nursery, across the hall from the master bedroom, and work, luxuries like sleeping late were few and far between. But neither one of them was complaining.

Her greatest joy, however, was Ethan's acceptance of her offer to join their lands, and his agreement to expand his herd. At first he'd been self-conscious, worrying about how it would look, since his several-hundred-acre operation was nothing compared to the thousands Kate had inherited. Also, Kate's land possessed the best pasture and water.

But when she reminded him that Shadow Ranch had no future without heirs, and that she would sell off all her horses, except for a few personal ones for pleasure—and to keep Jorge happy and out of mischief—he'd finally agreed...under the condition that it all now be called Shadow Ranch.

It had taken more convincing, but they'd talked John Mountain into moving into the cabin, and just recently they'd hired two other men to help with the work load, who would move into the bunkhouse.

Yes, fate was treating them with a new tenderness, Kate thought. She was even developing a cautious, but interesting, relationship with Ruth Taylor. Once Noble was released from the hospital and she had the full-time nurse to help her, she'd regained her strength and some of her previous self-esteem.

Kate made a point of bringing Darcy twice a month for a long visit. Noble had no perception of the child, but Ruth was blossoming into quite a grandmother, with the gentle help of her housekeeper, Norma. From the looks of things, it didn't appear as if the child would miss out on having a grandparent after all.

Best of all, though, last night, as they lay in each other's arms, Ethan had asked her what she thought about adopting a little brother or sister for Darcy. Kate was still basking in the warmth of that suggestion, and the lovemaking it had precipitated.

In fact, as she walked Ethan to his truck to say goodbye before he left to check on the crew over at the cabin, she was tempted to ask him to stay home to continue further "negotiations." The sound of an approaching vehicle had them both shading their eyes against the sun to peer at the truck with the overhead lights appearing around the bend.

Kate's heart did a little thump. She recognized the police vehicle, and when Ethan's arm tightened around her waist, she knew he was uneasy, too. Only the baby cooed with delight at the sight of more company.

"Aren't we getting paranoid?" Kate muttered, shooting her husband a quick, not quite amused, glance. "The sight of one of those, and automatically we anticipate bad news."

Ethan didn't reply, and he didn't step forward when Rafe Rawlings stepped out.

To cover for him, Kate offered a bright smile for the young, darkly handsome policeman. "Rafe, this is a surprise. What brings you out here?"

He tipped his hat to her and offered a crooked smile at the baby before sliding a more somber look at Ethan. "Sorry to disturb your day, Judge, Ethan. I was wondering if you might have seen Homer Gilmore around lately?"

Ethan stiffened, and his expression turned stony. "What are you accusing me of this time, Rawlings?"

The younger man held up both hands and vigorously shook his head. "Whoa—you have it all wrong, man. I'm not accusing you of anything. I'm not even here on official business. But I talked to Kane Hunter last night, and one of the first questions out of both of our mouths was whether the other had seen old Homer lately. Usually we can count on one of us having visited with him. Anyway, since you've got men covering a good stretch of land in this area, I thought you'd ask them to keep an eye out for the old guy, and to let one of us know."

Kate shifted the wriggling baby, who was intrigued with the policeman's shiny badge, glinting in the hot August sun. "Of course, Rafe. We'll be happy to."

Looking far more relaxed, Ethan added, "I'm going over to see the men now. Glad you caught me, because I'd like to help out if I can. I owe the old buzzard for saving at least one life." His words ended gruffly as he touched Darcy's baby-fine dark curls. He cleared his throat. "And I'm sorry for jumping to conclusions."

"Shoot. Can't say you don't have a reason to be cautious. If I was you, I might still be holding a grudge." Rafe extended his hand.

Overjoyed with the scene, Kate ducked her head to nuzzle the baby, and to hide the stinging in her eyes. She wasn't about to let it get around town that the Hanging Judge was turning into a softy.

But as soon as Rafe pulled away, and Kate called for him to say hello to Raeanne for them, she leaned into her husband's body and sighed. "I love you, Ethan."

He wrapped both arms around her and the baby and kissed one, then the other, on the crowns of their heads. "Keep telling me, love. Maybe in another thirty or forty years I may figure out what I did to deserve it."

"No problem," Kate promised.

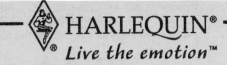

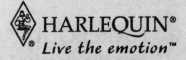

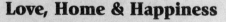
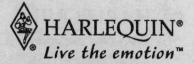

HARLEQUIN®
INTRIGUE®

BREATHTAKING ROMANTIC SUSPENSE

Shared dangers and passions lead to electrifying romance and heart-stopping suspense!

Every month, you'll meet six new heroes who are guaranteed to make your spine tingle and your pulse pound. With them you'll enter into the exciting world of Harlequin Intrigue— where your life is on the line and so is your heart!

THAT'S INTRIGUE—
ROMANTIC SUSPENSE
AT ITS BEST!

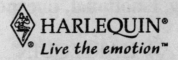

HARLEQUIN®
Live the emotion™

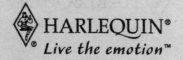